Caz Finlay lives in Liverp
children, and a grumpy d
probation officer, Caz has a
psychology of human behaviour and the reasons people do
the things they do. However, it was the loss of her son in
2016 which prompted her to rediscover her love of writing
and write her first novel, *The Boss.*

cazfinlay.com

f facebook.com/cazfinlayauthor
y twitter.com/cjfinlaywriter
BB bookbub.com/authors/caz-finlay

Also by Caz Finlay

The Boss

Back in the Game

HEAD OF THE FIRM

CAZ FINLAY

One More Chapter
a division of HarperCollins*Publishers* Ltd
1 London Bridge Street
London SE1 9GF
www.harpercollins.co.uk

This paperback edition 2020
First published in Great Britain in ebook format
by HarperCollins*Publishers* 2020

A catalogue record of this book
is available from the British Library

ISBN: 978-0-00-840509-0

Printed and bound in Great Britain by
CPI Group (UK) Ltd, Croydon CR0 4YY

Prologue

Zak Miller sat patiently on the stolen motorbike with the engine running while he waited for his target to approach. His heart thumped in his chest and the blood pounding in his ears seemed to reverberate off the sides of his motorcycle helmet as its soft leather pushed against his ears. He closed his eyes for a few seconds and focused instead on the rhythmic sound of his breathing – calm and steady, just like he'd been taught. What he was about to do was incredibly risky. It would change the landscape of the Liverpool underworld for ever. The ramifications would be felt far and wide and for years to come. Not only was his target one of the most dangerous and powerful individuals to ever walk the streets of Liverpool, it was also broad daylight, which ensured there were plenty of potential witnesses around. It was a calculated risk, and one that Zak was willing to take. Given that his target was particularly difficult to get close to, and was rarely alone, he didn't want to miss an opportunity to strike when he happened to know exactly where they would be.

Zak prided himself on being the very best at what he did, and he was getting very good money for this particular job. Money that would set him up for life. It would have to. He planned to disappear pretty quickly once this was over.

He could only hear the loud, rhythmic thumping of his heartbeat now as his target approached. Pulling down the visor of his helmet, he took the Beretta handgun out of his inside jacket pocket and edged the bike forward. A few more seconds and he would have a perfect shot. He watched as his intended victim smiled to themselves – they didn't have a fucking clue what was coming. As their paths crossed he raised the gun. By the time his target had noticed him, it was too late. He fired one clean shot straight through his victim's neck. Before they had even hit the floor, Zak hit the throttle and sped off out of sight.

Chapter One

THREE WEEKS EARLIER

Grace Carter looked up from her phone as her husband Michael walked over and sat on the sofa beside her.

'He's fast asleep now, just like his big sister,' he said with a grin, referring to their four-month-old son, whom he had just placed in his Moses basket.

She returned his smile as she put her phone on the coffee table in front of them. 'You are a genius, Michael Carter. He never settles that easily for me. You must have the magic touch.'

'Yeah. And that's not the only magic I can do with these hands, you know?' he said with a wink.

'Really? What other magic can you do? I can't recall.'

'What? You don't remember? It was only this morning, Grace.' He looked at his watch. 'Just over twelve hours ago in fact.'

Grace pulled his face to hers and kissed him. 'Oh yes, I remember now.'

He put an arm around her shoulder and she nestled against him. 'So how was work today?'

'Oh, you know what it's like. Everyone has a problem, but no one brings any solutions.'

'Speaking of problems and solutions, I heard another club got raided last night. Did you manage to find out any more about if and when they're likely to hit Jake's club?'

Michael shook his head. 'Not really. But it seems like the plod are insistent on raiding every club in town. You know they like to have a crackdown every so often. It keeps the mayor and the licensing board happy. So, it's only a matter of time before they target The Blue Rooms as well.'

'Well, you'd better tell the boys to keep their extracurricular activities to a minimum for a few weeks then,' she said with a sigh. 'We don't want any of our bouncers getting arrested. We're supposed to be legitimate now, aren't we?'

'I'll have a word with them tomorrow.'

Grace and Michael owned Cartel Securities, a successful business with security contracts across the country. Michael had started the firm himself a couple of years earlier, and at first he'd focused on the thriving Liverpool nightlife scene as well as one-off event management. The business was now considered the premier security company for Liverpool and Merseyside. However, it wasn't until they'd been married, sixteen months ago, that Grace had become a partner and had taken the business in a whole new direction. It had been both her and Michael's idea to try and keep the business legitimate. It had worked for the most part, and they'd secured themselves lucrative contracts with shopping centres, building sites and hospitals across the North West and North East.

If that wasn't enough to keep them busy, they were also co-owners of two successful Italian restaurants with Michael's brother Sean: one in the up-and-coming Baltic Market area, and one in the heart of Liverpool's Albert Dock. The latter, Sophia's Kitchen, was their flagship. Their pride and joy. It had cost them an arm and a leg to kit out with the finest furniture and state-of-the-art kitchens, but it had all been worth it. Now, Sophia's Kitchen was the hottest place to eat in Liverpool. Their weekends were booked months in advance and the place was permanently packed to the rafters. Grace had been involved in every detail until Oscar was born. Then she'd promised herself at least six months off to spend with Oscar and her daughter Belle. Michael had been happy to take over the reins while she did so, telling her to take all the time she needed. But, although she was technically on maternity leave, Grace was still busy making plans to open a wine bar in the next twelve months.

However, the legitimisation of the Carter empire appeared to have bypassed the younger generation, and together Grace's son, Jake, and Michael's twin boys, Paul and Connor, had taken over Grace and Michael's previous mantle of being the principal suppliers of cocaine, ecstasy and weed, as well as whatever else anyone needed to get their hands on, to the Merseyside area. This also involved using Grace and Michael's bouncers as dealers when the need arose, which was fine as a rule, except when the police and the licensing board were sniffing around looking for reasons to close places down.

The Blue Rooms was Jake's club, left to him by his father, Grace's ex-husband, Nathan Conlon. When Nathan had owned the place, it had been a seedy lap-dancing club – which had suited Nathan's character down to the ground. To Jake's credit, when he had first taken over, he'd turned the place into one of the most successful clubs in Liverpool. And with Jake's wife, Siobhan, at the helm, it had become one of the leading Liverpool nightspots. But since Siobhan had left work to have their daughter, Isla, a year earlier, the place had lost some of its class. It was still successful, but more often than not it was dogged by rumours of drugs and brawling, and more than once Grace or Michael had had to call in favours from the various officials they had on their payroll to stop the place from being closed down.

'Any chance that our kids will actually listen though?' Grace said with a sigh.

'Who knows?' Michael replied with a shrug. 'You do realise they're invincible, don't you?'

Grace laughed. 'Oh yes, of course. I forgot about that.'

'I remember when I used to think I was invincible. Seems like a lifetime ago now,' he said with a smile.

'Now you're all old and wise,' Grace said as she nudged him in the ribs. 'So they definitely won't listen to you.'

'Well, if they don't listen to me, I'll call in the big guns – you.'

They usually did listen to her, but all the same, Grace gave a sigh. 'I do worry about them though, Michael. What if one day they really do stop listening to us?'

Michael turned his head to look at her. 'They know what they're doing, Grace. They're not stupid. Young, and quite possibly a bit arrogant, but not stupid. They're not out there doing anything that we didn't do ourselves at one time or another.'

She nodded at him, but wasn't entirely convinced.

'And besides,' Michael added, 'they will always listen to you.'

Before she could respond, he silenced her with a kiss.

Chapter Two

Connor Carter closed his eyes and leaned back against the leather headrest in the back seat of his Range Rover, while his girlfriend, Jazz, rode him like her life depended on it. Despite being nine years older than him, she had the most incredible body he had ever seen. And she could do things with it that made his toes curl. Since he'd met her five months earlier on a night out in Manchester, he'd been completely besotted with her. The only potential blot on the landscape was that she was a married woman. And not just any married woman. But when he was with Jazz, Connor didn't care. He'd convinced himself they were too clever to get caught. They were always discreet. They used his car, or cheap hotels in the arse end of nowhere. Connor hadn't told anyone about Jazz except for Paul, and he would trust Paul with his life.

'Fuck, Jazz,' he breathed when they were finished. 'You're something else, girl. Do you know that?'

'I do my best,' she purred at him as she licked her lips.

The vibration of Connor's mobile phone in his pocket put an end to his post-sex haze. Jazz lifted her thighs off his as he reached into his pocket to retrieve it.

'What?' he snapped as he answered the phone to Gary Mac, one of his best soldiers.

'Sorry, Boss, but there's been a problem at the collection point. Someone must have known we were going to be there. They were waiting inside the container for us.'

'What? Is everyone okay? Is the gear okay?'

'We've got the gear. But Vinnie Black's been shot in the stomach.'

'Shit!' Connor snapped as he jumped up, sending Jazz sprawling onto the seat beside him. 'Sorry,' he mouthed to her.

'Where is Vinnie now?'

'The lads took the gear to the warehouse, and I dropped Vinnie at A and E. I left the stolen plates on the van, and I was in and out, Boss, so no one will know who dropped him off. But we couldn't just leave him like that.'

'No, of course you couldn't. Any idea who was behind it?'

'Yep. I'm back with the lads now and we've got two of the little fuckers.'

'Nice one, Gary. I'll call Paul and Jake and we'll be there as soon as.'

'Sound. We're at the warehouse.'

'Sound,' Connor replied and ended the call. He turned to Jazz. 'I'm so sorry, babe, but something's come up.'

'It's okay,' Jazz said with a sigh. 'I'd better be getting

back soon anyway before he notices I'm missing. Can you drop me back at my car?'

'Of course, babe,' he said before giving her one last kiss. Then, while Jazz got herself dressed, he dialled his brother's phone number.

Jake Conlon looked at the quivering man on the floor in front of him. Ian Thomas was a scumbag known locally as The Thrush, because he was so fucking irritating. He was a part-owner of a knocking shop, the aptly named Number 69 on the Dock Road, and with Jake and the Carter twins' permission he dealt drugs from there too – drugs that they sold him for a good price. He sold to the girls mostly and Jake supposed they needed something to get through the day when the likes of Ian Thomas and his mates were their clientele. The day before, Paul had received a phone call from one of the girls, Sasha. He and Connor had gone to school with her and she'd been a reliable source of information for them since she'd started working at Number 69 three years earlier. It was surprising the level of information that was divulged to the girls by some of the punters. So, seeing the potential business opportunity, the Carter twins had ensured that every girl in Number 69 had become their eyes and ears, and, by association, Jake's too. Sasha had told him that Ian had been taking the good-quality merchandise that they prided themselves on, and had been cutting it with all kinds of nasty shit. Two of the girls had become so ill they'd been hospitalised, and one had almost died. Paul had promised her that they would sort it as soon as they could – and so here they were.

'Please, Mr Conlon,' Ian snivelled. 'I didn't do anything with your drugs.'

'What? Are you calling my esteemed colleague a liar then?' He turned to Paul, who was sitting on the bonnet of Ian's battered Fiat Panda, holding a baseball bat as though it was his baby. 'He says it wasn't him, Paul. He thinks you're a liar.'

'No!' Ian wailed. 'I never said that. I never, Mr Carter.'

'Well, if it wasn't you, then who has been cutting our drugs with rat poison?' Paul said as he jumped off the bonnet and sauntered over to Jake and Ian.

'I don't know,' Ian cried. 'I don't know. But please, it wasn't me.'

'If it wasn't you, then you must know who it was. Because if you don't, that means you've been leaving our good-quality gear unattended. Either way, we're not happy,' Jake snarled.

Suddenly the sound of the *Z Cars* theme tune filled the air as Paul's mobile phone started ringing.

'All right, Con?' Paul said as he answered.

Jake listened to the one-sided phone call and realised there was something else requiring their attention.

Paul hung up the phone. 'As fun as it is to watch Ian piss himself, we don't have time for this, Jake,' he said sternly.

'Shame,' Jake replied.

Ian looked at his captors with a mixture of fear and relief

on his face. Jake smiled as he realised Ian had obviously misunderstood Paul's instruction.

Paul handed Jake the baseball bat. Ian scuttled backwards until he reached the brick wall and could go no further. He held up his hands in defence and let out a bloodcurdling scream as Jake brought the bat down. His hands and fingers took the brunt of the first blow so Jake struck him again for good measure, this time across his shoulders and chest. For his parting shot, Jake kicked Ian in the face, breaking his jaw.

'Your share of Number 69 is ours now, Ian. Don't go there again,' Paul reminded him as they walked away, leaving him howling in pain.

Chapter Three

Jake, Paul and Connor arrived at the warehouse on Canal Street together, to find Gary Mac with his two sons standing in a semi-circle. In front of them were two young lads, who looked no older than eighteen, strapped to chairs with cable ties and gagged with gaffer tape.

'Fucking hell. It looks like *Fifty Shades of Grey* in here,' Paul said with a chuckle.

'Are these the fuckers who tried to rob us?' Jake asked incredulously.

Gary and his sons nodded. 'There were two more but they got away,' Gary said.

'You get a look at them?' Connor asked.

'Only a fleeting glimpse. Didn't recognise them.'

'Thanks, Gary. You and the boys can get off now.'

Gary signalled his sons to follow him. 'Night, fellas,' he said on his way out.

Jake stared at the two young lads in front of them. Their

eyes wide in terror. Their legs trembling. One of them had a suspicious wet stain on the crotch of his jeans. Ordinarily, a scene like this would be right up Jake and the twins' street, and they would think nothing of making an example of anyone who tried to steal from them. But these two looked like a pair of terrified kids.

As if reading his mind, Connor spoke. 'What the fuck are we gonna do with these two?' he said with an exaggerated sigh.

Jake shrugged. 'Beats me, lad,' he said as pulled up one of the chairs and sat down. 'Paul? Any ideas?'

'We could just shoot them in the head?' Paul suggested, although Jake knew he had no intention of doing so. They had no guns on them for a start.

The two captive youths began to shake their heads furiously.

'Let's hear what they have to say for themselves then,' Jake said with a nod.

Paul approached the two youths and ripped the gaffer tape from their mouths.

'So?' Paul snapped.

Immediately the two of them started babbling. All Jake could make out were the words *sorry*, *melon* and *dare*.

'For fuck's sake!' Connor muttered and walked away.

'Oy!' Jake shouted as he stood up and walked over to them. 'You weren't fucking crying earlier when you shot one of our mates, were you? You pair of spineless little pricks.' He kicked one of the chairs, almost sending it toppling over. 'Calm the fuck down and tell us who you are and who you're working for.'

The one who'd pissed himself continued to cry but did so quietly, snot and tears pouring down his face. The other one, who had a mass of curly blonde hair, seemed a little more composed, so Jake focused on him.

'You! Curly! Tell us who you're working for,' Jake demanded.

Curly shook his head. 'No one,' he stuttered. 'No one, I swear.'

'Fuck off!' Paul snapped. 'You expect us to believe you and him, and your two mates who done a runner and left you in the shit, independently decided to rob our gear? Knew where it was coming in and ambushed some of our best lads? Do you think we're fucking stupid?'

'We didn't know it was yours,' Curly snivelled. 'We just thought we were going to nick a bit of weed from some lads. We had no idea what it really was, or that it was yours.'

By this point Connor had walked back over to them.

'This one's telling us some fucking porkies,' Paul said to his brother.

'He's not,' the other one suddenly wailed.

'Oh, I forgot you were even here. Stopped crying for your mummy now?' Jake said to him.

'I'm telling the truth. I swear,' Curly pleaded.

'Tell us what happened then. Everything. Including who shot Vinnie,' Connor demanded

Curly took a deep breath. 'Someone told us—'

'Who?' Jake snapped.

'We don't know his name. We met him in a pub in Birkenhead. We'd never seen him before.'

Jake raised an eyebrow at the twins. This was getting more ludicrous by the second.

'Look, I can explain, I swear. Just let me explain,' Curly pleaded.

'Go on then,' Jake replied. 'Let's hear your fairy-tale. But I want details, Curly. The more detail you give me, the more likely it is that you will live to see the light of another day.'

Curly licked his lips. 'Me and my mates, Jay'—he indicated the sobbing lad beside him at this point—'and Richie, were drinking in the Brass Balance pub in Birkenhead when we started to talking to this fella at the bar. We'd never seen him in there before.'

Jake opened his mouth to ask a question, but Curly pre-empted him. 'He was late thirties. Average build. Clean shaven. Brown hair. He was wearing a Hugo Boss tracksuit top. That's all I remember about him. He said he knew about this load of weed that had been left in a container near the docks, and how it was just sitting there for the taking. He said it was some real good-quality weed. Then, some lad who was a few years above us in school, Kenny Bailey, came in. Kenny's always been a bit of a nutter so when he heard what this fella was saying, he persuaded us to go and take this weed.'

'And you thought this was a good idea why?' Jake snapped.

'We were off our faces. We'd been doing coke and drinking Jaeger bombs all day. We just wanted some weed.' He sniffed. 'We weren't thinking at all.'

'So, you're telling me three of our best men were ambushed by a nutter and three stoners?' Jake barked.

'We didn't ambush them,' Curly went on. 'We thought this weed would just be lying there with no one guarding it. We weren't waiting for anyone. When we saw it was a container full of coke, we thought that maybe something wasn't adding up, but we were already in it up to our necks by then. We were just going to take some, but then your lads turned up and we panicked. Kenny shot one of them and then we ran.'

The lad beside him shook his head. 'I fucking told you not to go along with Kenny the Melon,' he wailed.

'Where can we find this Kenny the Melon?' Jake asked.

'The Brass Balance pub. He's always in there,' Curly said.

'Do you believe this pair of cretins?' Connor asked.

Jake shook his head. 'I don't fucking know. I think someone will be paying Kenny the Melon a visit though, don't you?'

'And find out if anyone knows who this fella in the Hugo Boss top is. If he exists!' Connor added and Paul and Jake nodded in agreement.

'Exactly how old are you two?' Jake asked.

'Eighteen,' Curly replied.

Connor shook his head and looked at Paul and Jake. 'We weren't this fucking green at eighteen, were we?'

'God, I fucking hope not,' Jake replied with a laugh.

'Right then, lads,' Connor said as he placed one hand on Jake's shoulder and one on Paul's. 'I'm goosed. And I don't think it's very fair if all three of us give these two little pricks a kicking, do you?'

Paul shook his head. 'Like using a sledgehammer to

crack a walnut, mate. Yous can get off. I can handle these two.'

'No, I'll stay,' Jake said with a smile. 'I enjoy watching you work.'

Paul shrugged. 'Sound.'

'I'm getting off then. I'll check on Vinnie, and tell Gary where he can find this Kenny prick.'

Ten minutes later, Curly and his mate stumbled out of the warehouse battered and bruised. They might have had a broken bone or two, but they had also had a very lucky escape. Jake, at least, was content that they would never try to take what was his again.

Chapter Four

G race walked into the kitchen as Michael was serving up generous portions of scouse to their three older sons, Jake, Paul and Connor.

'This smells fucking amazing,' Paul said as he almost stuck his face into the bowl.

'I haven't had scouse for weeks,' Jake said as he plunged his spoon into the hot stew. 'Thanks, Michael.'

'Not since the last time you all came for tea,' Grace said with a smile. Every few weeks one of them would phone up at the arse crack of dawn and ask if they could pop round for tea. When they were reminded they didn't need to ask, they followed up with a request for a pan of scouse. Grace had to admit, Michael made the best scouse she'd ever tasted. It was even better than her dad's had been, and that was saying something.

Grace sat on a chair at the big oak table. 'So, how are things boys? How is business?'

'Brilliant,' Paul and Jake said in unison as they stuffed their mouths.

'All right,' Connor replied with a shrug.

Grace noted the different responses but didn't push further. The lads would inevitably tell them everything anyway as the evening wore on.

'How is the new fella working out, Dad?' Connor asked before biting off a chunk of crusty buttered bread.

Michael sat down at the table with them. 'Carl? He's all right. A bit wet behind the ears, but he's up for a scrap. Sometimes a bit too up for it, but Murf and the lads will sort him out.'

'Good,' said Connor. 'He can handle himself in the gym, can't he, Paul?'

'Yep. Nearly knocked Jake out last week, didn't he, lad?' he said as he gave Jake a playful shove.

Jake almost spat his food out of his mouth in his effort to respond. 'No, he fucking didn't. Knobhead.'

Grace smiled at their good-natured banter. She loved to see the three of them together. They were step-brothers now as a result of her marriage to Michael, but they acted more like blood brothers.

'What about the trouble you had with those lads from Birkenhead?' Grace asked. 'Did you sort it out?'

'Yeah. It was just a bunch of kids trying to chance their arm. They had no idea who they were robbing off,' Jake answered.

'They won't be doing it again, anyway,' Connor assured her.

'Nope.' Paul laughed and shook his head.

'The club's doing okay too?' Grace said. 'I noticed when I looked at the books.'

Jake nodded. 'Yep. It's holding its own. It pays everyone's wages.'

'Did you sort out that problem I mentioned, Grace?' Connor asked. 'I couldn't work out how to balance the incomings and outgoing last month with that extra money we got in.'

'Yes. The books are straight now. Everything looks above board,' she replied.

'Brilliant. Thanks.'

Grace watched as the boys tucked into their food. It wasn't long before the talk turned to football and their beloved clubs. Jake and Michael were staunch Evertonians while the twins were diehard Liverpool fans, and the clubs' legendary rivalry never failed to spark some lively debates. She half listened to their conversation while her mind wandered to Connor's earlier response to her question about the business. It was a subtle change in his demeanour that she doubted anyone else in the room had even registered. She hoped that it meant nothing, but her gut told her that it was something.

Grace was putting plates into the dishwasher when Connor came into the kitchen. He opened the fridge and took out four beers.

'Everything okay, Con?' Grace asked him.

'Yeah. Why?' he replied.

'You just look like there's something on your mind, that's all. You didn't seem as convinced as Jake and Paul that things were going well. I know you're the one who does most of the boring paperwork stuff. Is something up?'

Connor placed the bottles on the worktop. 'You know when you get that feeling something's just not right, Grace?' he asked. 'I can't put my finger on it, but I just feel like something's off.'

'Any idea what?'

Connor shook his head. 'No. On the surface, everything looks great. We're doing better than ever. It's just a gut feeling I have.'

'Have you spoken to the other two about it?' she asked.

'Yeah. They just think I'm being paranoid. Maybe I am. There's always gonna be someone out to take what's ours, isn't there? It just feels like a storm is coming.' He picked up the beers and started to laugh. 'God, I sound like fucking Mystic Meg, don't I? Don't tell them two I said anything. Any excuse to take the piss.'

Grace laughed. 'Your secret's safe with me.'

Connor was walking out of the door when he stopped and turned around. 'What do you think, Grace? You ever just get a feeling about something?'

'All the time.'

'And what do you do?'

'In my experience, Connor, you should always trust your gut.'

'Thought so,' he said with a sigh. 'You coming back in?'

'Yes. Just clearing up a bit. I'll be through in a minute.'

He disappeared through the doorway. Grace watched

him leave the kitchen and leaned against the breakfast bar. On paper, at least, the boys' business was doing better than ever. The Blue Rooms was thriving and from the money they were turning over on a monthly basis, all of their other businesses were too. But, much like Connor, she also had an uneasy feeling. Perhaps it was because things seemed to be going a little too well, and she never trusted that. The boys had plenty of enemies. It was a given in their line of work. But no one ever challenged them, at least not overtly, and that made Grace cautious. In her experience, when you were the head of the firm, there was always someone trying to take you down. If there was a rival faction trying to take over their turf, then they were doing it in secret, and that was always more worrying. After all, it was much easier to deal with your enemy when you knew who they were.

Chapter Five

Michael Carter leaned back in the leather chair in his office as one of his head doormen, Jack Murphy, or Murf, as he was more commonly known, sat opposite him relaying a tale about one of the new bouncers being caught shagging one of the barmaids in the disabled toilets the night before.

'It's not even like he was on his break, Boss. He was supposed to be watching the room.'

Murf had been a bouncer for over twenty years. He was a professional and he didn't take kindly to young upstarts taking the piss. Michael was usually slightly more forgiving, but he trusted Murf and allowed him to run his door the way he wanted to.

'So, what do you want to do about it?' Michael asked, while suppressing a smile. He could imagine Murf's face turning a violent shade of purple last night as he burst in on young Carl, with his pants around his ankles and a barmaid's legs wrapped around his waist. 'Was the barmaid on her break at least?'

Murf stared at him open-mouthed. 'What? I don't fucking know. What the fuck's that got to do with it?'

Michael couldn't hide his amusement any longer and burst out laughing.

'Oh, fuck off,' Murf said with a laugh. 'You had me going there.'

'You need to calm down, Murf. You'll give yourself a stroke.'

'It just pisses me off when these cheeky little pricks walk around like they're God's fucking gift. They don't understand that we're a team, Michael, and every single one of them has a part to play in making sure we all go home in one piece at the end of every night.'

'So? Are you giving him the boot?'

'Well, that's why I'm here. What do you think?'

'I assume you gave him a good kick up the arse last night and docked his pay?'

'I gave him more than a kick up the arse,' Murf replied.

Michael shrugged. 'Personally, I'd give him another chance and see if he learns his lesson. But it's your door, Murf. It's your call. It's you and the lads he'd be letting down if he fucked up when you needed him, not me.'

Murf shook his head and smiled. 'You're just a big softie, really, aren't ya, Boss?'

Before he could reply, Michael looked up to see Grace walking through the open office doorway.

'There's not many people who would have the balls to

call my husband a big softie, Murf,' she said good-naturedly as she gave his shoulder a gentle squeeze.

'Grace,' he said, standing up to hug her. 'I didn't know you were coming in.'

'Neither did I,' Michael said with a smile as he stood up too. She walked over to him and he put an arm around her waist. 'To what do I owe this pleasure?'

'Your dad and Sue wanted to take the kids for a few hours, so I thought I'd drop by and see what was going on,' she said with a shrug.

'Can't bear to be away from the place, eh, Grace?' Murf said.

'Nah. She can't bear to be away from me, that's all, can you, love?' Michael said with a wink, before giving her a kiss and offering her his seat.

Grace sat down at the desk. 'So what on earth has happened to make Murf think that you're a big softie then?'

Grace listened as Murf relayed the story of Carl the bouncer and the barmaid from the previous night and soon the three of them were laughing so hard, Murf almost fell off his chair.

'Oh, I do miss this,' Grace said when they regained their ability to speak. 'No one can tell a tale quite like you, Murf.'

'You know you can come back any time you like. Don't think I don't know you're always keeping an eye on me anyway,' Michael said with a smile.

'But Oscar—'

'Oscar would be fine. Try a day or two and see how you feel.'

'It would be great to have you back, Boss,' Murf added. 'Someone to keep this fella on his toes.' He nodded towards Michael.

'Maybe I'll think about it,' she replied. The truth was Grace was torn over her decision to return to work. As difficult as it was at times to be the one who always had to make the tough decisions, it was a role that she had made her own, and one that she had found harder to let go of than she'd expected. There was no escaping the fact that this was her world and she belonged here, but she was also a mum to two young children whom she adored and wanted to protect from all of the potential dangers in the world. She and Michael had chosen the lives they led, and they had acquired more enemies over the years than she cared to admit. There was no one better equipped to protect her children from harm than she was. But being back at the helm and keeping a watchful eye on Jake and the twins was good for all of their sakes. 'Maybe in a couple of weeks,' she added with a faint smile.

'Whenever you're ready, love,' Michael said and kissed the top of her head.

Murf was looking at them both with a smile on his face.

'What are you fucking grinning at?' Michael said to him.

'I'm just glad you two finally came to your senses and got together, that's all,' he said.

'And I'm the big softie? You soppy old bastard,' Michael said to him good-naturedly.

'You know me, I'm all heart really, Boss,' Murf said as he

stood up. 'I'll give that Carl kid one more chance then. If he fucks up again, he's had it.'

'Sounds like a plan,' Michael replied.

'I'll be off then. I need to sort the lads' wages. Leave you two lovebirds in peace.'

'It's nice to see you, Murf,' Grace said to him.

'It's nice to be seen,' he replied.

'Close the door on your way out,' Michael said.

Murf gave a mock bow as he walked out of the office and closed the door as instructed.

As soon as they were alone, Michael sat on the desk beside Grace and pulled her up into his arms. 'This is a *very* nice surprise,' he said as he brushed her hair behind her ear. 'I thought the most exciting part of my day today was going to be listening to Murf's sordid tales of bouncers and barmaids.'

'Well, I'm happy to be of assistance,' Grace whispered in his ear. 'Just what exactly were Carl and that barmaid caught doing again?'

'Murf already told you,' he replied with a smile. 'Weren't you paying attention?'

'Obviously not. I was too distracted by how good you look in that suit.'

'Well, maybe I should give you a practical demonstration?' he growled in her ear.

'Hmm, now there's an idea,' she replied with a grin as he took her face in his hands and kissed her.

Chapter Six

Half an hour later, Grace had said goodbye to Michael and was walking through the offices of Cartel Securities, looking for Murf. She found him in his usual spot in the break room, chatting to Edna the cleaner over a mug of coffee. They both looked up as she walked into the room.

'Hello, Grace, love,' Edna said as she approached her and pulled her into a warm hug. 'Murf mentioned you'd popped in. It's lovely to see you.'

Grace returned Edna's hug. 'Thanks, Edna. It's good to see you too. How's things?'

'Oh, I can't complain, girl,' she said with a grin. 'I'd better get on and finish cleaning this place though. I'm meeting our Marg in the Bingo at two. This fella would keep me gassing for hours.' She gave Murf a nudge in the ribs.

'Behave yourself. It's you can't stop your nattering, Ed,' he replied good-naturedly.

Edna giggled like a schoolgirl before fluttering her eyelashes and disappearing in a waft of Chanel N°5.

'You're such a bloody flirt, Murf,' Grace said with a smile.

'Me? It's all Edna,' he protested with a twinkle in his eye. 'I swear if she were twenty years younger, my Carol would have a fight on her hands.'

Grace sat down at the table opposite him.

'So, how's things been, Murf? Other than your bouncers getting caught with their pants round their ankles?'

'It's all good, Grace. Business is great. But, you already know that.' He eyed her suspiciously over the rim of his coffee mug as he took a swig.

Grace nodded. 'You've been working The Blue Rooms?'

'Yep. I always do.'

'Anything unusual happened there lately?'

'It's a nightclub. Unusual stuff happens there all the time. Are you thinking of anything in particular?' he replied with a frown.

'No. I've just got a feeling, that's all. Everything seems to be going a little too well, and you know that makes me twitchy.'

'I can understand that. But things are ticking along nicely, Boss. And there's been no bother at the club. Well, nothing out of the ordinary anyway.'

'Okay. But keep your eye out for anything fishy going on, would you?' she said as she stood up.

'Of course, Grace. Always,' Murf assured her.

'Thanks.'

Grace said her goodbyes for the second time and left the

office. As she climbed into her car, she couldn't shake the feeling that something wasn't quite right. Was it simply that she was such a stranger to happiness that she couldn't trust it to last? Or had her conversation with Connor the night before caused the growing uneasiness she was suddenly experiencing? No, she'd been feeling like this for a few weeks now, but she couldn't put her finger on what it was. An occasional shiver down the spine as though someone had walked over her grave, or a sudden sense of dread in the pit of her stomach, with no idea where it had come from. At first, she'd put it down to the tiredness of looking after a new-born and a toddler. But her chat with Connor had brought it the fore again. Perhaps she wasn't just tired? Or perhaps both she and Connor were paranoid for no reason?

Whatever the truth of it, her returning to work was now looking more imminent than she'd expected.

Chapter Seven

Connor Carter sat back in his seat and closed his eyes as his brother Paul drove the two of them home. They each had their own apartment on the same landing of a block on Liverpool's waterfront.

'What's the matter with you tonight, face-ache?' Paul asked him.

'Nothing. Why?'

'You've been moody for weeks, Con. I thought a pan of scouse at Grace and Dad's last night would snap you out of it.'

'I'm fine,' Connor said with a sigh.

'You're not. Is it this bird you've been seeing? Is she giving you grief? Coz if she is, bin her off, lad. She's fucking married anyway.'

Connor glared at his brother. 'It's nothing to do with Jazz.'

'So, there is something then?'

'Just fucking leave it, will you, Paul?'

'Con. It's me, Bro. You can tell me anything. And you usually do. What's up?'

They stopped at some traffic lights and Connor felt his twin brother's gaze burning into him.

'This had better not be about Isla. Is it?' Paul asked.

Connor glared at him. 'Course it's fucking not. Why would it be?' he snapped.

'All right. Keep your fucking hair on.'

'If you must know, I can't shake this feeling that something's about to go down. Something just feels off. I know you and Jake think it's fucking hilarious when I mention it, but I can feel it, Paul. Someone, somewhere, is fucking us over.'

'Well, if you think that, let's do some housekeeping then.'

'What?'

'It's about time we did the rounds and made sure everyone is doing what they're supposed to. Might as well start now. It's only half eight. Phone Jake and tell him to meet us at Eric's gym.'

After Connor had phoned Jake, he spent the rest of the drive looking out of the window. It was true he did have a bad feeling about something. Maybe it was all the sneaking around with Jazz? The guilt of seeing a married woman? Nope, definitely not that, he decided. He didn't feel an ounce of remorse or regret about his relationship with Jazz.

As much as he would never admit it to Paul, he had

been thinking about Isla a lot. His niece. The daughter of his best mate – Jake. At least that was what everyone thought. But shortly before Isla's conception, Connor had made an incredibly stupid mistake and screwed Jake's then girlfriend, Siobhan. She'd announced she was up the duff a few weeks later, and then Jake had married her shortly after. Connor had stood by and let it all play out, knowing there was every chance Siobhan's baby was his, but unable to say anything because of the huge fallout it would cause in his family. He'd watched one of his best mates marry a woman he didn't love because he thought it was the right thing to do. Connor had tried to forget about it all, and had convinced himself that the child was Jake's. He'd only been with Siobhan once – surely the odds were in Jake's favour.

Then Isla had been born and as soon as he'd seen her, Connor had been convinced that she was his own flesh and blood. He saw her every week at his dad and Grace's house, and each week he thought about how she was starting to look more and more like him. He wondered how nobody else had noticed the resemblance and lived in constant fear of someone picking up on it and asking awkward questions. He'd tried staying away for a few weeks, but everyone had given him so much grief about missing family Sunday dinners that he'd given up soon after. The guilt of that was what was eating away at him. He was sure it was only a matter of time before someone found out. There was no one he could talk to about it. The possibility that he might be Isla's father was a secret so explosive he could never let it out. Paul knew about his encounter with Siobhan – he and Connor told each other everything – but it wasn't a topic that was usually up for discussion. On the odd occasion Connor had brought it up, Paul had shut him down, probably because it made him feel disloyal to Jake, and Connor could understand that, so he'd stopped mentioning it altogether. But keeping it all to himself was killing him. The one person who would know exactly what to do, the one person, apart from his dad, whose advice he sought on almost everything, was Grace. And there wasn't a chance in hell he could ever risk her finding out.

Chapter Eight

'Come on, Jake, stop dicking about on your phone and get out here. It's fucking freezing,' Connor shouted from the garden of Nipper Jackson's semi-detached house in West Derby. 'You said this cunt would be in.'

Jake Conlon grinned as he put his phone into his coat pocket and slammed the car door shut. 'He is. Trust me. He's just not expecting a visit tonight, that's all. He'll have taken one look at your ugly mugs and barricaded himself in.'

'Well, it's definitely about time that we met the elusive Nipper then, isn't it?' Connor snapped as he shuffled his feet in the cold. 'Let's get in there and tell him to get the fucking kettle on.'

Jake laughed as he walked past Connor and Paul Carter. Using his fist, he banged loudly on the front door. 'Nipper. It's Jake,' he shouted. 'Let us in, it's fucking Baltic out here.'

A few seconds later, the sound of heavy bolts being drawn back signalled Nipper had heard Jake's request. He popped his head around the door and eyed the three of them warily. 'Sorry, Jake, I didn't know who it was,' he mumbled.

'Not a problem, Nipper,' Jake said as he pushed past him through the doorway and into the warm house.

Paul and Connor followed him inside while Nipper watched silently.

'Any chance of a brew, lad?' Jake asked.

'Yeah, we nearly froze our nuts off waiting for you to answer the fucking door,' Connor snapped.

'Sorry, lads,' Nipper said again. 'Course I'll make a brew. Come through.' He signalled for them to follow him through to the kitchen as he walked past them.

Nipper filled the kettle and put it on to boil. He looked at the three men sitting in his kitchen. He knew now that the two men he'd never seen before were the Carter twins, and they were as terrifying a sight as their reputation suggested. Nipper only usually dealt with Jake, although he'd been working for all three of them for the past three months. He was their counter – responsible for collecting, counting and distributing all of their considerable cash. They had it coming in from everywhere. Some days he could barely keep on top of it. But he did and he could account for every single penny. There wasn't a chance in hell he'd ever leave himself open to being accused of robbing from this lot.

Not that he needed to steal their money. They trusted him and they paid him well for his services. It was a role he'd fallen into when his brother, and predecessor, had been sent down for six years. Now Nipper lived in constant fear of having his own collar felt, and having to do a long stretch because he would never grass his employers up. At first he'd been terrified that the huge quantities of cash he often had in the house would make him a target for thieves, but he'd soon learned that there wasn't a man alive who would dare take anything from Jake Conlon or the Carters – not a sane one, at least.

'I wasn't expecting you tonight,' Nipper said as the kettle boiled behind him. 'Is anything wrong?'

'You tell us,' one of the twins snarled at him.

Nipper shook his head vigorously. 'Not that I know of. Everything's good from my end.'

'Take no notice of Connor.' The other twin, who Nipper now knew must be Paul, laughed. 'He's got a cob on because his bird has stood him up.'

'Fuck off,' Connor replied although Nipper sensed it was in good humour.

'My colleagues here thought it was about time they met you face to face,' Jake said. 'Paul and Connor Carter,' he said as he nodded towards the twins. 'And also because we need to make a significant withdrawal.'

'No problem. How much?' Nipper replied. They'd had their usual fifty grand each earlier that week, deposited at Jake's club, The Blue Rooms, as usual, and they didn't normally take extra. There was only so much money a man could spend without drawing too much attention.

'Half a mill,' Paul answered nonchalantly, as though he was talking in pennies.

'Not a problem. That will clear me out though, lads,' Nipper said.

'There'll be more coming tomorrow,' Jake said. 'Plenty of it.'

'We need you to count and parcel it up as soon as you get it,' Connor warned him. 'There's people need paying as soon as.'

Nipper resisted the urge to tell Connor he knew what he was doing. Instead he turned his attention to the kettle which had now switched itself off. He took three mugs from his kitchen cupboard and made his visitors a hot drink.

'I'll go and get your money while you finish those,' Nipper said as he left the three most terrifying men in Liverpool in his kitchen sipping tea while he went to his loft to retrieve half a million quid for them. He was just grateful his wife and kids were staying out for the night. His wife, Shirley, knew full well what he did, but he didn't think she'd take kindly to having her house invaded at ten o'clock on a Saturday night.

'I told you he was all right,' Jake said to the twins as they sat in Nipper's kitchen. 'Just over five hundred grand is exactly what he should have right now, and he's trotting upstairs to get it like the good little soldier he is. Why did you think he was having us off all of a sudden?'

Connor shrugged. 'Just a feeling. Something feels off, lads. And I can't put my finger on it.'

Jake shook his head. Now they were stuck with five hundred grand that they didn't need right now, which was going to have to be kept somewhere, and all because Connor had a feeling that Nipper, or someone, was ripping them off. Connor was becoming increasingly paranoid and suspicious. It seemed the better they did, the more edgy

Connor became, when for Jake it was the complete opposite. They were considered untouchable in Liverpool now. They had a loyal workforce who were paid well, enough of the filth in their pockets to ensure that none of those pricks ever bothered them, and more money than they could spend in two lifetimes. Life was good. It was time to start enjoying it a little. But Connor seemed to be becoming moodier by the week.

Chapter Nine

Paul threw the holdall into the back seat of Jake's car and climbed in next to it.

'Where are we gonna keep this little lot then?' he asked Jake and Connor as they got into the front seats.

Jake shook his head. 'I can't take it home. The wife will think it's a licence to go on another fucking spending spree. I keep telling her she needs to rein it in a bit, but that woman doesn't know the meaning of the word subtle.'

'We could leave it at the club?' Paul offered.

Jake shook his head. 'There's already a shitload in the club. I can't fit any more in the safe. It needs to go elsewhere.'

'Maybe you should get a bigger safe?' Connor suggested.

'Or maybe we should have just left it with Nipper,' Jake replied. 'You know, the guy we pay to take care of our cash?'

'Oh, fuck off,' Connor snapped at him, sensing the dig. 'I'll take it then.'

'Settled,' Paul said with a smile, trying to defuse the tension that had been lingering in the air all evening. 'Fancy a drink then, lads?'

'Can't.' Jake shook his head. 'It's Isla's birthday tomorrow. I was supposed to be home hours ago and I promised Siobhan I'd help with the balloons and all that.'

'Not for me either, I'm knackered,' Connor replied.

Paul sat back in his seat and sighed. 'You two are a right pair of fucking bores today.'

Jake laughed. 'It's my kid's first birthday, mate. What do you expect me to do?'

'I know,' Paul conceded.

'You two are coming tomorrow, aren't you?' Jake asked.

Paul rolled his eyes, but there was no way he would miss it. 'Course, mate,' he said.

'Con?' Jake nudged him with his arm.

'Yeah, course,' Connor said.

'Good. The party starts at one.' Jake said.

Paul watched his brother and his best mate carefully as they drove on in silence. Jake seemed happier than he'd been in a while. To the outside world, Jake seemed to have it all. He adored Isla and he and Siobhan were the perfect couple – on paper anyway, and Jake seemed to enjoy playing the role of the married man. Although Paul knew that the recent spring in Jake's step was nothing to do with Siobhan or Isla.

Jake pulled up outside Eric's gym where Connor had left his car earlier.

'You coming, Bro?' He turned to Paul in the back seat as he unfastened his seat belt.

'Nah. I'm going for a drink.' Paul smiled as he handed his brother the holdall full of cash.

'I'll drop him off in town,' Jake said.

'I'll see you tomorrow at the party then,' Connor said as he climbed out of the car and slammed the door.

'What's the matter with him?' Jake asked as he put the car into gear and pulled away from the kerb.

'Fuck knows,' Paul said with a shrug, feigning ignorance. The truth was, Connor obviously had something more on his mind than his belief that someone was ripping them off, and Paul was afraid he knew exactly what it was.

'Where do you want dropping?' Jake asked when they stopped at the traffic lights.

Paul leaned forward in his seat and placed his hand on Jake's shoulder. 'You're not really going straight home, are you?'

Jake sighed. 'I should. I promised Siobhan.'

'You don't have to stay out late,' he said. 'Just a few hours. You can sort the balloons and shit in the morning.'

Jake relented. 'Just an hour. Tops.'

'An hour's all I need, mate,' Paul replied with a grin.

Chapter Ten

J ake climbed out of bed and started picking his clothes up off the floor. Paul lay back with his arms above his head and a grin on his face as he admired Jake's naked body.

'Shit! It's fucking one o'clock,' Jake said as he pulled his jeans on. 'Siobhan's going to go fucking mental.'

'Tell her you were on a job,' Paul said dismissively.

'Just like that?' Jake snapped at him. 'I'm going to get earache for days for this.'

'Hey. It's not my fault you can't keep your dick in your pants, lad,' Paul said with a laugh.

Jake looked at him, lying in bed without a care in the world. No responsibilities. No ties to anyone or anything. He went around screwing who he liked, when he liked, without any thought for the consequences. But, to Jake, he was like a drug. No matter how hard he tried, he just couldn't stay away from him.

'It's all your fucking fault,' Jake said. 'I was going home until—'

'Until I dragged you here against your will?' Paul interrupted him. 'You could stay the night, you know?'

Jake shook his head. 'You know I can't.'

'Shame.' Paul grinned. 'I like waking up with a warm body next to me.'

'Yeah,' Jake said as he picked up his shirt. 'I bet you fucking do.'

Paul suppressed a grin. 'Don't tell me you're jealous, mate?'

'Fuck off!' Jake shot back.

'You're the one who's married,' Paul reminded him.

'Yeah I know,' he said as he finished buttoning his shirt. 'But you're the one who'll fuck anything with a pulse.'

'But I'd give 'em all up for you,' Paul said with a wink.

'Oh you would? Really?' Jake said, picking up a stray pillow and throwing it at him. 'Now stop taking the piss and let me get home before my missus sends out a search party for me.'

'Go on then,' Paul said with a wave of his hand. 'Get lost and let me watch *Venom* in peace. You'll only spoil the ending anyway.'

'We really need to stop doing this, Paul,' Jake said as he opened the bedroom door.

'Whatever you say, Jake,' he replied.

Paul lay in bed and flicked through the television channels

after Jake left. His mind raced and he couldn't focus on the film. He and Jake had been on and off for two years. When his dad and Grace had got married, they'd sworn they'd stay just friends. Being step-brothers just made the whole thing feel even more awkward and wrong. They'd stuck to their agreement too – for a while. But they'd been back on again for the past six weeks.

Paul didn't do relationships. He didn't like to be tied down to anyone. But like it or not, he was tied to Jake Conlon, and there wasn't a single thing he could do about it.

———

Jake Conlon climbed into his car and started the engine. It would be almost two o'clock by the time he got home. Siobhan was going to have his bollocks on a skewer. Not that he could blame her. As much as he always enjoyed his time with Paul, sometimes the guilt was overwhelming. Siobhan was a good woman. She was an amazing mum, and she deserved so much better than him.

Jake smiled as he thought about his daughter. Big brown eyes and beautiful dark curls. She had him wrapped around her little finger. He would do absolutely anything for her. He thought back to the night Siobhan had told him she was pregnant. He'd been planning to break things off with her, then she'd hit him with that bombshell. Less than a year later they were married in a massive do at Liverpool Town Hall – his mum had pulled some strings to get the venue at short notice. A shotgun wedding, his in-laws had affectionately called it. He'd never intended to marry Siobhan; he loved her, but not like a husband should. But she had given him a beautiful daughter, and for that he would always be grateful to her. He would always be there for her, even if it meant he had to keep so many secrets that it sometimes felt like his head would explode.

Now his daughter was about to turn one and Jake felt like he had been sleepwalking through the past twelve months of his life. To the outside world, he had it all. He was the happy, devoted family man with a beautiful wife and daughter. He and the Carter twins were at the top of their game. Money. Respect. Power. But the only time he felt like he was being the real him was when he was with Paul. He knew they could never be together. Not really. Not out in the open. But sometimes he wondered what it would be like if they could. He could still be a dad to Isla. His mum and Michael would get over the shock eventually. If he could just get out of his marriage, then maybe it could work?

Jake sighed as he put his foot down on the accelerator. It was a fucking ball-ache having to live two separate lives. There was no way out of his marriage. Siobhan wouldn't divorce him. She was a good Catholic girl from a traditional family. Besides, she loved spending his money too much.

Chapter Eleven

G race looked around the crowded kitchen of Jake and Siobhan's large detached house and smiled to herself. She had always dreamed of having a big family, but being an only child and losing both of her parents so young, as well as her marriage to Nathan Conlon, had put paid to such notions – or so she'd thought. Now, here she was, in the midst of all these people, children, grandchildren, grandparents, brothers and sisters, nieces and nephews, and she loved them all. She was finally a part of the family she'd longed for and it made her happier than she had ever dreamed possible.

'I think the milk monster needs a feed,' Michael said in her ear as he walked up behind her.

Turning around, she took their wriggling son Oscar from his arms. His cherubic little face was beginning to turn a familiar shade of puce and she knew they had mere seconds before he let the entire kitchen know how much he needed a feed – and loudly. 'Let's go and find somewhere nice and quiet then, my little man,' Grace said softly to him as she cuddled him to her. She left the kitchen and went upstairs to Isla's nursery, where she could nurse Oscar in the rocking chair, whispering to him all the way as he began to become increasingly agitated.

Sitting in her granddaughter's nursery, feeding her son, Grace looked around the room. She could hardly believe Isla was one year old today. How the time had flown. She'd been shocked to learn she was becoming a grandmother at the age of forty-two, but that had soon turned to excitement once Siobhan's bump had started to grow. While some women might resist any involvement from their mother-in-law, Siobhan had always encouraged it, inviting Grace along to some of her scans and ante-natal appointments. Grace had learned that Siobhan wasn't particularly close to her own mother, Theresa, and thought what a shame it was that Theresa had missed out on so much of Siobhan's pregnancy. When Siobhan and Jake had got married when Isla was just two months old, Grace had finally met Theresa and Siobhan's father Harry, and found them to be friendly enough, but they seemed to keep very much to themselves. They saw Isla once a month when Siobhan took her for a visit, but beyond that, they didn't seem to show much interest. Their loss, Grace thought. Siobhan was an incredible woman and Isla was quite simply adorable. With big brown eyes and dark curls, she looked so much like her aunty Belle. If Grace ever took the two girls out together, they were often mistaken for sisters.

Leaning back in the chair, Grace stared at the contented face of her son and felt a warm rush of love for him. She was so lucky to have her three children. All of them were incredible in their own way. All of them were healthy. And most importantly, all of them were happy. Grace had few memories of her own mum, who'd died when she was a toddler. When she'd fallen pregnant with Jake at the age of nineteen, she'd been terrified she wouldn't know what to do. That seemed so long ago now – a different lifetime. Smiling to herself, she supposed that she wasn't doing such a bad job after all.

Michael walked into the garden of Jake and Siobhan's house and found Connor sitting alone at the patio table.

'What are you doing out here on your own, Con? It's freezing.'

Connor shrugged. 'It was getting a bit noisy in there, that's all.'

'Well, it is a kids' birthday party.' Michael laughed but Connor didn't join in. 'What's going on with you lately? Is it this woman you're seeing?'

'How do you even know about her?' Connor said.

'Well, I didn't really. I suspected you had someone on the go though. You're permanently glued to your phone.'

'It's nothing to do with her anyway,' Connor replied defensively.

'Well what then? Has something happened between you and Jake?'

'No. Why?' Connor bristled.

'Because you seem especially on edge around him, that's why.'

'No, I don't,' Connor protested.

'You do. And look at you now. You're fidgeting like a crackhead waiting for his next fix. What the fuck is going on, Son?' Michael asked.

Connor hung his head and Michael wondered what the hell his son was hiding.

'You really don't want to know, Dad. Trust me,' Connor said as he stood up and started to walk away.

Michael grabbed him by the arm. 'There is nothing you can't tell me, Con. I'm your dad. Whatever it is, you can talk to me about it.'

'I'm warning you, Dad. This is something you really don't want to know. Because once I tell you, you can't un-know it, and it's going to put you in a fucking impossible position.'

'If it's anything to do with you, then I want to know. No matter what it is.'

Connor shook his head. 'No, Dad. Not this. I can't...'

'Connor. Please? You're starting to freak me out. What could possibly be so bad that you can't tell me?'

Connor stared at him then nodded. 'Okay then. Have you ever noticed how much Isla looks like Belle?'

'Yeah. So?'

'But Belle looks like you, doesn't she? Even Grace has said none of her kids look like her.'

Where the hell was Connor going with this? 'Yeah. So what? What the hell are you trying to tell me?'

'I think Isla is mine, Dad.' Connor swallowed.

'What?' he snapped. 'How?'

Connor shrugged. 'Siobhan and I... It was just before she got pregnant with Isla. The dates all fit.'

'Jesus Christ! What the fuck are you kids trying to do to me?' Michael said as he ran his hands through his hair.

'I warned you that you wouldn't want to know,' Connor said.

'Son'—Michael shook his head—'what the hell were you thinking? This is a fucking shit-storm waiting to happen. Does anyone else know?'

Connor shook his head. 'No. Well, only Paul. He knows that me and Siobhan were together anyway, but he doesn't know that I think Isla is mine. Look, Dad, no one ever needs to know. I just need to work this through in my head and then I can forget about it.'

'And you think this will all just magically go away then, do you? Michael said.

'It might. I just need to get through these next few weeks. I think Isla's birthday has stirred all of this shit up for me. I'll work it out and then everything can go back to normal,' Connor pleaded.

Michael started to pace up and down the garden. 'Between you and your brother, I'm surprised I'm not fucking hairless,' he sighed. 'Grace will bloody kill me if this ever comes out and she finds out I know.'

'I know that. I know I've put you in a difficult situation and I'm sorry, but you asked.'

'I know, Son.' He put an arm around Connor's shoulder

and gave him a hug. 'You're a fucking idiot, you know that, don't you?'

'I know, Dad,' Connor sighed against his shoulder.

Michael looked up at the house and saw Siobhan watching them from the kitchen window. He wondered if she suspected Isla was actually Connor's child, and a part of him hoped that it gave her sleepless nights. He wasn't a vindictive man by nature and he knew that it took two to tango, but it hurt him to see his son in such turmoil. Now that Connor had mentioned it, the resemblance between him and Isla was clear. How had nobody else seen it and asked questions? Because it was too bloody awful to even imagine, that was why. If it wasn't bad enough that Paul and Jake had once had a thing for each other, now this. Connor had been right about putting him in an impossible position. There was no way he could tell Grace about this, but keeping something so big from her was unthinkable.

Connor straightened himself up. 'We'd better get back inside before someone misses us, or sees us hugging in the garden,' he said with a faint smile.

Michael nodded. 'Let's go.' They headed up the steps to the back door and Michael wondered how on earth he was going to keep this monster of a secret from his wife. His wife whom he'd promised he would never keep secrets from. His wife who was one of the smartest people he had ever met, and who knew him better than anyone. If he told her, she would have to tell Jake. Then she would be compelled by her innate need to protect her family and drive herself crazy trying to fix everything for everyone. But she couldn't fix this, and it would break her. Her loyalty would be torn, just as Michael's was right now, and he couldn't bear to do it to her.

As he walked back into the kitchen and saw her waiting for him, with a smile on her face, and their son in her arms, he knew in his heart that one day she would find out, and she might never forgive him.

Chapter Twelve

Grace smiled as she looked at her sleeping children on the back seat of the car. Turning in her seat, she switched the radio to Smooth FM and sang along to Phyllis Nelson's "Move Closer" as Michael drove them home.

'Are you okay?' she asked Michael when the song had finished.

He turned his head to look at her and gave a weak smile. 'I'm fine. Why?'

'You just seem a bit quiet. And you didn't sing the chorus with me,' she said with a laugh.

'I enjoyed listening to you sing. I didn't want to spoil it with my tone-deaf wailing.'

'I love your tone-deaf wailing,' she replied.

He took her hand in his and raised it to his lips, kissing her fingertips. 'I'm good,' he assured her.

'It was a nice party,' Grace said. 'Isla seemed to enjoy herself anyway.'

'Yeah. And Belle.'

'I love it when the whole family gets together,' Grace said with a contented sigh.

They sat in silence for a few minutes, listening to the radio, before Grace spoke again. 'Do you think Connor is seeing someone?'

'He's always seeing someone.'

'I mean someone special?'

'What makes you think that?'

'He kept checking his phone every ten minutes, and then when it finally rang, he slipped off outside with a strange look on his face.'

'Could have been anything,' Michael replied with a shrug.

'Looked like the face of a man in love to me,' she said. 'Or at least in lust.'

'Probably the latter knowing Connor.'

'Hmm. I'm usually right about these things.'

Michael turned to her. 'You're usually right about most things.'

They stopped at some traffic lights and Grace watched her husband, his eyes fixed on the road ahead. He ran a hand through his hair and sighed.

'Are you sure everything's okay?' Grace asked him again.

He smiled at her. 'Yeah. I'm just tired. I want to get home.'

'Okay,' she said. But she didn't quite believe him. There was something on his mind and for some reason he wasn't telling her what it was. That was so unlike him. They didn't keep secrets from each other – not any more, at least. It had been one of the conditions she'd told him was a deal-breaker when she'd accepted his marriage proposal. They'd only been seeing each other for a few months, but given their history, it had felt like a lifetime. So, when he'd dropped down on one knee one night after dinner, and presented her with his mother's engagement ring, Grace had said yes, on the condition that they were always completely honest with one another.

After Nathan, she had promised herself she would never get married again. She didn't want to be tied to another person, or depend on them for her happiness. Her first marriage had been a daily battle of survival, and she never wanted to go there again.

But then Michael Carter had changed all of that. He was a man worth breaking her rule for. Even when she'd first met Nathan, and he'd been charming and romantic and promised her the world, there had always been an edge to him. Grace had never felt entirely herself in his company, as though she always had to be on her best behaviour. It was something she found hard to describe, but even before the first time he'd hit her, there would be times he'd come home and be in the kind of mood that would make the hairs on the back of her neck stand up. Michael was bigger and taller than Nathan had been, and Grace had no doubts about the level of violence he was capable of, particularly after her kidnapping almost two years earlier. But, despite all of the years she had known him, all of the arguments and disagreements they'd had, as friends, co-workers and lovers, she had never once felt uneasy around him. Even when he found out that she had been lying to him about his not being Belle's father, and had gone mental, she had never felt threatened by him. Instead, he made her feel safe, and whilst that had taken some time to get used to, it was a feeling that she treasured.

'Why are you staring at me with a grin on your face?' Michael said to her.

'I was thinking of the night you proposed to me,' she replied.

That seemed to snap him out of his sombre mood and he looked at her with a genuine smile on his face this time. 'I honestly thought you were going to say no.'

'Then why did you ask me?' she said with a laugh.

'Well, if you remember, I'd plied you with wine first, which does make you a bit giddy. And then I thought, fuck it, life's too short,' he said with a flash of his eyebrows.

'I love you, you know?' she said, conscious that she didn't say it enough to him, whereas he told her almost every day.

'I know,' he said softly. 'I love you, too.'

Grace sat back in her seat. Maybe he was just tired. Maybe her suspicion was brought on by the wonderful day they'd had and the fact that she still couldn't trust that happiness lasted. Perhaps, this time, it would.

Chapter Thirteen

Carrying a sleeping Oscar in his car seat on her arm, Grace climbed the rickety wooden steps to Nudge Richards' Portakabin. Nudge was an old friend. He didn't have many friends himself, on account of his job as the best fence in Merseyside (he'd discovered it wasn't good for business to show favouritism), and also because he was a huge, hairy gorilla of a man, with questionable hygiene at times, and he didn't attract people easily. There was something about him though that Grace had always liked. He had a good sense of humour, he was discreet and he was fiercely loyal. Grace had helped him out of a situation years earlier which had prevented him losing everything, including quite possibly his head, and he had never forgotten it. He'd remained loyal to her ever since, and whilst he was usually a model of discretion, he also knew everything and everyone, and he bent his rules for Grace and her alone.

Grace pushed open the creaky door and peered inside.

'You in, Nudge?' she asked. He was expecting her but she still proceeded with caution. As well as being a bit of a gambler, Nudge also had a penchant for women – the cheaper and looser the better. Once before, Grace had visited him and found him and his lady-friend in a very compromising position. She'd felt the need to bleach her eyeballs afterwards.

'Grace,' she heard him bellow from the other side of the room, as he walked towards her, kettle in hand. 'I was just putting a brew on.'

Grace smiled before holding a finger to her lips and nodded towards Oscar, who was still fast asleep.

'Oh, sorry, love,' Nudge said quietly. 'Want one? I've washed the cups.' He laughed. It was a standing joke between them that she'd only accept a drink from him if he scrubbed the cup first. He owned a scrapyard and didn't see why his office shouldn't replicate the rest of his yard. But for Grace, he made an exception.

'Yeah, go on. I'm parched,' Grace said as she placed Oscar's car seat on the desk and sat on the chair.

Nudge finished making the tea before placing the two mugs on his desk. He peered inside Oscar's car seat. 'He isn't half coming on. Spit of his dad, isn't he?'

'Yep,' Grace replied with a nod. 'I didn't get a look-in with any of them, did I?'

'Oh, I don't know. I see more of you in Belle as she gets older. And where is the lovely Belle today?' Nudge asked as he took a seat opposite her.

'Nursery. Only two days a week. She started two weeks ago. I thought it was probably best to get her used to going before she has to start school next year. I was worried she wouldn't settle, but she loves it. Comes home telling me all about the fun she's been having all day. Probably much more exciting than sitting at home with me, eh?'

'Ah. It'll do her good, no doubt,' Nudge replied.

'So? Anything interesting happening?' Grace asked as she picked up her mug and blew on the steaming tea to cool it.

'Not much, to be honest, Grace. All's quiet on the Western Front. Seems Jake and the twins have got everything sewn up and running smoothly.'

'For now,' Grace said before taking a sip of her tea.

'Forever the optimist?' Nudge said with a laugh.

'Well, you know as well as I do that things never stay the same for long round here. It seems the better you're doing, the more people want to take it from you.'

Nudge nodded. 'I suppose you're right there. You can never take your eye off the ball, and you, my dear, never do. Aren't you supposed to be on maternity leave?'

'I am! This is a social call,' Grace replied, even though that wasn't entirely true. While she was visiting Nudge for a catch-up, she could never switch off entirely from her previous responsibilities as head of the firm. Because of that, she liked to keep herself apprised of any developments she might need to know about, and Nudge always seemed to have the lowdown on the comings and goings of the Liverpool underworld.

'Oh, well in that case, I'm honoured,' Nudge replied with a laugh. 'I hope those lads appreciate you always looking out for them, Grace.'

'I don't do it for the appreciation, Nudge. Besides, I wouldn't say it's keeping an eye out for them. They're big boys, they can handle themselves. I just like to keep my ear to the ground, that's all.'

'Well, I'm happy to keep my ear to the ground for you. I enjoy our little chats.'

'Me too,' Grace said with a smile.

Nudge took a big gulp of tea. 'I suppose you heard those Johnson brothers are out in a couple of weeks though?' he said as he wiped his mouth with the back of his hand.

'I hadn't heard, no. I forgot they were inside, to be honest. They got a hefty sentence, didn't they?'

'Yeah. Craig and Ged did anyway. Eight years each. Billy did five, while Bradley got off scot free.'

Grace nodded. The Johnson brothers could have been big players if they had only been a little smarter and not blindly followed their eldest brother, Bradley, who was as stupid as he was dodgy. Craig and Billy actually had something about them, but the two eldest, Bradley and Ged, were walking egos who seemed too self-obsessed and arrogant to see the bigger picture and consider that their younger brothers could actually lead them and therefore make any real money. 'Yeah, I remember that,' Grace replied. 'I always thought that was a bit suspect, to be honest. He was in the thick of it, and he walked away without even a slap on the wrist.'

'Seemed a bit fishy to me too,' said Nudge. 'I bet he was a grass.'

'Against his own brothers though?' Grace said with a shake of her head. 'That's low.'

'Not for Bradley Johnson,' Nudge snorted. 'He's a horrible little fucker. He'd sell his kids for the right price. You know I love a little flutter, Grace, but this fella's something else. Would bet on an egg and spoon race if he could. He's a fucking sore loser as well. Mean bastard when he wants to be. You'd think he'd have gotten used to losing by now, he does it so often.'

'I didn't realise he was a gambler. I always wondered why him and his wife never seemed to have a pot to piss in. I assumed he was being careful so he wouldn't get nicked. I thought he must have had at least some of the money that went missing from the job his brothers went down for?'

'Nope. It's because he goes through money like the clap in a whorehouse. And as for the money from that job, I reckon Sol got it all, otherwise, why would Bradley still be breathing?'

Grace had forgotten it was Sol's job. The Johnson brothers had never worked in Merseyside since they'd tried to muscle in on her business years earlier. No doubt assuming they could because she was a woman. Michael had dealt with them for her, and whatever he had done, had ensured she never heard from any of them again. Grace had worked with Solomon Shepherd too, back in the day. For a long time, he and Grace had had an arrangement that had been beneficial for both of them. Sol was now the top dog in Manchester and any business connection Grace had with him had been severed when she'd moved to Leeds before Belle was born. Sol had been the instigator of her coming back to Liverpool. He was the one who'd told her that Jake was in trouble, and he'd seemed to expect some sort of recognition or reward for that, but Grace had stayed well away from him, and had warned Jake and the twins to do the same. Sol was into absolutely everything now – things that she would never allow herself or any of her family to become involved in.

'You're right. There's no way Sol would have let him off with that. So, Bradley's penniless then?'

'Yep. He spends it twice as fast as he can earn it.'

'Good to know, Nudge,' Grace said with a grin. 'You really are a mine of information.'

Nudge smiled appreciatively. 'Well, I'm glad to be of service, Boss. Fancy another?' he said as he held up his empty mug.

Grace glanced at Oscar, who was still fast asleep, and probably would be for another half hour at least. As much as she enjoyed chatting to Nudge, she couldn't chance having to feed her son in Nudge's grotty Portakabin, and with Nudge looking on – pretending not to look, but being unable to anyway. She enjoyed a strictly platonic relationship with Nudge, and would rather keep it that way.

'I'm sorry, I can't. This little milk machine will wake up for a feed soon, so I'd better get home. I'll pop in one day next week though. I'll leave the baby with Michael so we can have a proper catch-up.'

'Sounds good to me. I'll see you next week,' Nudge said as he stood up to show Grace out.

'See you, Nudge. Thanks for the brew,' Grace said as she gave him a hug.

'My pleasure. And give Michael and the boys my best, won't you?'

'Of course.'

Grace gave little thought to the Johnson brothers as she drove home. They had never really been on her radar and the fact that two of them were getting out of prison shortly was of little consequence to her. Hopefully they would remain out of her and her family's way, as they always had done. She couldn't help wonder again about her conversation with Connor earlier that week, though, and the uneasiness he'd described. It was a feeling she was all too familiar with. Things had been going too well for too long, and in Grace's experience, it was only a matter of time before something happened to change that.

Chapter Fourteen

Jake looked up as Paul and Connor came bounding through into his office at The Blue Rooms.

'How did it go, lads?' he asked.

Paul grinned and sat on the chair opposite Jake. 'Go on, tell him, Con.'

'It was fine. It's all sorted,' he replied with a groan.

Paul started to laugh as Connor sat on the leather sofa in the corner of the room.

'Then what's up with Chuckles here?' Jake said, indicating Paul.

Connor glared at his brother but Paul didn't heed the warning.

'We saw Kenny the Melon,' Paul said, stifling his laughter. 'We had a word with him. Slapped him around a bit. He didn't have a clue what he was doing or who we were, so we were just going to mess with him a bit, you know, pretend we were going to pull his teeth out or something. But then...' At this point, Paul burst into a fit of laughter.

'It's not even fucking funny, Paul,' Connor barked.

Jake, who was smiling at this point, urged Paul to go on and finish the story.

It took Paul a while to compose himself before he could finally speak. 'But then he shat on Connor,' he snorted before literally doubling over with laughter as tears streamed down his face.

Jake stared at them both. 'What? How did that even happen?' he asked through his own laughter.

'He didn't exactly shit on me,' Connor snapped. 'He shit *himself* when we told him we were going to cut him up and throw him in the Mersey. He was wearing these baggy fucking shorts, so some of it went on my shoe. That's all. He didn't shit on me!'

Jake looked down at Connor's shoes.

'I fucking threw them away! And my keks too. Dirty bastard!' he snapped.

'Where is he now then?' Jake asked.

'We left him there in the street, covered in his own shit,' Connor replied.

'That's hilarious, Con,' Jake said as he started to laugh harder. 'You'd better hope word doesn't get out that the quickest way to take out the Carter twins is to shit on them.' This caused Paul to become hysterical again and soon Paul and Jake could barely speak for laughing.

'You're a pair of fucking clowns,' Connor said, although Jake could see the hint of a smile on his lips. There was something about Paul's laughter, in particular, that was infectious.

It took a good ten minutes for Paul and Jake to stop laughing entirely and when they did Connor spoke again.

'In all seriousness, while I'm not bothered about Kenny or them lads we caught the other night, I am bothered that someone knew where our stuff was and blabbed about it. Whoever this mysterious fella in the pub was, he basically goaded them into nicking our gear. Do you think we have a leak?'

Jake shook his head. 'Nah. More likely someone who works on the docks saw our container and the fact that it was set aside, assumed it was full of weed because it's come from the Dam, and blabbed to some young lads in the pub to give himself a bit of kudos.'

'Yeah. That's more likely,' Paul agreed. 'If he'd known anything about our operation, he'd have known what was really in that container.'

'I think it was a case of wrong place, wrong time,' Jake said.

'I still think we should check out how our Wirral business is doing,' Connor suggested. 'It wouldn't hurt to pay Stu Poynter a visit, would it?'

'No, I suppose not,' Paul said.

'If you insist,' Jake replied. 'It would give me a chance to meet Stu anyway.' Stu was responsible for ensuring their operations in Wirral ran smoothly, which included keeping all of their dealers in line, as well as handling any possible takeovers. It was a job that they paid him, and the small army he recruited to assist him, handsomely for, and one that he'd always done well. Nevertheless, it was always good to remind their employees who was really pulling the strings.

'Tomorrow then?' Connor suggested.

Jake and Paul nodded.

'I'll give him a ring then and let him know we'll be round,' Paul said.

Chapter Fifteen

'Stu? Are you in, lad?' Paul Carter shouted up the stairs of Stu Poynter's open-plan house in Heswall as he let himself through the unlocked door.

'Yeah. Come up,' was the reply.

Jake watched as Paul jogged up the stairs and frowned. There was something about the way that he did it, as though he'd ran up and down them many times before. Connor sat down on the sofa and stretched out his legs. Jake followed suit and sat on the armchair, keeping an eye on the stairs for Paul and Stu's return. A few moments later the two of them came bouncing down the stairs laughing.

'What's so funny?' Jake asked.

Stu shook his head. 'If I told you, I'd have to kill you.'

Jake scowled at him. 'What the fuck did you just say to me, you little cunt?'

Stu looked at Jake in surprise as Paul replied for him. 'Calm down, Jake. He's just messing.'

'We were just laughing about something that happened years ago,' Stu said apologetically. 'It's not even that funny.'

Paul frowned at Jake as he sat next to Connor on the sofa.

'So, how are things up here in sunny Wirral going then?' Connor asked. 'Everyone behaving themselves?'

'Yep.' Stu perched on the arm of the sofa. 'It's going well. We've had no bother from anyone for a while. Business is good,' he said as he lit himself a joint. He took a long drag before handing it to Paul. 'Want some?'

'No, thanks,' Paul said.

Stu shrugged, but didn't offer the joint to anyone else, which only annoyed Jake further. Not that he'd have taken it, but that wasn't the point.

'In fact, we could probably shift more, if you've got it?' Stu said.

'Sound. We'll make sure there's some extra in this week's drop then?' Connor said.

They made some small talk before Jake suggested it was time to leave. As they reached Stu's garden gate, he shouted after them. 'Paul. Have you got a minute?'

'I'll just be a sec,' Paul said to Jake and Connor before walking back to Stu's front door. Jake watched the two men chatting and laughing for a minute before Stu handed Paul a small package. Paul put it in his pocket and jogged back to the car with a smile on his face. He climbed into the back seat and Connor started the engine.

'What was that about?' Jake asked.

'He gave me a bag of some of our finest quality weed.

The lads have just harvested a fresh crop, so he thought we might want to sample the merchandise.'

'Is that all?'

'And he wanted to know if I fancied going to a party later.'

'And do you?' Jake said as he felt the anger bubbling beneath his skin.

'Not that it's any of your fucking business, Susan, but no, I don't,' Paul snapped.

'Oh, will you two give it a fucking rest,' Connor shouted at them before turning up the radio to such a volume that any further conversation was cut dead.

The atmosphere in the car on the journey back was tense, and in the time it took to reach The Blue Rooms the three men barely said a word to each other. It wasn't until they were in the privacy of Jake's office that Jake spoke.

'Are you fucking around with Stu?' he snapped at Paul.

'What the hell?' Paul replied.

'Oh, for fuck's sake!' Connor mumbled.

'I asked you if you're fucking Stu?' Jake shouted.

'No, I'm not,' Paul replied.

'But you want to?'

'Fuck off!'

'Jesus Christ. Will you two get a fucking grip!' Connor shouted. 'I don't have the sodding energy for this. Sort out your screwed-up love lives in your own time, and preferably out of my earshot. Because in case you hadn't noticed, we are trying to run a business here.'

'Don't fucking tell me. It's him.' Paul pointed at Jake.

'Me? You're the one fucking one of our dealers.'

'What did I just fucking say?' Connor snarled. 'Will you two pack it in? I'm going to get a drink. And when I come back in here can you two have sorted yourselves out? You pair of fucking tarts.' He shook his head as he left the office.

Jake sat on the chair behind his desk and Paul opposite him. They sat in stony silence for a few minutes until Paul finally spoke.

'There's nothing going on between me and Stu, you know. He's not even gay.'

Jake stared at him but didn't respond.

'I've known him for years, that's all. I don't see much of him but we have a laugh together. That's all. I did bang his ma once though,' he said with a grin.

'His ma?'

'Yep. I was only sixteen. But she was a right goer. My dad went mental at her when he found out,' he said with a laugh.

'You're a fucking slag,' Jake replied, smiling.

'And proud of it. Anyway, as funny as it is to see you getting all jealous and hot under the collar about me and Stu, what's going on with you? Between you and Connor, you're a right pair of moody gits lately.'

'Just the usual,' Jake said with a sigh. 'Siobhan's been giving me grief about staying out late the other night. I can't fucking stand living like this, mate. It's fucking exhausting.'

'Then leave her.'

'Just like that?'

'Yes! People get divorced all the fucking time, Jake. You're in a mess of your own making. You know that as well as I do. And only you can get yourself out of it.'

Jake stared at him. 'Everything's just so fucking easy for you, isn't it? Just leave her. You haven't got a clue what it's like to be married or have kids.'

Paul sighed. 'I fucking give up with you, Jake. I don't know what you want me to say then. If you're not gonna leave her then fucking suck it up.'

Jake stared at him. Paul was right, but he wouldn't admit it. Sooner or later though, something had to give. Living this double life was taking its toll on him in more ways than one. He was finding it increasingly difficult to keep Siobhan happy while also lying to her almost every day. He'd felt it more acutely since he'd started up with Paul again and knew that any happiness he found with Paul was coming at great cost to his wife and child, and this only exacerbated his feelings of guilt. But he couldn't divorce Siobhan. He had an image to maintain. To the outside world he was a happy family man with a gorgeous wife and a beautiful daughter, and he couldn't lose that. It offered him the perfect smokescreen for who he really was, and it gave him the perfect excuse to turn down the constant stream of women who threw themselves at him.

'You coming to mine when we're done here?' Paul said to him, his voice softer now.

'Yeah,' Jake replied. Despite everything he'd just said, he couldn't say no.

Chapter Sixteen

P aul walked into the living room of his flat, with Connor close behind him, and threw the bag of weed onto the coffee table before taking off his jacket and throwing it onto the armchair. Connor put down the large takeaway pizzas he was carrying, kicked off his shoes and sat on the sofa.

'Beer?' Paul asked him.

'Yeah. Where are the Rizlas?'

Paul nodded towards his jacket. 'In my pocket. If you're building a joint, make sure you put enough of the good stuff in. It's not like we haven't got enough to go round, is it? Stu gave us a bag full.'

'You fucking build one then, you ungrateful bastard,' Connor said with a smile.

A few moments later, Paul returned to the living room with two bottles of Budweiser, placing them on the coffee table as he sat on the armchair opposite his brother.

'So what were you and the arl fella talking about the other day then?' Paul asked as he rolled himself a joint.

'When?' Connor replied with a frown as he tucked into a slice of meat feast pizza.

'At Isla's party?'

'I can't fucking remember. It was days ago, lad. Why?'

Paul shrugged. 'Looked like you were getting all emotional sitting out there in the garden.'

'Aww, feeling left out, were you, Bro?' Connor said as he started to laugh.

'Fuck off, you knob!' Paul said as he picked up a slice of pizza from the open box in front of him and threw it at Connor.

Connor ducked and the pizza landed behind the sofa. 'We were just talking about Isla being one. Him marrying Grace and becoming a grandad and all that shit.' Connor shrugged.

'Him being a grandad?'

'Yeah.'

'Did you happen to mention that you think he'd be Isla's grandad even if he hadn't married Grace?'

Connor stopped eating his pizza and glared at his brother. 'You always tell me to shut up when I mention Isla. So why the fuck would you bring it up now when Jake will be here in a minute?'

'I'm bringing it up because you've been walking around with a face like a slapped arse for the past few weeks, mate. And, other than that married bird you've been knocking off, I can't think of anything else that might be bothering you.

So, which is it? The bird or the fact you think you might be Isla's dad?'

'Just leave it alone, Paul.'

'Did you tell him?'

'Tell who?'

'Tell our dad what you fucking did?' Paul snapped.

Connor nodded.

'Oh, nice one, Con. You've proper landed him in the shit there,' Paul said. Selfishly, his most pressing concern was that Jake was one step closer to finding out the truth, and the impact that would have on their relationship. Paul wasn't sure if Jake would ever forgive him, and the thought of that made his chest physically hurt.

'He knew something was wrong, Paul. What was I supposed to do?' Connor replied.

'Erm, you lie. Like us normal people do.'

'I've never been able to keep stuff from him. You know that. It's like he knows what we're thinking or something.'

Paul shook his head as he lit the end of his joint. 'What if he tells Grace, and she tells Jake? Do you have any idea what you've done? You've launched a hand grenade right into the middle of our family. You're a fucking idiot, Bro. You need to let this Isla thing go. She's Jake's kid. Go and have some kids of your own to fuck up.'

After Paul took a long drag, he passed the joint to Connor. Taking it from him, Connor started to laugh. 'You've got a fucking cheek calling me an idiot when you're still fucking around with Jake.'

'Yep, I know,' he said as he blew out a long stream of smoke. 'We're a pair of lost causes, mate.'

'Good job we've got each other then.'

A knock at the door put an abrupt end to their conversation. 'That'll be Jake,' Paul said as he stood up.

'Yeah, so no more deep and meaningful stuff, eh, you big fairy?'

Paul stuck two fingers up at him as he headed for the front door.

Chapter Seventeen

Paul stretched his arms above his head and yawned. Looking at the clock he saw it was only just after midnight, but weed always made him tired.

'I am absolutely fucked, lads.' He said to Connor and Jake, who were looking equally worse for wear on his couch.

'Yeah. It's been a long day.' Connor nodded, sleepily. The copious amount of weed they'd all smoked that evening had made them more relaxed than usual.

'I'm getting off,' Connor said as he stood up and almost stumbled over.

Paul laughed. 'You're fucking wasted, Con. Good job you only live down the hall.'

'I know,' Connor giggled and soon the twins were doubled over with laughter, each of them almost unable to breathe.

Jake smiled at them but didn't join in with the laughter.

Weed usually made him feel thoughtful and melancholy, whereas it turned the twins into a pair of laughing clowns.

'Right, I'm off. Night, lads,' Connor said when he'd finally regained his senses.

'Night, Bro,' Paul said.

'Night, mate,' Jake added.

Once Connor had left, Paul and Jake sat in silence for a moment. Paul took a swig of beer and was about to turn off the television when Jake spoke.

'I can't do this any more, Paul,' he said.

'Do what, mate?' Paul said with a frown. 'Get stoned?'

'Don't be fucking soft,' Jake snapped, seemingly annoyed that Paul couldn't read his mind. 'Do this. Live this double life. Keep seeing you and be married to Siobhan.'

'So, what are you going to do then?'

'I should leave her, shouldn't I?' Jake said.

Suddenly, Paul felt much more sober. 'Well, only you can decide that, mate.'

'I think I have to. I just can't do it any more.' Jake's eyes filled with tears.

'Fucking hell, Jake,' Paul said as he shook his head. 'Are you sure?'

'One hundred per cent. I can't keep lying to her, Paul. I can't keep lying to myself. Most nights I dread going home. If it wasn't for Isla, I wouldn't. And then when I get home, Siobhan's there waiting for me. Waiting for something that I can't give her. It's fucking exhausting. And it's killing me.'

'Well, I wasn't expecting you to say that, mate,' Paul said as he ran a hand through his hair.

'I'm not expecting anything from you,' Jake said defensively.

Paul stood up and crossed the room to sit next to Jake on the couch. 'I never said you were, lad. But are you really sure you want to do this? Once you tell her, there's no going back.'

Jake shrugged. 'I don't even know if I can. Maybe it's the weed talking?'

'Why don't you sleep on it and decide what to do in the morning?'

'Yeah. Sounds like a plan. I'll go home in the morning when my head's a bit clearer.'

'Are you going to stay the night then?' Paul asked.

'Yeah.'

Paul didn't say anything further, but instead took Jake's hand and pulled him up from the couch before heading to the bedroom.

Jake opened the front door of his house and prayed that Siobhan and Isla were still asleep. It wasn't quite seven o'clock, which was when they usually got up. He could sneak into the living room and pretend he'd slept on the couch.

Stepping into the house, he heard Isla's laughter and groaned inwardly. He tiptoed down the hallway but it was too late: just as he reached the stairs, Isla and Siobhan came out of the kitchen, Siobhan carrying two bowls of cereal, and Isla her favourite teddy bear.

'Jake!' Siobhan said sharply, but not so much that it would startle Isla. 'Where have you been?'

'I had too much to drink and stayed at Paul's, babe,' he said sheepishly. Although he'd decided that he needed to leave Siobhan, he didn't know when, or indeed if, he'd muster the courage to do it. He'd talked it over with Paul before he left and decided it was something that he'd have to build himself up for. He might give it a few weeks and see if he was ready to tell her. But not today.

'Paul's?' Siobhan snapped at him.

'Yeah. I slept on his couch,' he found himself saying, adding to his statement unnecessarily. Because in his mind, as far as Siobhan was concerned, where else would he have slept?

'Toons, Daddy,' Isla squealed, interrupting them both, as she held her arms out for Jake to pick her up. He responded to her request, picking her up and cuddling her to him, relieved to have her between him and Siobhan's icy stare.

'Toons, Daddy!' she said again, reminding him that she wanted to watch the cartoons.

'Okay. Okay.' He laughed as he gave her a kiss on the cheek. 'Cartoons for my Isla,' then he turned from Siobhan and walked away, chatting to Isla and making her giggle with delight, while Siobhan followed dutifully behind.

Chapter Eighteen

Siobhan was just getting out of the bath when she heard the vibration of her mobile phone on her dressing table. Wrapping a towel around herself, she walked into the bedroom to answer it. As she glanced at the screen she saw a number she didn't recognise, but answered anyway in case it was Jake, who occasionally used a burner phone.

'Hello?' Siobhan said.

'Siobhan! I'm so glad you've kept the same number,' a familiar female voice replied.

'Jenny? Is that you?' Siobhan asked as a smile started to spread across her face. 'It's so lovely to hear from you.'

Jenny Lyon had been one of Siobhan's best friends all through high school and college. After college she'd gone to New York to work in her uncle's law firm. The two women had kept in touch for a while, then life had got in the way and they hadn't spoken for over a year, since before Isla was born.

'How is married life? How is your baby girl? I saw some photos of her on Instagram. She's beautiful,' Jenny said.

'Married life is great,' Siobhan lied. 'And Isla is amazing. But tell me about you. Are you still living it up in New York?'

'No, I'm home. I came back last week. New York was amazing, but I missed Liverpool too much. I'm a home bird at heart, I suppose, and I don't think I'm cut out for being a paralegal if I'm honest.'

'Oh, wow! I can't believe you're back,' Siobhan said as she sat down on the bed.

'Well, I definitely am,' Jenny said with a laugh. 'And I've really missed you, Vaunie. I'm so sorry I was crap at keeping in touch, but the working hours over there were crazy.'

'Don't worry about it. I missed you too,' she replied as she swallowed the lump in her throat.

'How about meeting up soon then? It would be good to see Jake too, and meet that gorgeous daughter of yours.'

'Yes, that would be lovely. Although Jake's super busy. Maybe we could go out, just the two of us? Have some cocktails.'

'Ooh, drinks and dancing. That sounds like a much better idea,' Jenny giggled. 'When and where?'

'I'll need to sort a babysitter, and check with Jake. But soon. Very soon.'

'Sounds like a plan then. Oh, it's so good to hear your voice, Vaunie,' she replied. 'Look, I'll have to run, Mum and Dad are taking me out for a Chinese. But we'll speak soon, okay? Let me know when you can get out. I'm footloose and fancy free so I can do any night.'

'I will do. Bye, Jen.'

'Bye, Vaunie.'

Siobhan placed her phone on the bedside table and smiled as a tear rolled down her cheek. Jenny had been a good friend to her over the years. They'd gone through all of their teenage dramas and heartbreaks together and had mended many a broken heart over a bottle of wine or vodka stolen from Jenny's parents' well-stocked kitchen. It was a shame that they'd drifted so far apart and hadn't spoken for so long. Speaking to Jenny had reminded Siobhan that she wasn't just Jake's wife, or Isla's mum. She was Vaunie too – a funny, kick-ass woman, who had once literally drunk the student union dry of tequila. She'd been hiding away for too long, letting go of good friends like Jenny. Trying to be the perfect wife, while her husband was decidedly imperfect. She thought about how much she'd changed in the recent years and how naïve she'd been to think that getting pregnant would change Jake and who he was. She had never wanted to accept that he was gay. There was a time he had been attracted to her too, and she had convinced herself that he must like both men and women. But she had made a huge mistake in pressuring him to marry her. Perhaps she should have told him the truth about her and Connor, and the possibility that Isla was Connor's child? That was a thought that Siobhan never gave much headspace to, mostly because she tried to forget that she and Connor had ever happened. It had been a stupid, reckless mistake and one she never cared to repeat.

She didn't regret for a minute having Isla though, even though she did feel incredibly alone as a new mum. Well, now she knew she wasn't alone. She had friends, and family, who loved her and saw her for who she really was.

Maybe there was still a chance to remind her husband of that too?

Chapter Nineteen

Siobhan checked in on Isla and confirmed she was still sound asleep. Fastening the belt of her silk robe tightly around her waist, she crept downstairs to check on dinner. Jake had promised to be home by eight-thirty and, given his behaviour the night before when he'd stayed out all night without telling her, she suspected he'd actually stick to his word for once.

Walking into the kitchen, she lifted the lid on the pan of potatoes before removing the pieces of steak from the fridge. Aside from a pan of scouse, which Siobhan could never seem to make just right, Jake's favourite meal was steak and mashed potatoes. Her phone call with Jenny had started her thinking about the woman she used to be, before she'd become a wife and a mother. When she used to turn heads wherever she went, and she was witty and funny. When Jake used to actually talk to her, or even listen to her. When he used to make love to her. Despite everything, she still found him attractive and when he was in a good mood, she still saw glimpses of the man she had fallen in love with. She couldn't even remember the last time they'd had sex, and whilst she knew he had other tendencies these days, there had been a time when he had made her feel desired. She wondered if it was something she'd done to make him turn away from her so completely. In public, he played the adoring husband, but in the privacy of their home it was a very different matter. Perhaps she paid too much attention to Isla, and not enough to her appearance? Had she forgotten how to be a woman while trying so hard to be a good mum? If Jake still had any kind of romantic feelings towards her then she needed to know. Perhaps then there was still a chance for them? She didn't want to give up on her marriage so quickly if she thought there was even a remote possibility of saving it.

Going to her bedroom, she opened the bottom drawer of her fitted wardrobe and picked out some of her most expensive, and sexiest, La Perla underwear. Trying it on, she was relieved that it still fitted. If his favourite meal and his wife in revealing underwear didn't at least put a smile on Jake's face, then their marriage was doomed.

It was eight-forty when Jake strolled through the door of the kitchen. Siobhan had heard his key in the lock and had just added the filet mignon to the sizzling frying pan.

'Sorry, I'm a bit late, babe,' Jake said as he approached her and gave her a peck on the cheek. 'Is that for me?'

'Yes. I thought I'd cook your favourite.'

'Oh,' he replied.

'What? It's still your favourite, isn't it?'

'Yeah. It's just that I ate something before with the lads, that's all.'

Siobhan felt her cheeks flush hot.

'But it's okay. You know me, I can always eat,' he said as he put an arm around her waist. 'Just don't give me loads, will you?'

Siobhan shook her head and blinked back the tears as Jake walked away from her and started to unbutton his shirt. 'I'm just going to get changed,' he said to her before disappearing upstairs.

Siobhan wiped her eyes and took a deep breath.

———

By the time Jake came back into the kitchen, Siobhan had plated the food and was sitting waiting for him.

'This looks lovely, babe,' he said as he sat down, feeling a pang of guilt for eating with Paul earlier. He was stuffed full of curry and wasn't sure how much food he could physically force down him.

'Thanks. I wanted to treat you to a decent meal. I feel like I've been neglecting you lately,' she replied with a smile.

'Neglecting me?' Jake said with a flash of his eyebrows. 'Don't be daft. You pay me plenty of attention.' *Too much*, he thought to himself, but didn't dare say.

'Well, I'm glad you think so, but I feel like we've kind of lost our way a little lately. Don't you?'

Jake frowned at her. He'd had a long day and wasn't in

the mood to be dissecting his marriage right now. 'What do you mean, lost our way?'

'I mean, we're so focused on Isla, that we don't seem to have enough time for each other, that's all,' she said.

The guilt that seemed to permanently eat away at him now rose to the fore and he swallowed the mouthful of steak he'd just put in his mouth. 'Shouldn't we be focused on Isla?' he said.

'Yes, of course. But that doesn't mean we can't make time for each other too,' Siobhan said as she allowed her robe to slip open and reveal a glimpse of her fuschia-pink lace bra.

Jake stared at his wife. He didn't like feeling guilty, it was an emotion that didn't sit well with him and who he was. So, he did what he always did, and buried it under his primary emotion – the one that always bubbled just beneath his skin.

'Is that what this is really about then? The meal and the underwear?' he snapped. 'You're just trying to make me feel bad for not paying you enough attention!'

'No. That's not it at all. I just thought—'

'You thought what?' he snarled. 'That a bit of steak and a flash of your knickers would stop me from going out to work? That's where I go, you know, Siobhan. To work. To keep you and our daughter. To give you the lifestyle you both deserve,' he said as he stood up from the table.

'Jake, that's not what I'm trying to do,' Siobhan pleaded.

Shaking his head, Jake stormed out of the kitchen and upstairs. His heart pounded in his chest and he felt like he was going to vomit. His head spun from all the lies he constantly had to tell. Despite everything, he did love Siobhan and he hated what he was doing to her. But the alternative was to reveal what he really was – and he couldn't do that. Could he? All he knew was what he'd told Paul last night was true – he couldn't go on doing this for much longer.

Siobhan sat on the sofa with a large glass of wine in her hand and tears streaming down her face. She was completely useless. She couldn't even cook a nice meal for her husband without it turning into an argument. How the hell could she meet up with Jenny, who remembered her as fun Vaunie, not this miserable shell of a woman she'd become? Then she'd be the talk of their old friends. She could just hear them all now, gossiping about her and talking about how far she had fallen. Well, she couldn't argue with them, could she? She was a stupid cow. Stupid for getting herself involved with Jake bloody Conlon. She was wiping the tears from her face when Jake walked into the sitting room and sat beside her.

'I'm sorry, babe,' he said softly as he put an arm around her shoulder. 'You tried to do a really nice thing for me, and I threw it in your face.'

'I just wanted us to spend some time together,' she said with a sniff. 'I wasn't trying to have a go at you.'

'I know. I'm sorry I went off on you. I'm just a bit stressed out, that's all. Work is doing my head in. But I shouldn't take that out on you. I am really sorry, babe.'

'Okay,' she said with a nod. She didn't entirely believe him, but it was easier to be around him when he was like this, and she didn't want his mood to change again.

'Come to bed, eh? You look knackered, and I could do with a good night's kip,' he said as he took the glass of wine from her hand and then pulled her up from the sofa.

Feeling like she couldn't refuse, Siobhan followed him to their bedroom.

Chapter Twenty

G race placed Siobhan's mug of coffee on the table beside her and watched her daughter-in-law as she cradled Oscar. He had big brown eyes and dark curls and, just like all of her other children, was the image of his father. Oscar nestled contentedly into the nook of Siobhan's arm as she ran her fingertips across his chubby cheek.

'Not broody are you?' Grace laughed as she took a seat on the armchair.

Siobhan looked up at her, her mouth a ring of surprise. 'You must be joking. I've got my hands full with just the one,' she said, indicating her head towards Isla, who was playing happily with her three-year-old aunty Belle. Despite the two-year age gap, the two girls adored each other and would play together with dolls and building blocks for hours. Siobhan had become a regular fixture in the Carter household. Every Monday and Friday afternoon she came around with Isla and stayed for dinner. Then on Sundays, the whole family would arrive for a slap-up roast dinner. The thought of her new hectic family lifestyle made Grace smile. She had always wanted a big family – and now she certainly had one.

'Ah, she's no bother at all,' Grace said.

'Not when she's here with Belle. But she gets bored on her own.'

'All the more reason to have another one then?' Grace grinned at her and then immediately regretted her remark when she saw the look of panic flash across Siobhan's pale, freckled face. She'd noticed the change in Siobhan in the past few months. Gone was the feisty, confident woman who could hold her own in any situation, and in her place was a woman who came across as quiet and shy, and who often appeared lost in her own thoughts. Grace wondered if she was suffering from post-natal depression, but the one time she'd mentioned such a thing, Siobhan had got very upset and seemed so incredibly offended that Grace hadn't wanted to bring it up again.

'Any thoughts about whether you'll go back to work?' Grace said in an attempt to change the subject.

Siobhan shook her head. 'I want to, but Jake doesn't think it's the right time. He thinks I should wait until Isla starts school at least.'

Grace frowned. 'And what do you think?'

Siobhan shook her head. 'I really don't know what I think any more.'

Before Grace could probe any further the door to the living room burst open.

'Daddy!' Belle squealed as she looked up. Flinging her

doll onto the sofa, she ran into Michael's arms and he scooped her up high into the air before giving her a kiss on her cheek. Isla followed suit and toddled over to him. 'Ganga,' she shrieked as she lifted her arms to signal she wanted picking up too.

With Belle in one arm, Michael picked up Isla too and began to swing the pair of them around until they were shrieking with laughter. Oscar stirred on Siobhan's lap, but, used to the noise of a busy house, soon snuggled himself back to sleep.

Grace smiled at her husband and he winked at her in response. 'How was work?' she asked.

He shrugged. 'The usual. Nothing exciting.'

'Did the lads have any trouble with that new firm I told you about, Sable Securities?' Despite being on maternity leave, Grace had always kept an eye on the competition, and her recent uneasiness that something was untoward had made her even more curious than usual. Sable Securities were a new firm. Grace had been looking into them. They were taking over the doors that Cartel Securities didn't run and she wondered whether it was a matter of time before they pushed their luck.

Michael placed the two girls on the floor and walked over to Grace before kissing her on the head. 'Nope. It was all fine, love. They haven't been near any of our premises.'

'Did you tell Murf to keep his wits about him anyway?'

Michael smiled as he sat on the sofa next to Siobhan. 'Murf has been in this game for as long as I have. He knows the score, Grace.'

'I know.' She shook her head. 'It's just—'

'That you're a control freak?' Michael laughed as he finished her sentence for her. 'That you can't switch off from it all, despite your insistence that you wanted nothing to do with work for at least six months?' He grinned at her, his brown eyes twinkling.

'All right,' she said as she lifted her hands in mock surrender. 'Not another word.'

'You're the only one who imposed this work ban on yourself. I can see you getting twitchy to come back already.'

'But Oscar's not even five months old yet,' Grace said.

'So?' Michael replied. 'Just come back part-time then?'

Grace shrugged. As much as she adored her children, she did miss working. 'Maybe just a day or two a week for now?'

Michael nodded. 'Sophia said she'd watch the kids if we ever need her to. You know how much she adores them, and with her girls at school all day, I think she gets a bit lonely.'

'I thought she was going to start covering the lunch in one of the restaurants?' Grace asked.

Sophia was married to Michael's brother, Sean and Grace adored her. The two women had only been discussing the possibility of Sophia working in the restaurant a few days earlier and Grace knew that her sister-in-law was looking forward to getting back to work herself after years of being at home with her children.

'I think Sean was just worried about her having nothing to do while he was at work all day. Anyway, if she does, my dad and Sue will have the kids. Or I will. We'll sort something out. Just don't feel like you can't go back to work, that's all I'm saying.'

As though he'd heard the conversation, Oscar woke up and began to protest loudly. Michael took him from Siobhan. 'Is he due a feed?'

Grace checked her watch. 'Yes. There's some expressed milk in the fridge.'

'I'll sort this little milk monster out then, and leave you ladies to it.' He smiled as he stood up.

'Thanks, love,' Grace replied as she watched her husband carrying their son out of the door. She couldn't deny that it would be good to get back to work, even if it was just a few days a week. The trouble with her job, though, was that it was difficult to limit a working week. She knew that as soon as she returned, she'd find it hard not to take the helm again. She was no longer cut out for taking a back seat. But being at home, fretting about what was and wasn't happening in her absence, wasn't exactly ideal either. She'd have to make a decision soon, to either step back or get stuck back in.

Siobhan had watched Grace and Michael's exchange intently, and with a pang of jealousy. She saw the way Michael looked at Grace and realised that her own husband would never look at her that way. She had married a man who would never love her the way she needed him to, the way every husband should love his wife. She had known Jake was gay and she had married him anyway. No, she had practically forced him to marry her. Now she realised she had quite possibly made the biggest mistake of her life.

Chapter Twenty-One

Siobhan dropped Isla's changing bag on the kitchen table and placed her daughter in her high chair.

'Shall we have some dinner, Isla?' she asked as she took a tin of beans from the cupboard. Beans were currently Isla's favourite food and one she was guaranteed to eat. Siobhan had been thinking about going back to work ever since she'd left Grace's house earlier, and was wondering how to broach the subject with Jake. She couldn't cope with a battle of wills with Isla over dinner time too.

Another positive outcome of her visit to Grace's was that she'd agreed to go out with her old friend Jenny later that evening. Up until today, Siobhan thought she couldn't face hearing all about Jenny's exciting adventures and comparing them to her own miserable life. But seeing how happy Grace was in her marriage, something had sparked in her. So, when Jenny had sent her a text message asking if she fancied some cocktails, Siobhan had agreed. Jake had promised to be home by six to do Isla's bedtime, and since staying out with no notice a few nights ago, had been largely keeping to his word. He could look after Isla on his own for a change.

'Bees, mummy,' Isla said with a clap of her hands, snapping Siobhan from her thoughts. 'Bees.'

'Yes, bees.' Siobhan smiled as she shook the tin of beans in her hand.

As she was emptying the contents of tin into the saucepan, Siobhan's mobile phone started to ring. Glancing at the screen, she saw it was Jake.

'Hi, Jake,' she said when she picked up.

'Hiya, babe. Look, I've got to work tonight. We've got a job to do in Scotland.'

'Scotland? What are you doing up there?'

'Just some business,' he replied.

'So, when will you be back?'

'Some time in the early hours. I'll be home by the time you and Isla wake up. You'll hardly even have time to miss me.'

'For God's sake, Jake! I was hoping to go and see Jenny tonight!'

'Jenny who?'

'Jenny Lyon! Who went to school with us. I told you she's back from America and she'd got in touch.'

'Oh, I'm sorry, babe. I didn't know you were going tonight. You never mentioned it. Look, ask her to come round instead. You can show her your fancy house. Ask her to bring a bottle and you could treat yourselves to a nice takeaway?' he offered. Did he expect her to be grateful that she could *treat* herself and her friend to a takeaway?

'Oh, just forget it,' she said with a sigh. 'What's the point anyway?'

'For fuck's sake, Siobhan,' he snapped at her. 'What the fuck do you want from me? I have to work. How else could I keep you in designer fucking handbags?'

'How dare you! I haven't bought a handbag in over a year,' she said instinctively, then felt angry that she was even attempting to defend herself.

'Whatever,' he said dismissively. 'I'll see you both tomorrow. Give Isla a kiss from me.'

'Yeah. Bye,' she said and hung up before he could answer. God, how could she have even thought for a second that they had anything worth saving? Jake was a selfish, narcissistic, egotistical bastard who clearly had little regard for her, and despite all his talk of his love for his daughter, had lately done little to actually demonstrate that.

As she stared into the saucepan of bubbling beans, a few silent tears started to fall down Siobhan's cheeks. What the hell had her life become? Growing up poor, she'd been blown away by Jake and his money. She'd been blinded by the flash lifestyle he'd offered her and had thought it was something that once she'd had a taste of, she couldn't live without. But now she realised that all the money in the world didn't keep you warm at night, or comfort you when you'd had a crappy day. From the outside she had the perfect life. She was the envy of the other mums in the baby groups she frequented, and the Facebook messages from her schoolfriends always hinted at the easy life of luxury she lived, but it was all a massive lie. It was she who should be envious – and she was. She envied the other mums their adoring partners who shared the parenting. Jake had made a good show of that for a while. For the first eight months of Isla's life he had doted on their little girl, but he was never really there for them both. Not any more.

'Bees, Mummy!' Isla squealed again.

Siobhan straightened her back and wiped the tears from her face with the back of her hand. Tomorrow was a brand new day. Turning to her daughter, she forced a smile.

'Yes, baby. Your bees are coming.'

Chapter Twenty-Two

Paul looked up from the newspaper as Jake walked into the kitchen. They'd got back from their job in Scotland at 1am and then had spent two hours talking about how Jake was going to tell Siobhan it was over. Paul had heard it all before, of course, but there was something about the way Jake spoke this time that made Paul think he might actually go through with it.

'Morning, handsome,' Paul said.

'Morning,' Jake responded gruffly.

'Fancy going down to Maria's café and grabbing some breakfast?'

'Yeah.' Jake sat on the chair opposite Paul. 'In a bit.'

'You okay?' Paul asked softly.

Jake looked up at him and smiled. 'Yeah, mate. Better than I've been in a long time.'

Paul returned his smile. 'Are you really going to do it today?'

'I have to, Paul. I can't keep living like this.'

'What about Isla?'

'I'm still her dad. Nothing will change that. Siobhan wouldn't keep her from me. She can't anyway. I'll have solicitors crawling all over her if she even tries.'

'So, when are you telling her then?'

'Today. As soon as I get home.'

Paul took a swig of his coffee. 'Good.'

'So, where does this leave us?' Jake asked.

'Wherever you want it to,' Paul replied softly.

'I want to be with you, Paul...'

'But?'

'I'm not ready for the rest of the world to know about us. Not yet.'

'We have to tell Connor though. And my dad—'

'And my mum?' Jake interrupted with a roll of his eyes.

'They'll understand, Jake. Eventually. Even if they're not happy about it. What are they gonna do? Disown the pair of us?'

'I hope you're right,' Jake said as he took the mug from Paul's hands and downed the last of the coffee.

Jake watched Paul silently as he read the newspaper. It was yesterday's *Liverpool Echo*. Paul always read it from cover to cover as part of his morning ritual. Jake realised that he knew more about the man sitting opposite him than he did his own wife. He felt a pang of guilt as he thought about telling Siobhan that he wanted a divorce. He should never have asked her to marry him. There was a reason he knew so little about her daily routine, and, as ashamed as he was to admit it, it was because he wasn't interested in it. He had no interest in her, and he knew that was unfair to her. He assured himself that leaving her was the best thing for her too. She deserved so much better than him. He was doing it for her really. He was doing her a favour. The more he convinced himself of that fact, the more the guilt ebbed away. He would miss living with his daughter, but he'd make sure he got shared custody. Well, a few nights a week at least. His leaving Siobhan wouldn't damage his relationship with Isla – he would make sure of that.

Jake smiled to himself. He had it all worked out. This time tomorrow he'd be a free man. Free to see Paul, the man he had come to love more than he ever imagined possible, whenever he wanted. Free to come and go as he pleased. Siobhan would be upset – who wouldn't be? But she'd get over it.

'You gonna get dressed then?' Paul said, snapping Jake from his thoughts. 'I'm starving and I haven't got anything in to eat.'

'Yeah,' Jake said as he stood up. 'I'll only be a minute.'

Jake walked through the flat into Paul's bedroom and collected the rest of his clothes from the bedroom floor. His stomach churned as he started to get dressed and he realised he probably couldn't eat a bite if he tried. He'd let Paul go to the café on his own. He needed to speak to Siobhan before he changed his mind.

Jake walked back into Paul's kitchen. 'I'm going to go home and tell her now,' he said. 'Before I chicken out.'

Paul put down his paper and walked over to him, putting a warm hand on the back of his neck. 'You can do this,' he said to him.

Jake swallowed and nodded. 'I know.'

Paul pressed his forehead to Jake's. 'I love you,' he said quietly.

Jake closed his eyes. Paul had never told him that before, and he'd never told Paul either. It was an unspoken truth between them. One they'd never dared acknowledge before.

'I love you too,' Jake whispered.

Chapter Twenty-Three

Paul sat at the table in Maria's café opposite Connor and tucked into the large cooked breakfast in front of him.

'You'd think you were starved the way you're shovelling that in, lad,' Connor said with a laugh.

'I'm a growing boy,' Paul replied.

'So, what time did Jake go home last night?' Connor asked.

Paul shook his head while he finished chewing and then took a large swig of his tea. 'He didn't. Well, not until this morning anyway.'

'Fucking hell. Siobhan is going to go mental at him.'

'Well, I think that'll be the least of her worries, to be honest.'

'What do you mean?' Connor said as he frowned at his brother.

'I mean, he's planning to tell her he's leaving her.'

Connor almost spat out his coffee. 'Fuck! No way?'

'Yep. That's what he told me this morning, anyway. Said he can't stand lying any more and he's going to tell her it's over.'

'What? He's going to tell her he's gay?' Connor whispered.

'No! Don't be fucking soft. Jake can barely admit that to himself. He's just going to tell her he's leaving her.'

'And how do you feel about this?' Connor asked, his voice full of concern.

'Nothing to do with me really, is it?' Paul replied with a shrug

'Of course it's to do with you, you knob. You're the reason he's leaving his fucking wife.'

'He'd have left her anyway, Con. If it wasn't me, it'd be for someone else.'

'But it is for you, isn't it? So, how do you feel about it? You're not exactly great at monogamy, are you?'

'Says the guy who's fucking the married woman,' Paul replied with a raised eyebrow.

'Yeah, she's married, not me,' Connor snapped. 'Besides, her husband is a cunt.'

Paul nodded. 'Well, you're right there.'

'So?' Connor asked. 'You and Jake?'

Paul smiled. 'Well, it certainly makes things more interesting, doesn't it?'

'You'll have to tell me da, and Grace,' Connor added.

'Yeah, we know.'

'I hope he's worth it, Bro?' Connor warned.

'Oh, believe me, he is,' Paul replied with a grin.

'Well, just don't fuck it up,' Connor said. 'Because if you two fall out, it'll cause world war fucking three.'

Paul looked at his plate. Connor was right, of course. His dad and Grace were going to go apeshit when they found out about him and Jake. Especially Grace. At least his dad knew they'd once had a thing together. But before he'd proposed to Grace, his dad had asked Paul if there was anything going on between them any more, and Paul had sworn that there wasn't. It had been the truth at the time. And now they were step-brothers and everything was ten times more complicated than before. It was an incestuous shit-storm of potentially epic proportions, but all Paul could think about was how being with Jake made him feel, and sometimes that was all that seemed to matter.

And if he and Jake couldn't make it work? If it all ended horribly? What the fuck would they all do then?

Chapter Twenty-Four

Siobhan picked up the remote control and idly flicked through the channels on the television as she wondered where on earth her husband was. He'd promised he'd be home before she and Isla were awake. He'd been staying out more and more lately and she knew he was seeing someone. She could almost overlook the occasional one-night stand – almost, but this recent thing was obviously more serious. She could tell. Woman's intuition? The way he took extra care of his appearance before he went out. Leaving the house with a spring in his step and coming home in a mood, as though he didn't want to be there any more. Did he think she was stupid?

Perhaps she was.

She had been stupid to think that getting him to marry her would change him. At the time, getting pregnant had seemed like the surest way to make him commit to her – to secure their future together. Now she realised that all she'd done was to tie herself to a man whom she would never be enough for. Someone who could never love her the way she deserved.

Jake's life had barely changed since they'd had Isla. He still got to leave the house every day and run his precious club, while she was always stuck at home playing mum. While Siobhan loved her daughter dearly, she just wasn't cut out for being a stay-at-home mum, especially when her husband was never around. She had little time to herself, and when she did dare to ask for some, Jake had the barefaced cheek to ask her a hundred questions about where she was going and who she'd be with. She felt like a prisoner. She was trapped inside a dead marriage, with a man she wasn't even sure she loved any more. She wasn't sure how much longer she could live like this before she lost the plot and had a complete breakdown.

Now it was time to consider her options. There was no way she was walking away from her marriage just yet, not without some decent compensation. If Jake wanted to keep his dirty little secret, then he would have to buy her silence. She knew, on paper, their assets were considerable enough – Jake had the club, and together they owned the house, and had kept their flat on near the Albert Dock. If she divorced him and claimed what she could legally, it would be plenty, but she knew that it wouldn't even make a dent in his wealth. And she intended to take every penny she could. After all, she had earned it. She needed to plan her escape. And the first step was to get herself some concrete proof of his extramarital liaisons, and who he was having them with. Once she had that, she would hit him where it hurt.

Unable to find anything on television to hold her

attention, Siobhan threw the remote onto the sofa. She would speak to Grace on Sunday when they went for dinner. Siobhan adored her mother-in-law and she was the only person Jake paid much attention to. Maybe Grace could persuade Jake to allow Siobhan to get back to work – even part-time hours would do her for now, it would at least make the next few months more bearable. It was Grace who had groomed Siobhan to take over The Blue Rooms. It was a job that Siobhan enjoyed, and one she'd been bloody good at too – until her pregnancy had made it impossible to continue. God, how stupid she was to think that having a baby would be the answer to all of her prayers. How bloody wrong she'd been. If she could go back in time and speak to that naïve, stupid little girl who believed that money was the answer to everything, she'd tell her how very wrong she was, and give her a quick slap for good measure.

The sound of the front door closing snapped Siobhan from her train of thought. She checked her watch and noticed it was 11am. Fortunately, Isla was taking a nap in her cot, because Siobhan was going to give her lying, cheating husband what for. She'd had enough of his antics. She'd had enough of him making her feel like she was the problem. It was time for him to accept some responsibility for a change.

'What time do you call this, Jake?' she snapped as he entered the living room.

'Siobhan,' he started. 'We need to talk.'

'Too right we do,' she seethed at him as she stood up. 'Where the hell have you been?'

'I've been at Paul's—'

'Paul's?' she interrupted him. 'Again? I should have fucking known,' she shouted, not caring now if she woke Isla or not. It was a kick in the teeth. After all that time, he was still screwing about with Paul Carter. Right under her nose? They must have thought she was a bloody idiot. She bet they had a good old laugh at her expense while they carried on their disgusting little affair. God, she wanted to murder the both of them.

'Siobhan, I want a divorce,' he said quietly as he stared at her.

Siobhan thought she must have misheard him. 'A divorce? You want to divorce me?' she said with a snort.

He nodded. 'It's not working.'

'Well, maybe it would if you weren't fucking around with Paul Carter,' she screeched.

'What?' Jake said as he frowned at her.

'Don't think I don't know about you two and your dirty little secret,' she hissed.

He stepped towards her. 'You have no idea what you're on about, Siobhan. This is the shock talking.'

'Shock? It was a shock two fucking years ago when I first found out. Now it's just bloody pathetic, Jake. You're pathetic!' she spat.

Jake edged closer to her. 'You don't know what you're saying, Siobhan. So shut the fuck up before you say something we both regret.'

'The only thing I regret, Jake, is marrying you! You lying, cheating, bastard! You're a shite husband, and a worse fucking father.'

She saw the temper flash across Jake's face and although

ordinarily she would have felt afraid, in that moment she felt only satisfaction that she had got to him, and hurt him as much as he had hurt her. 'That's right,' she spat at him. 'You're useless. Of course, you are, considering the role model you had. You're just as bad as him.'

'Don't you fucking dare,' he hissed at her. 'I love Isla. I'm her dad, Siobhan, and no matter what you do or say, you will never stop me seeing her.'

'Oh, really?'

'Really.'

'Well, we'll see about that!'

'And what's that supposed to mean? If you even try and stop me seeing her, I'll have solicitors tying you up in knots so fast, you won't know what's hit you. I'll have you declared an unfit mother if I have to. So just watch your step,' he said as he glared at her.

Siobhan stared back at him. This man had caused her so much pain and heartache she could barely stand to look at him, and now he was threatening to take her daughter away from her. She knew that Jake had the means to make a case against her – he knew people who would lie for him for the right price, or simply because they were too terrified not to. Well, she would never let that happen.

'It means, Jake, that no court in the land would give you custody of Isla,' she said to him as she walked away from him, not wanting to be in striking distance when she delivered her next piece of information.

'Oh? And why's that?'

'Because she's not yours,' she said.

'What?' he said as the anger flickered across his face,

confirming to her that he'd heard exactly what she said.

'I said she's not your daughter.'

'You lying fucking slag.'

'That's rich coming from you!'

'You're a lying fucking bitch,' he shouted as he strode across the room towards her, kicking one of Isla's teddy bears aside as he did so.

Siobhan instinctively recoiled from him, edging towards the door. She felt her pulse quicken. Her heart pounding against her ribcage. She had gone too far now. Her desire to hurt him, to damage his precious relationship with the Carter twins, and her desperate need to ensure that he never took Isla from her, had made her feel invincible for a moment. Now, she realised she was not. She had seen Jake angry before. She had seen him go off on people – but never at her. Not until now. She considered herself a tough woman when she had to be. She took no crap from anybody, but right now she was terrified. She shook her head as she continued to edge towards the door. 'Jake, please?'

'Don't fucking Jake me,' he spat. 'Whose is she then?' he snarled as he pushed his face into hers.

Siobhan's racing heart started thundering so hard she could barely hear herself think. 'I was just messing about, Jake. I just wanted to hurt you.'

'Stop lying! Don't you fucking dare try and take me for any more of a mug than you already have. I asked you whose is she. If she's not mine, then whose?'

'She's yours,' she whimpered.

He didn't respond immediately and she thought for a

second that she had convinced him to back down. At least now she would have some time to think. That was when she felt his hand around her throat, gripping and squeezing her until she was struggling for air. He lifted her off the ground with ease. Her legs scrabbled beneath her as she struggled to make contact with the floor. He glared at her and all she could see in his eyes was pure hatred.

'I will ask you one more time, Siobhan, who is Isla's real father and if you lie to me I swear I will snap your fucking neck.'

Siobhan blinked at him, trying desperately to think of an answer – a lie – but none came to her. Her throat screamed in pain as her lungs gasped for breath, burning through the lack of oxygen. He was going to kill her if she didn't answer him soon. Not sure if answering him would make him release his grip, or kill her, she gave the only answer she could – the truth.

'Connor,' she gasped.

Jake let her go and she dropped to her knees, clutching her throat and gasping for air.

'Connor? My Connor? Connor Carter?'

The tears rolled down Siobhan's face. 'Yes,' she sobbed.

Jake staggered backwards, shaking his head. 'No! You're lying,' he said.

Siobhan shook her head.

'You're a lying fucking whore,' he snarled. 'I'm done with you. If I ever see your miserable face again, I'll fucking kill you.'

The next thing Siobhan heard was the slamming of the door.

Chapter Twenty-Five

Paul and Connor drove to The Blue Rooms after their breakfast at Maria's café.

'Did Jake say he'd meet us here?' Connor asked Paul as they let themselves into Jake's office.

'Yeah. As soon as he's done what he needs to do at home, he'll come straight here.'

'I wonder if he's told her yet?' Connor asked as he sat down in the leather chair that was usually occupied by Jake.

Paul looked at his watch. 'I hope so. How do you think she'll take it?'

'She'll probably smash the telly over his head,' Connor replied with a laugh. 'Either that or she'll burst into tears and hang onto his leg so he can't leave.'

'Women, eh!' Paul said with a shake of his head. 'Too much like hard work. Is it any wonder I prefer men?'

'Oh yeah, coz Jake is much easier to handle, isn't he?' Connor snorted.

'He is if you know how,' Paul said with a wink.

Connor shook his head. 'I don't want to know, Bro.'

Jake floored the accelerator and sped through the streets of Liverpool towards the town centre and The Blue Rooms. Siobhan had to be lying. Otherwise nothing made any sense. Connor and Siobhan? It couldn't possibly be true. Connor would never lie to him. But why would Siobhan say that if it wasn't true? To drive a wedge between him and the twins, that was why. He needed to speak to Connor and find out the truth for himself.

Striding through The Blue Rooms, Jake burst into the office at the back of the club to see the twins waiting for him. They looked at him as he strode in. There was something about the way they looked at him. Suddenly, he felt like he was a stranger bursting into there, and not the man whom only that morning they had considered their brother. Now he felt like the enemy. Was he?

'Is it true?' Jake asked, looking directly at Connor.

'Is what true?' Connor said, a look of bewilderment on his face.

'About you and Siobhan?' Jake snarled.

Connor's face paled as he turned to look at Paul, and Jake knew that Siobhan had told him the truth.

Turning back to Jake, Connor started to talk. 'Look, Jake—'

Propelled by an indescribable rage, Jake launched himself across the room and over the desk at Connor who put his arms up in defence. Bringing his right hand back,

Jake swung it towards Connor's face with every ounce of strength he had. Before the punch connected, Paul grabbed his arm and pulled him back, wrapping him in a bear hug. 'You don't want to do this, mate,' Paul said softly in his ear.

Mate! The word meant nothing to him any more.

Shrugging Paul off, Jake spun around and glared at him. 'You knew, didn't you?'

Before Paul could answer, Connor started talking again. 'Just calm the fuck down, Jake, and we can sort this out.'

Jake lunged for Connor again, but was once again stopped by Paul.

'You pair of lying, two-faced cunts,' Jake spat as he shrugged away from Paul once more.

'Jake,' Paul said.

'Fuck off!' Jake snapped. 'Fuck off out of my club. If either of you ever set a foot in here again, I'll kill the fucking pair of you.'

Connor stood up and walked towards Paul. With a final glance at Jake, the two of them walked out of the office. Jake watched them go before slumping to the floor with his head in his hands. His whole world had just crashed down around him. There was no one he could trust. They were all a shower of lying, back-stabbing cunts. There was only one person who had never let him down. Only one person who had ever really had his back. Taking his mobile phone out of his pocket, he dialled her number.

Chapter Twenty-Six

G race paced anxiously up and down her hallway, worried that she'd wear a groove into the oak floor if Jake didn't arrive soon. He'd sounded so upset and angry on the phone, but he'd refused to tell her why, except to say that he couldn't trust anyone any more. She knew that wasn't true, but had no idea what could have caused him to make such a statement. Obviously, something terrible had happened. She'd popped her head into the study to ask Michael if he knew anything about what might be going on, but he was deep in conversation about work, so she'd left him to it. Oscar was fast asleep having his afternoon nap and Belle was in nursery, so she didn't even have her youngest children to distract her. All she could do was wait for Jake's arrival. Her stomach almost dropped through the floor when she finally saw Jake's shadow approaching through the stained glass of the front door.

Opening the door before Jake could knock, she saw his tear-stained face and pulled him inside.

Grace placed her hand on Jake's shoulder as she followed him into her living room. She'd never seen him looking so upset and her stomach churned at the thought of what he was about to tell her.

'Sit down, Son,' she said as they neared the large, comfortable sofa.

He shook his head and walked over to the cabinet where she kept the expensive bottles of brandy she and Michael had bought on their last holiday. He took out one of the open bottles and a crystal tumbler and started to pour himself a glass.

'Want one?' he asked Grace.

She shook her head. 'No, thanks. What's wrong, Jake? Tell me what's going on.'

Jake took a large swig of brandy and looked at her. She was sure he was about to speak when the door opened and Michael strolled in.

'I need to go into work,' he sighed. 'Should only be for an hour. There's been a mix-up with some of the lads' wages.' Upon seeing Jake in his agitated state, he frowned. 'All right, mate. What's up?'

Grace watched as her son stared at Michael for a moment, as though sizing him up.

'You knew, didn't you?' Jake snapped.

Michael stepped closer to him. 'Jake…'

'You fucking knew!' Jake shouted.

Grace rose from her seat. 'Knew what? What the hell is going on?'

Michael looked towards her and was about to speak

when Jake launched himself across the room and punched Michael in the jaw, causing him to stagger backwards.

'Jake?' Grace screamed. 'What the hell are you doing?'

'You fucking bastard,' Jake shouted as he lunged for Michael again. This time, Michael was ready for him and he managed to overpower him, pushing him down onto the sofa.

'What the hell is going on?' Grace shouted at the pair of them.

'Ask your husband,' Jake snarled. 'He's the one been keeping secrets.'

Grace turned to look at Michael but before she could speak he cut her off. 'Me keeping secrets? What about you? You've been keeping a pretty fucking big one of your own, haven't you, Jake? Don't you think Siobhan knows all about you carrying on behind her back? After all, it's been going on since before you even got married. Have you considered that's why she went looking elsewhere?'

Jake bounced up from his seated position. 'You fucking cunt,' he spat, almost foaming at the mouth. 'I'll fucking kill you,' he said as he went for Michael again.

This time, Grace caught him by the arm. She wasn't sure if she'd just misheard, but she could have sworn Michael accused Jake of cheating on Siobhan. 'Will one of you tell me what the hell is going on before I slap the pair of you myself?'

Jake turned to her and his face crumpled. He started to shake his head and she pulled him to her, wrapping her arms around him as he started to sob. She glared at Michael who stood looking on wordlessly.

After a few moments, Grace pulled Jake away from her and held his face in her hands. 'What's going on, Jake?' she said softly.

He sniffed and she was reminded of him as a small boy. Her heart almost broke to see him in such obvious pain. 'Isla's not mine, Mum,' he sniffed.

'What? Of course she is,' Grace replied.

Jake shook his head. 'No, she's not. Siobhan told me herself. Ask your husband if you don't believe me.'

Grace felt her heart sink through her chest and onto the floor. If she wasn't holding onto Jake she wasn't sure she'd remain upright. She glanced at Michael. What the hell did this have to do with him?

'So who is her father then?' she asked, dreading the answer.

'Connor,' Jake snarled.

Grace was ashamed to admit that the first emotion she felt was relief. For an awful moment, she'd thought that Jake was implying Michael was Isla's father. But Connor! That was almost as bad. 'Connor? Our Connor?'

Jake stepped back from her and wiped his eyes. 'Yeah,' he snarled. 'And he knew all about it.' He nodded towards Michael.

'Is this true?' Grace asked her husband.

'It's not that simple,' Michael replied.

'I never said it was simple,' Grace snapped at him. 'I asked you if it was true.'

'Connor *might* be Isla's dad,' Michael said. 'But Siobhan and Connor aren't the only ones keeping secrets, are they, Jake?'

'Fuck off!' Jake growled as he walked towards Michael.

'For God's sake, will one of you tell me just what the hell is going on here?' Grace shouted. 'What secrets?'

'Tell her,' Michael said to Jake.

Jake turned to her, his face dissolving into tears. 'I think I'm gay, Mum.'

The shock hit her like a slap to the face, but she pulled him to her. It was the last thing she'd expected to hear, but she would deal with her own feelings later. Right now, she had to be there for her son. 'Why didn't you tell me?' she asked.

Jake shrugged. 'I couldn't.'

'You can tell me anything. You know that,' she said softly as she wiped the tears from his cheeks with her thumbs.

Grace was aware of Michael scowling in the background. 'What?' she snapped at him. 'Did you know about this too?'

Suddenly, she saw the anger flash across Jake's face again then and he stepped back from her.

'Yes, he fucking did,' Jake snapped. 'I've got to go, Mum. I need to sort my head out.' Then he was walking out of the door faster than Grace could follow him.

'Jake,' she said after him. 'Talk to me.'

'I'll ring you tomorrow,' he shouted before slamming the front door behind him.

Grace glared at her husband, noticing his obvious discomfort. 'So?' She folded her arms and glared at him. He'd better be able to offer some sort of plausible explanation for everything that had just happened. Because surely all of this was some kind of huge misunderstanding?

Michael swallowed and took a step towards her. 'I think you should sit down.'

Grace sat on the sofa, thankful to feel something solid beneath her legs, while Michael perched on the coffee table in front of her. She took a deep breath to steady her breathing and try to calm the thunderous beating of her heart in her chest. She unclenched her fists and stared at her husband, waiting for him to speak.

'Connor told me at Isla's party last week that there was a chance he could be Isla's biological father,' he said as he lowered his gaze to the floor.

'What? How?'

Michael looked up again with a slight frown on his face.

'I'm not asking you for a biology lesson! I mean how could your son possibly be Isla's father?'

'Apparently, they slept together around the time Isla was conceived. It was just the once, but as we both know, once is enough.'

The reference to Belle's conception when Michael had been married to his second wife, Hannah, didn't escape Grace's attention, and was no doubt designed to elicit some empathy, but it didn't, so she ignored it. 'So for a whole week you have known that Isla might not be Jake's daughter, but could in fact be Connor's child, and you didn't think it pertinent to tell me?'

'Grace,' he said with a sigh. 'It's not that simple.'

'You are a fucking hypocrite, Michael Carter,' she shouted at him as she jumped up from her seat, recalling the way he'd treated her when she'd kept the fact that he was Belle's father from him. 'The grief you gave me for keeping secrets. When we got married we promised each other we would never keep any secrets from each other again. And you choose to keep this one?' she shook her head.

'For fuck's sake, Grace,' he snapped. 'Can't you see I was in an impossible situation? Connor is my son. What did you expect me to do? How could I tell you and ask you not to tell Jake? I couldn't put you in that position. Do you think I was happy knowing something that big and not being able to tell you about it?'

'All I know is that you have kept this from me. Every minute of every day since you found out.'

'Grace—' he started.

Then she remembered Jake's other revelation, and his anger when he'd told her that Michael knew about that too. Dear God, could this get any worse? 'And you knew about Jake being gay too?' she asked.

'Yes.'.

'How? Did he tell you?' Surely that was the only way he would know? She had always considered herself close to Jake. He and Michael got on well enough, but still, why would he tell Michael and not her?

'No. I walked in on him and Paul.'

'Paul?' Grace almost shrieked. 'Our Paul? Your son?' She could hardly believe what she was hearing. It was all such a mess she could barely make sense of it.

'It was ages ago. Before we got married, obviously. They haven't been together for a long time now.'

Grace shook her head. Her blood thundered around her body, pounding in her ears and making it hard to think clearly. Within the space of a few hours, their close-knit family had been torn apart and she was wavering between feeling so angry she might implode, or as though her heart was about to break. She felt like she had been air-dropped into some American soap opera. She had to have been – because this was not how families who claimed to love each other behaved. 'So, you've all been lying to me, all this time?'

'I can explain everything, Grace,' he said as he walked towards and reached out his arm.

'Don't you fucking touch me,' she snarled at him. Then she grabbed her car keys from the table and walked out of the house, slamming the door as she went.

Chapter Twenty-Seven

G race drove around for hours through the streets of Liverpool and realised she had nowhere to go. She owned numerous properties throughout Merseyside but they were all rented out to tenants. Siobhan and Jake's house was out of the question for obvious reasons. Her accountant, Ivan, was now semi-retired and spending six months of the year in France. Her friend Libby had got married and moved to Manchester with her wife, Maria. Almost everyone else she knew, or was close to, was a member of the Carter family. And she wasn't ready to explain what the hell had just gone on. She could barely comprehend it herself.

Her instincts took her to her old stomping ground in the south of the city. She drove past the site of her old pub, The Rose and Crown, and noticed they were building on it now. She was glad. The ruins of that pub had been painful to see. It had played such an important part in her life for so long – at times both her sanctuary and her prison. The place she had grown up in with her dad after her mum had died. It had been left to her at the age of eighteen when he'd passed away. She'd lived with her ex-husband Nathan Conlon in the flat above, and they'd spent some happy times there, before he'd revealed himself to be the monster that he truly was. She had raised Jake in that pub, marked his first fourteen birthdays by blowing out the candles on his cake in the poky little kitchen. It had broken her heart to lose the place, but she had burned it to the ground herself in an attempt to finally break free of her ex-husband Nathan. He'd survived the fire, but not the bullet she'd put in his chest the following day.

———————

Before long, Grace found herself at a familiar house in Childwall. She walked up the path and knocked on the door.

After a few moments, the hulking figure of John Brennan appeared. Grace had known John for over twenty years. He had once been the right-hand man of her ex-husband, and despite the fact that Grace had killed Nathan, she and John had managed to develop a friendship of their own. More recently, he had started working for Grace after he'd helped her to track down one of the men responsible for the kidnap and attempted murder of Jake and Michael over two years earlier.

'Grace? What are you doing here?' he asked with a look of concern on his face.

'I'm sorry, John. I know it's late. But I couldn't think of

anywhere else to go. Can I come in?'

'Of course,' he said as he opened the door and invited her into his hallway. 'Is everything okay?'

'Not really. But I'd rather not talk about it, if that's okay?' she replied.

He smiled at her. 'Whatever you say, Boss. Brew?'

'Oh, I'd love one John,' she said and gave him a half-hearted smile in return.

'Make yourself at home,' John said as he indicated his living room. 'And I'll stick the kettle on.'

Grace sat on John's sofa and looked around the cosy living room. He had numerous photographs dotted around, of what she assumed must be his family. He had three sisters, whom Grace had never met, but whom he talked about often, and so many nieces and nephews that he often joked he'd lost count. As far as Grace was aware, there was no one special in John's life. He had girlfriends but none of them seemed to last very long. She assumed that was John's decision because he was generally considered a good catch. He was funny, smart, good-looking if you liked that big and brooding look, had good manners and a nice smile. In fact, Nathan had nicknamed him the Smiling Assassin. Grace suddenly realised that she could well have interrupted something and hadn't even thought about that when she'd knocked at the door. She'd simply thought of someone whom she could turn to in a time of need, which John always was, and she'd do the same for him.

A few moments later, John came into the room carrying two steaming mugs of tea and handed one to Grace.

'Thanks, John,' she said.

'So, you sure you don't want to talk about it?' John said, raising one eyebrow.

'Oh God, John. Where would I even start?'

Chapter Twenty-Eight

Bradley Johnson pulled the collar of his Hugo Boss tracksuit top up over his neck against the cold wind on Otterspool prom.

'No need to fucking count it, Jock,' he snapped as he looked around the car park, which was deserted except for the two of them and Bradley's youngest brother, Scott. 'It's all there. Apart from the ten grand that Mr McGrath agreed I could keep for a down-payment on new premises.'

Jock laughed good-naturedly as he zipped up the black leather holdall that was resting on the bonnet of the silver Mondeo estate. 'Oh, I know, lads. Mr McGrath would have all of our bollocks on a skewer if it wasn't.' He winked as he slung the bag over his shoulder. 'Nice doing business with you, boys. I'll be back in touch when we have some merchandise.'

'Same deal as last time?' Bradley asked.

Jock looked him over as though considering his offer. Bradley knew that Jock didn't have the authority to negotiate prices, and that Alastair McGrath had already briefed him on any future deals. After a few seconds, Jock shrugged. 'Let's see how you get on shifting this little lot first. If you can take this much every month, then you can keep the same deal.'

Bradley nodded. 'We'll shift it. Don't worry.'

Jock grinned. 'We'll see. It's a buyers' market. And haven't Jake Conlon and the Carters got it all sewn up round here?'

Bradley sensed Scott bristle beside him and spoke before his brother even had a chance to open his mouth. 'Don't worry about us, Jock. We can look after ourselves.'

Jock laughed again as he pulled his vape from his coat pocket and took a long drag. 'That's good to hear, boys. I'd hate for our little business arrangement to come to an end before it's even really begun.'

'It won't,' Bradley assured him. 'That shower of flash pricks don't scare us, eh, Scott?'

Scott looked up at his big brother and shook his head. 'No,' he mumbled.

'I'll be in touch in a few weeks then,' Jock said as he opened the boot of his estate and put the holdall full of money under the false bottom, before replacing the fishing gear he carried around in the back as a decoy. 'Try and keep yourselves out of too much trouble 'til then.'

Bradley grinned. 'Not a chance, mate.'

They watched Jock's car as it pulled out of the car park until his brake lights disappeared into the darkness. 'That went all right, didn't it?' Bradley said with a grin. 'This is going to be the start of something big for us, kid.'

Scott shook his head. 'I don't know, Brad. Are you sure you know what you're doing? We could be stepping on some dangerous toes here.'

Bradley glared at Scott. He was the baby of the family and it showed. He was by far the youngest of the five Johnson brothers, with eight years between him and the second youngest, Billy, and sixteen years between him and Bradley. Twenty years earlier, he'd been a happy surprise to their mother, who'd thought she couldn't have any more kids, and as a result he'd been mollycoddled from the moment he was born. He was a clever little fucker, but he had no common sense at all. Scott had wanted to go off to Cambridge and ponce about doing a Maths degree, but after their parents had died, Bradley had become the head of the family, and he'd insisted that Scott join the family business and earn his keep, just like everybody else had to.

'Don't be such a fucking quilt,' Bradley snapped at him. 'I've already told you, this is the time for us to make our move. Craig's out tomorrow and Ged will be too in a few days. Once they're back we're going to be fucking unstoppable. Just how it was always meant to be before that cunt Sol Shepherd got them sent down.'

Scott sucked the cold air through his teeth. 'I'm just saying, Jake Conlon and the Carter twins are no mugs, Bro. They're a gang of fucking psychos.'

Bradley pulled his brother into a headlock and ruffled his hair. 'So are we, sunshine. So are we.'

Chapter Twenty-Nine

The following morning, Grace walked through the living-room door and threw her car keys onto the sideboard. Sensing movement from the corner of the room, she glanced across to see Michael sitting in the armchair, an empty glass in his hand and a half empty bottle of brandy by his feet.

'Where the hell have you been?' He snapped.

'Out,' she snapped back.

Rising from his chair, he crossed the room in a few short strides. 'No shit, Sherlock. Where?'

Grace could smell the alcohol on his breath. Michael very rarely drank more than a couple of beers. A glass of wine with a meal, a short if he was celebrating. She'd only seen him drunk on a handful of occasions. She studied his face. He was angry. She couldn't blame him. She knew he must have been worried sick about her, but wasn't that why she'd done it? To hurt him?

'With an old friend,' she said dismissively. 'Not that it's

any of your business. We don't tell each other everything, do we? Isn't that our deal now?'

'For fuck's sake, Grace,' he snapped at her. 'I'm sorry. But, I couldn't tell you. How do you not get that?'

'You made me a promise that you would never to lie to me, Michael,' she started before shaking her head and walking away from him.

He stared after her, the anger in his face slipping away. She supposed he could hardly argue with that.

'Where are the kids?' she asked.

'My dad and Sue came to take them out for the day first thing.'

'Oh, good.'

'Have you spoken to Jake?'

Grace shook her head. 'No. He's not answering his phone. Have you talked to the boys?'

'Well, I spoke to Connor.'

'And what did he have to say for himself?'

'Not much. He's gutted about it all. But what do you expect him to say?'

'Erm, how about sorry for fucking up everyone's life? That might be a good start.'

Michael bristled. 'And you think this is all on Connor, do you?'

Grace shrugged. 'Him and Siobhan.'

'And your precious Jake isn't responsible for any of it?' he sneered.

Grace glared at him. She didn't appreciate the sarcasm or the tone. 'Jake is the one who's been lied to about his own daughter. Connor was supposed to be his best mate and he slept with his wife—'

'She wasn't his wife then,' Michael interrupted her.

'Oh, for God's sake. Does that even matter?'

'What about Jake? He was cheating on Siobhan before they were married and still is. He's fucking gay, Grace, and he never thought to mention that to the woman he was marrying! No wonder she got fed up of him.'

Grace stared at him. She felt so many emotions, anger, sadness, betrayal, that she didn't know which one to deal with first. It was true that Jake had lied to Siobhan, but from the limited information she had, it seemed like he'd been lying to himself for much longer. It made her heart physically hurt to think that he'd been forced to carry such a secret all alone for so long, and hadn't felt able to confide in her of all people. Hadn't she always been there for him? Hadn't she proved beyond a doubt that she loved him unconditionally? Then there was Michael. The man for whom she had finally let down her guard, and whom she had trusted implicitly. It had taken a lot for her to do that. Her marriage to Nathan had damaged her in ways that Michael couldn't even comprehend – and he had lied to her too. Despite how much she loved him, she wasn't sure that she could ever forgive him for that.

Sinking onto the armchair, Grace put her head in her hands. She was so used to solving everyone's problems, but she couldn't see any way out of this, at least not one that didn't involve losing some of the people she loved most in the world. 'What the hell are we going to do?' she said quietly.

Michael placed a hand on her shoulder and she shrugged him off. After a few seconds, she stood up and took her car keys from the sideboard.

'Where are you going?' Michael asked in exasperation.

'To find my son,' she replied.

Chapter Thirty

Grace drove into the almost deserted staff car park of The Blue Rooms and turned off the engine. Jake's BMW was the only other car there, confirming her suspicions about his whereabouts. She tried not to dwell on how sad it was that he had nowhere else to go. His rift with the Carter brothers was going to hit him as hard as his inevitable split from Siobhan. She couldn't even imagine how he was processing the fact that he might not be Isla's father, and what that would mean for all of them. She could barely wrap her head around any of it herself.

Using her key, Grace let herself into the back entrance of her son's nightclub. The automatic lights flickered to life as she walked down the hallway towards Jake's office. The door was closed. The place was deathly quiet, such a difference from its evening atmosphere. As she placed her hand on the doorknob, Grace felt a chill and for a split second, she dreaded what she might find on the other side of that door. Pushing it open, she saw the figure of her son, slumped across his desk. Her heart leapt into her chest and she rushed over to him.

'Jake,' she shouted.

His head snapped up and he looked at her groggily. 'Mum? What are you doing here?' he mumbled.

Grace closed her eyes and let out a long slow breath. 'Jesus Christ, Jake. I thought you were...'

'What? You thought I'd top myself over that little slut?' he sneered.

Grace shook her head. 'No. I thought, maybe...' She trailed off. She didn't know what she thought. Her mind didn't feel quite as sharp as it had been just twenty-four hours earlier.

Jake sighed and sat back in his chair.

'Have you been here all night?' Grace asked, noting the smell of alcohol fumes emanating from his body.

'Mostly.' He shrugged. 'Nowhere else to go, have I?'

'You could have stayed with me.'

'And that lying twat of a husband of yours?' Jake snapped. 'I don't fucking think so, Mum.'

Grace suppressed the urge to remind him that he had a nerve calling anyone a liar. But as annoyed as she was with him, she tried to focus on the pain he must be feeling. His whole world had come crashing down around his ears – and she knew exactly how that felt. So instead she sat down on the chair on the opposite side of his desk. 'What are you going to do?'

'About what?'

'About everything? Isla? Siobhan?'

Jake shook his head. 'Fuck all! Fuck the fucking lot of them,' he barked.

'But there's every chance Isla might still be your daughter, Jake. And even if she's not…'

'What? She's still my niece?' he snorted. 'I'll tell her I'm her uncle Jake, shall I?'

'No,' Grace snapped at him. 'But you adore that child, and she adores you. She never asked for any of this, and all she knows right now is that her dad isn't there. Whatever happens at the end of all this, she is the innocent party here.'

'And what about me?' Jake said to her. She was reminded of him as a petulant child.

'I don't think you can play the innocent victim card, Son, do you?' She raised an eyebrow at him. 'I know you're hurting. What Siobhan and Connor did is unthinkable, but let's not pretend you haven't been sneaking around lying to people too.'

Jake glared at her. 'So what was I supposed to do? Tell everyone I'm gay? Yeah, right.'

'Yes,' Grace said. 'If that's the truth.'

'That's easy for you to say, but you're not me, Mum. You don't understand.'

'Then explain it to me. Tell me how lying to everyone, and marrying Siobhan, was easier than admitting the truth.'

'I was going to tell her,' he snapped. 'When I was in hospital the night she told me she was pregnant. I would never have married her otherwise. Don't you see that? And do you know what's even worse? She already knew about me. She'd seen me with Paul, but she tricked me into fucking marrying her anyway. And the kid wasn't even mine,' he said with a growl before picking up the almost empty bottle of whisky from his desk and pouring himself a glass. 'She ruined my fucking life for nothing.'

Grace shook her head. Was anyone capable of telling the truth in this family? 'She was wrong, Son. No one can argue with that. But Isla isn't nothing. She may still be your flesh and blood, and even if she's not, she's still one of us.'

Jake glared at her as he downed the glass of whisky in one. 'No, she's not. So, if she's not mine, then you're going to have a tough choice to make, aren't you, Mum?'

Grace shook her head and stood up to leave. Jake was drunk and there was no sense to be talked into him today. He needed some time to calm down and some space to think.

'Who will it be? Me or the Carters?' Jake said as he leaned back in his chair. 'Your real family, or your new one?'

Grace looked at him and felt like her heart was going to break in two. She wanted to tell him to stop being so ridiculous, but how could she when there was a part of her that wondered if things could ever be the same again? She would never choose between her children but, like it or not, there were going to be some difficult choices to be made, no matter who Isla's father turned out to be.

Chapter Thirty-One

C raig Johnson squinted as he stepped out of Walton prison and into the bright sunlight. Four years over – at long fucking last. Doing his time hadn't been hard, but it had been bloody boring. They'd kept him and his older brother Ged apart for most of it. Ged was due to be released from Strangeways the following day. He'd been kept in Cat A for most of his sentence because he hadn't learned the fine art of keeping his head down and not starting fights with every poor fucker who looked at him sideways.

As he looked across the busy main road, Craig could see his eldest brother Bradley waiting for him, standing beside a shiny silver Mercedes, which was glinting in the sun.

Slinging his holdall over his shoulder, Craig waited for a break in the traffic before jogging over the road. 'Nice motor.' He grinned at Bradley.

'I know. It was about time I got myself a decent one and I thought it was only fair for you to be driven home in style.' Bradley laughed as he gave Craig a giant bear hug. 'It's nice to see you, Bro,' he said with genuine affection.

'It's nice to be seen,' Craig replied, throwing his bag into the back seat of the car.

'Where to then, lad? The world is your lobster.'

Craig thought about what he'd missed most – decent drugs, alcohol that didn't burn a hole in your gullet, and sex. Especially sex. He contemplated going somewhere he could get all three at the same time, but he had an appointment with his Probation Officer later that afternoon, and he knew better than to piss her off on his first day out. She was a heartless bitch and he had a suspicion she'd have him recalled back to prison in a heartbeat given half a chance. Besides, he knew his missus Gemma was waiting at home for him. She'd even packed the kids off to her ma's for a few hours so they could have some time alone.

'Take me home, mate,' he said with a sigh. 'And don't spare the horses.'

Resting his head against the cool leather headrest, he took a cigarette from the open packet in the centre console of the car. 'Am I allowed to smoke in this posh motor?' he asked.

'Course you are, you daft cunt,' Bradley replied.

Craig took his lighter out of his pocket and lit the cigarette before taking a long drag. 'So how did your meeting with Alastair McGrath go?'

Bradley grinned at him. 'Better than expected. He gave us a good deal. And we've already shifted some of the gear. Easy money, mate.'

Craig nodded. 'I told you he was a good bloke.'

'I didn't actually meet him. Spoke to him on the phone, but he sent his right-hand man, Jock, to drop off the gear.'

'Makes sense. I don't think he likes to get his hands dirty these days.'

Craig had done a stint in Frankland, where he'd met Alastair McGrath, a Scot who'd married an Essex girl and had made a considerable name for himself working for her father, who'd then left him the family business when he'd popped his clogs. Alastair had been released a few months before Craig, but he had been untouchable on the inside. He was the top dog and Craig had made it his mission to become indispensable to the man himself. He'd told Alastair all about his brothers and their plan to become big players in Liverpool and it had paid dividends. Alastair had been looking to establish some connections up North and the Johnson brothers were happy to help him out.

'You did good getting in with him, Craig,' Bradley said. 'Really good.'

'Thanks, Bro.' Craig couldn't help but feel a swell of pride whenever his older brother, his hero, paid him a compliment. He'd never got on as well with his other brothers as he did Bradley. Ged had been born with a massive chip on his shoulder, and had taken it out on his younger brothers until they'd been big enough to stand up to him. Billy was a bit of a loner, who for the most part kept his thoughts and feelings to himself, and Scott had always been a mummy's boy. Craig would kill for any of his brothers, but he would die for Bradley.

'I'm glad you're out, mate. I felt like I'd lost my right arm with you inside,' Bradley said.

'Well, your right arm is back and ready to get stuck in, as soon as I've been home and seen to the wife.' Craig grinned.

'Good. I could do with some help sorting out a few little scrotes who've been avoiding paying me what they owe. They're over in Birkenhead. Fancy a little drive later?'

'Sounds good. But I've got to see my PO at three.'

'Sound. I'll pick you up from yours at half seven.'

'Is Billy coming?'

Bradley shook his head. 'Nah. Let's just me and you go. Like the old days.'

'Sound, Bro,' Craig replied, recalling how he and Bradley had once had a lucrative, if short-lived, career taxing local dealers, before they'd had a hiding from Michael Carter for stealing from the wrong person. That ensured they'd burned their bridges in Liverpool. Back then, if you fucked with Grace Sumner, you were screwed. Fortunately for them, Bradley's then girlfriend, now wife, Tina, was from Manchester and her brothers had connections to Sol Shepherd, so they'd managed to land themselves an even better gig selling drugs for him. They knew as long as they stayed out of Liverpool, and out of Grace Sumner and Michael Carter's way, they'd be sweet. Soon they'd been doing so well, they'd had to enlist the help of Ged and Billy. The Johnson brothers had coined it in until one of Sol's trusted inner circle had turned out to be a grass and had thrown them all under the fucking bus. Him and Ged had got eight years each, Billy just five, while by some miracle Bradley had been lucky enough to avoid having his collar felt at all.

Craig smiled as they drove through the streets of

Liverpool towards his house in Old Swan. Their partnership with Alastair McGrath was going to make them untouchable. They weren't just the Johnson brothers any more. Now they had some serious backing behind them. If Alastair wanted to branch out into the North-West, then Craig and his brothers would ensure that they rode his coat tails all the way to the top.

Chapter Thirty-Two

Arriving back at home, Grace kicked off her shoes and walked along the hallway to the living room. She'd driven around for a few hours after speaking to Jake, thinking about how she could fix the whole mess they'd all got themselves into. But no solutions had presented themselves and she was as confused as ever.

Michael was sitting on the sofa when she walked into the room. When he saw her enter, he stood up and walked over to her. Thankfully he appeared to have stopped drinking and was looking considerably more sober than when she'd left earlier that morning.

Grace looked at her husband. She saw the tears pricking his eyes and the agony on his face, but as much as her instinct was to offer him some words of comfort, she couldn't bring herself to do it. She was too hurt herself to try and deal with his pain too.

'Grace, please?' he started. 'What can I do to prove to

you how sorry I am? What will it take for you to forgive me?'

'I don't know,' she sighed.

'You must understand I was in an impossible situation, Grace.'

'I know you were. I really do. I know you were torn between your loyalty to your son and your loyalty to me, but that doesn't make it any easier to deal with the fact that the people I love and trusted most in the world have been lying to me. I feel like my whole world has been tipped upside down and you were all just waiting for it to happen.'

'I know that, but...'

Grace shook her head. 'Do you know what? I could have handled the others lying to me. I could have dealt with the whole fallout of this entire shit-storm if I'd just had you on my side. If only you had been honest with me. That's what hurts me the most.'

'I know—'

'No!' she snapped. 'No, you do not know. You don't know at all. You have no idea what it took for me to let myself fall in love with you. To agree to marry you.'

'What?' he said with a frown. 'I didn't realise it was so fucking difficult for you to marry me.'

'Well, it was. Do you have any idea what it feels like to have to survive a marriage where the person who swore to love and protect you is actually a monster whose sole purpose is to destroy you and everything that is good in your life? Do you know what it was like to have to protect myself and Jake from Nathan every single hour of every single day?

Because there was no one else to do it. And even when I was finally free of him, I was so terrified to let anyone else in get that close to me again. I was so damaged that the thought of doing that was incomprehensible. But then, something incredible happened, and you finally got through my armour. I trusted you. I gave you everything I had, and then you broke that trust by lying to me. This has broken me, Michael.'

He stared at her. 'Grace,' he whispered.

'Stop!' she snapped, unable to look at him any longer for fear she might say something she'd regret. 'Look, I just need some space.'

'What does that mean?'

'Just leave me be for a while. I'm not going anywhere. I don't expect you to go anywhere, the kids would be devastated. But I just want some space to think.'

'About what?' He sounded exasperated now.

'Us. This mess, and how we're going to fix it.'

'It's not our mess to fix. It's for our kids to sort out. Our grown-up sons who are perfectly capable of looking after themselves and making decisions, stupid fucking decisions I'll grant you, but we need to let them sort this out themselves.'

'And you think they'll do that? This could tear our whole family apart.'

'It won't,' he sighed.

'If one of you had just told me. Maybe I could have—'

'What? Stopped this? I know you're good, Grace but even you couldn't have prevented this. Our kids fucked up. The three of them. And they have to take responsibility for that. You have to stop trying to fix everything for everyone.'

Grace glared at him. 'Spoken by a man who has never been left to pick up the pieces.'

'That's not fair, Grace.'

'Fair? None of this is fair. What about poor Isla? The poor kid doesn't know if she's coming or going.' She shook her head. It was all too much to even think about.

'Where does this leave us?' Michael asked.

She shrugged. 'I honestly don't know.'

The sound of the doorbell brought their discussion to an abrupt end, much to Grace's relief. She left the room to answer the door, leaving Michael standing alone in their living room.

Chapter Thirty-Three

Siobhan opened the front door and burst into tears as soon as she saw her friend Jenny standing there on her doorstep. She had phoned her thirty minutes earlier after putting Isla to bed and asked her to call round.

'Hey,' Jenny said as she stepped into the hallway and pulled Siobhan into a hug. 'What's wrong?'

'Everything,' Siobhan sniffed.

'Well, let's open this and you can tell me all about it,' Jenny replied as she held up the bottle of rosé she'd brought with her.

Siobhan wiped the tears from her face. 'Sounds like a good idea,' she said with a faint smile.

With an arm around each other's waist, the two women walked down the hallway and into the kitchen.

Siobhan looked at Jenny, who stared at her open-mouthed.

Siobhan had just relayed a blow-by-blow account of the incident the previous day when she'd told Jake he might not be Isla's father, and filled in all of the backstory too. Jenny had once been her best friend, and Siobhan was sure she could still trust her to be discreet, although part of her was beyond caring. She needed someone to talk to, and she felt like there was no one else she could confide in.

'Wow!' Jenny said as she poured them both another glass of wine. 'And I thought my time in New York was eventful.'

'What am I going to do, Jen?' Siobhan said as she took the proffered glass of wine from her friend's outstretched hand.

Jenny shook her head. 'Damned if I know, girl. You're in a right mess, aren't you?'

Siobhan nodded. 'I sent for one of them DNA tests today.'

'Well, that seems like a good place to start. Find out the truth and then work from there.'

'Yes, but how do I get the DNA samples from Jake or Connor?' she said with a sigh.

'Well, you only need one, don't you? If Jake isn't Isla's dad, then Connor is. Or is there someone else?'

'No!' Siobhan shrieked. 'What do you take me for, Jen?'

Jenny laughed. 'I'm just making sure. No one could blame you. Jake obviously wasn't satisfying your needs. So you were perfectly entitled to look elsewhere. He was!'

'That may be, but that doesn't help me figure out how to get their DNA sample. I can't bear to ask either of them,' she said with a shudder.

'What about asking Grace?' Jenny suggested.

'Grace? Are you serious?'

'Why not? You said you always got on well—'

'Yeah, before I slept with her stepson behind her son's back!'

'She's a better bet than those two though, isn't she? She's a woman. She must understand how hard it was for you being married to a gay man, whether he was her son or not.'

Siobhan shook her head. 'I really don't think she'll see it that way. She adores Jake. He's her son – and no matter what he was, or is, what I did is unforgivable.'

'Didn't she lie about Belle's dad though?'

'Yes. But that was completely different. Grace and Michael spent one night together when she got pregnant with Belle. Michael was married and she didn't want to ruin that for him. She lied, but it was for a good reason.'

'Seems like she ain't no saint to me,' Jenny said with a raised eyebrow.

'You don't know her,' Siobhan said with a wistful shake of her head. 'She's amazing. And I really miss her,' she sniffed.

'Well, if you want to know the truth, seems like it's either her or one of the potential fathers. Which is it to be?'

Grace considered Jenny's question. She had no idea what reception she'd get from Grace if she turned up at her house unannounced. But, what she did know was that it would be a whole lot better than any reception she'd get from Connor or Jake.

'You know what? You're right. I'll go to Grace. I'll ask

my mum to watch Isla for an hour tomorrow, and call round.'

Jenny nodded. 'That's settled then.'

Siobhan stared at her friend as her lower lip started to wobble. 'What if she refuses to see me?'

Jenny stood up and walked around the breakfast bar. Putting her arm around Siobhan, she pulled her close. 'She won't,' she said soothingly.

Siobhan gave Jenny a faint smile, but she didn't feel quite so confident about the reception she'd receive from Grace. There was no saying how she would react. Siobhan wasn't even sure exactly how much Grace knew about the whole situation. Did she know that Siobhan had slept with Connor? Had Connor told everyone the details of their tawdry night together? God, the thought of Grace knowing intimate details of her sex life made her want to curl up and hide away. Nevertheless, any shame she felt was vastly overshadowed by the fear that she could potentially be on the receiving end of the legendary wrath of Grace Carter. Grace was fiercely protective of her family, particularly her children, and Siobhan also felt an acute sadness that she might never again feel the safety and security that came with being a member of that family.

Chapter Thirty-Four

Bradley Johnson pulled up outside his younger brother Craig's terraced house in Old Swan and beeped the horn of his Mercedes to let Craig know he was there. A few seconds later he watched as his brother opened the door and then disentangled himself from his two daughters, Cheyenne and Jade.

'I'll be back in a bit, girls,' he shouted as he bounced down the path, rolling his eyes and grinning at Bradley as he did.

'God, I've only been home for a few hours and I'm glad to be out of there already,' Craig said, laughing as he climbed into the passenger seat. 'Can't be doing with all them females and their raging hormones.'

Bradley nodded in sympathy. Craig's daughters were a few years older than his, and he was dreading Keisha and Carly getting older. At nine and seven years of age, they were already a handful. Unlike his son, Bradley Junior, who was coming up to thirteen and was as good as gold.

'How was your meeting with your PO?' Bradley asked.

'All right.' Craig shrugged. 'She gave me a list of rules to follow and told me about some job club I'm supposed to go to next week.'

Bradley laughed. 'Did you tell her to stick her job club up her arse?'

Craig shook his head. 'Can't, can I? I have to at least to pretend to play the game. Anyway, tell me where we're off to on this glorious Monday evening?'

'Off over to the dark side. There's a couple of lads who have been selling some gear for us round Birkenhead. They were good as gold at first, and then they started being a day late paying. Now they've been dodging my calls all weekend, and I think it's about time they learned that we are not men to be messed with.'

'Sound.'

Bradley smiled as he pulled into the Wallasey tunnel. It was good to have his favourite brother back by his side. He liked working with his other brothers too, but he and Craig had always had a special bond – an understanding. However, together the Johnson family were unstoppable.

———

Just over twenty minutes later, Bradley pulled up outside the almost vacant block of flats in Birkenhead where Kev and Colin lived. Opening the boot of his car, he took out a small crowbar.

'What's your poison?' he asked Craig, as they looked over the array of tools in the boot.

'This'll do me,' Craig said as he picked up a sledgehammer.

Bradley nodded. 'Let's go and remind our friends why they need to pay on time then.'

They jogged up the steps to the second floor and knocked on the door of Kev and Colin's flat. When there was no answer, Bradley jimmied the lock with the crowbar and the two Johnson brothers burst into the flat to find Kev and Colin Jones comatose on the sofa, surrounded by various drug paraphernalia.

'Fucking hell. They're wasted,' Craig said in disgust.

'Fuck!' Bradley snapped. 'We could kick seven shades of shite out of them and they wouldn't feel a thing.'

Craig shook his head. 'What you doing letting this pair of crackheads sell our gear, Bro?'

Bradley frowned at his brother. 'Well, I didn't know they were crackheads, did I? Obviously, they looked all right when I spoke to them. Big Geoff said they were okay, and it's not like we have much choice right now. Conlon and those fucking twins have got most of the Wirral sewn up as well. We've got to start somewhere, haven't we?'

'Alastair won't like this,' Craig said quietly.

'Fuck Alastair!' Bradley shouted. 'Besides, who's gonna tell him? I'm not. Are you?'

'Course not.' Craig shook his head. 'But how much do they owe us?'

'Ten grand,' Bradley replied.

'Ten grand?' Craig snapped. 'For fuck's sake, Brad.'

'That's pocket change to Alastair McGrath. He's not gonna miss it. Besides, we can make it up elsewhere.'

'Whatever you say, mate,' Craig replied sarcastically. 'And what about this pair of cunts?'

Bradley kicked one of the sleeping men in the face and he groaned but remained otherwise motionless as the blood started to pour from his nose. 'Have a quick look round and see if any of our gear's left. If not, let's just torch the place.'

'What? With these two in it?'

Bradley nodded. 'Don't you think nicking ten grand off us is something we need to send a message about? If it gets out that we let this pair of lowlifes get away with nicking from us, we're never going to make our mark. We need to send a message, Craig. You never used to be so squeamish.'

'I'm not squeamish,' Craig snapped. 'But there are other flats here. There could be kids in them. Or someone's old granny for all you know.'

'Most of the flats in this block are empty. But if you're that worried, we'll give the neighbours' doors a bang on the way out.'

'You're the boss,' Craig said with a shrug.

Bradley took some of the old newspapers and magazines and arranged them in a pile on the old couch, before pouring the dregs of a bottle of vodka onto the carpet. Taking one of the lighters from the coffee table, he lit the pile of paper and watched as it quickly caught fire. The flames were already spreading across the couch when Craig walked back into the room.

'None of our gear is in here. Looks like they fucking took it all themselves,' he said with a look of disgust.

'Let's get going then,' Bradley ordered.

The two of them walked out of the flat and closed the

door on the burning rooms behind them. As promised, they banged loudly on the neighbours' doors as they passed, before running down the steps and climbing into Bradley's car.

As they drove back through the tunnel to Liverpool, Craig started to wonder whether torching the Joneses' flat, with them inside, had been the right thing to do. If he'd been in charge, he would have gone back tomorrow when they were sober, given them a good kicking, and then ensured the Joneses remained indebted to them for all eternity. They would have spent the rest of their miserable lives working to pay off that ten grand debt. As it was, now Craig and Bradley had lost their drugs and their money, and had absolutely no chance of getting any of it back.

'You all right?' Bradley said as Craig stared out of the window.'

'Yeah,' he replied. 'I just wonder if we should have handled that differently, that's all.'

'You're not going soft on me, are ya, lad?'

'No! But we could have used them. Got our money back somehow.'

'No chance, Craig. Did you see them? A useless pair of oxygen stealers. We've done the world a favour getting rid of them.'

'Whatever,' Craig said and went back to staring out of the window. He was used to Bradley's way of working even though he sometimes didn't agree with it. His eldest brother had always been impulsive, preferring to ask for forgiveness rather than permission ever since they were kids, but Craig wasn't sure that kind of thinking got you far with the likes of Alastair McGrath. Craig had worked hard to get into Alastair's inner circle while he'd been inside, earning his respect and trust. This was a huge opportunity for the Johnson brothers and there was no way Craig was going to allow anyone to fuck it up for them. Not even Bradley.

Bradley stared at the road ahead and tried his best to ignore Craig's bad mood. Instead he thought about what a stroke of luck it had turned out to be that Kev and Colin were wasted when they'd arrived. Instead of the two grand in debt they actually owed, now Bradley had been able to pin the whole ten grand on them. It was one less thing for him to worry about. At least Craig would have his back trying to recoup the missing money and he no longer had to do it alone. Bradley hadn't meant to gamble away ten grand of Alastair McGrath's money in the casino the week before. He'd intended to double his money, and he'd been on course to until they'd changed the croupier on him, and Bradley's luck had disappeared with her. If he'd have just had a couple of hundred quid left, he could have won it all back, and more. But luck hadn't been on his side.

Alastair McGrath had agreed to give Bradley ten grand as a deposit on a little terraced house in Bootle. It was being sold by an old acquaintance of his and Bradley had planned to make it the base of the Johnson brothers' operations. They couldn't be having too many drugs coming in and out of their own houses with the kids hanging about, or the possibility that the plod might come sniffing around. Alastair had agreed that it was good business and would only help to maximise profits in the long term. Bradley could have tripled that money on a good night in the casino, and Alastair would have been none the wiser, but now he would have to find a way to scrape the money together from somewhere. Craig would help him think of something though, Bradley was sure of that. His younger brother was loyal to a fault; it was one of the things he admired so much about him. He felt a pang of guilt for lying to Craig about Alastair's money, but Bradley had been lying to his family for years, and the more he lied, the easier it became. Besides, lying to Craig was an infinitely better option that allowing Alastair McGrath to find out that he'd lost ten grand of his money. Whilst the brief twinges of guilt would ease, the fear that someone would slip into his house in the middle of the night and slit his throat wouldn't have been so easily allayed.

Chapter Thirty-Five

Paul Carter climbed out of his car and pulled up the collar of his jacket. Walking through the staff car park, he reached the entrance to The Blue Rooms and nodded to the bouncers on the door.

'All right, lads,' he said as he walked through them.

'All right, Boss,' they murmured back to him. While most of them looked him in the eye, a few others fidgeted nervously and averted his gaze, suggesting to Paul that they been witness to, or heard about, his and Connor's spat with Jake the night before.

Paul walked through to the back office, wondering what reception he was likely to get. He wasn't expecting a warm welcome, but hoped that Jake would at least listen to what he had to say.

Paul pushed open the office door and saw Jake sitting at his desk with a half-empty bottle of whisky in front of him.

'What the fuck do you want?' Jake growled at him.

'I'm just here to talk to you, mate,' Paul replied.

'Mate?' Jake said with a snort. 'You must be fucking kidding. You're no mate of mine. Mates don't stab you in the back. Mates don't do what you did.'

'Jake,' Paul said as he took a step towards him, his hands raised in surrender. 'I know you're angry—'

'Angry?' Jake bellowed. 'That's a fucking understatement!'

'I know,' Paul said quietly.

'No! You don't fucking know, Paul. What Connor did is fucking despicable.'

'I know.'

'But you still covered up for him?'

'What was I supposed to do, Jake?'

Picking up the bottle of whisky, Jake started to pour himself a large glass. 'I bet the two of you had a right laugh at me, didn't you?'

'No, of course we didn't.'

'I don't fucking believe you, Paul. How could you do that to me? How could you let me marry her, knowing that Isla wasn't mine?' He slumped in his chair and downed the glass of whisky in one.

Paul had asked himself that same question over and over again and the only answer was his loyalty to his twin. 'Siobhan said she was yours, Jake. Connor believed her. They only slept together once. But we should have told you. I'm sorry.'

Jake looked up at him with bloodshot eyes. 'Sorry?'

'More than you could imagine.'

'You know what, Paul?'

'What?'

'Fuck off!' Jake shouted as he launched his empty glass at Paul's head. Paul ducked just in time, allowing the glass to hit the wall behind him and shatter.

'Okay. I'm going,' Paul said as he backed out of the office.

'And don't fucking come back, you traitorous bastard,' Jake shouted after him.

Paul climbed into his car and rested his forehead on the cool leather steering wheel. How could it be that in twenty-four hours his whole world felt like it was falling apart? It felt like all of the people he loved most in the world were at each other's throats. He already missed Jake so much it felt like there was a gaping hole in his chest. He missed his dad and Grace, and being able to pop into their house whenever he felt like it – to ask for their advice, or just to eat their food. He missed his little brother and sister and how they always smiled whenever he walked into the room. It was Sunday in a few days and it would be the first one he hadn't spent with his family for as long as he could remember. Everything was fucked and he didn't have a clue how to fix it.

Chapter Thirty-Six

Ged Johnson walked through the hallway and into the kitchen of his childhood home. Since his beloved mum had died, his eldest brother Bradley and his wife Tina had moved in and now called the place their own, along with their three kids, Bradley Junior, Keisha and Jade. They'd offered to put Ged up for a while when he'd got out of the nick, but the constant noise and chaos of the house would have soon started to drive him nuts, so he'd sorted his own little flat near Everton Brow. Still, he, like his three younger brothers, came to the house on Bournemouth Street almost every day. It was the family seat, the base of the Johnson brothers' operations. Tina always made them some grub while they talked business.

Ged smiled as he saw all four of his brothers sitting around the kitchen table. They were waiting for him. They would never start without him, and today he had some belting news to share with them all. News that was about to change their lives and would finally cement their rise to the top.

'You're late, lad,' Bradley said as he took his feet off the chair he'd had them resting on to allow Ged to sit down.

Ged picked up a bacon butty from the pile on the plate in the centre of the table and grinned. 'I've been busy.'

'Doing what?' Bradley snapped.

'Yeah, what?' one of his younger brothers, Craig, added.

Ged sat in his chair and smiled at them all. He enjoyed being the centre of attention for a change. Growing up, Bradley had been the golden child. His mum and dad thought the sun shone out of his arse. His youngest brother, Scott, was the baby who everyone had to look after. He, Craig and Billy had had to jostle for position and attention. He was only a year younger than Bradley, but it was Bradley who was always first in the queue for everything. Ged had to make do with his brother's castoffs.

Well, today he was going to be the star of the show whether Bradley liked it or not.

'I was down the bookies this morning and I bumped into Mickey Newhall. He was telling me that Jake Conlon and the Carter twins have had a massive fallout, and I mean a big one.'

Bradley waved his hand in dismissal. 'Mickey Newhall is a fucking quilt who gossips like an old tart. Take no fucking notice of him.'

Ged frowned. 'Mickey heard them come to blows himself. Jake told the Carters never to go near his club again.'

'It won't last. They're fucking family. Grace Sumner is

married to Michael Carter. Do you think the pair of them will stand for their kids being at odds?'

'Well, I asked around and Grace and Michael aren't happy about it, obviously. Caused a bit of trouble in paradise by all accounts. But the lads still won't speak to each other. Jake even asked Mickey if he knew anyone who could sort some shooters for him. You know the Carters always took care of that. I'm telling you, Brad, they're at fucking war.'

Bradley regarded his younger brother. There had always been a rivalry between the two of them. Their dad had thought it funny to encourage it, while their mum had been too scared of him to put a stop to any of his nonsense. Bradley always felt an underlying animosity from Ged, and although he loved his brother, Ged's seemingly constant need to outdo him annoyed him at times. But even Bradley had to admit, if what Ged was saying was true, it was a stroke of luck that had come at exactly the right time.

'All right, Ged. Suppose your information is right.'

'It is,' Ged snapped.

'Well, if it is, this is like a fucking gift from the gods, lads. We'd be stupid not to capitalise on those little fuckers being at each other's throats.'

'What do you mean?' Scott piped up.

'I mean that we are going to strike while our enemies are weak. What better time to take over than when the enemy is distracted and too busy bickering with each other to pay any attention to what we're doing? We're going to make sure that Jake Conlon and the Carter twins become nothing more than a memory.'

Ged nodded his agreement, with Craig and Billy following suit.

'They won't have a clue what's fucking hit them,' Craig said, laughing.

'Bunch of arrogant wankers,' Billy joined in.

Soon, four of the five Johnson brothers were grinning from ear to ear as they started to discuss how they would put their new plan into action. It was only Scott Johnson who remained quiet while he sipped his now cold mug of tea and watched his brothers. The bacon butty he'd consumed fifteen minutes earlier was threatening to make a reappearance and only the thought of the look of disgust that would appear on Bradley's face stopped him from throwing up all over the table. His brothers were crazy. Whilst they liked to remind him at every opportunity just how much he had to learn about the family business, he was the only one who could see that taking on Jake Conlon and the Carters was a suicide mission. Even if they were at war with each other, they were still dangerous and ruthless men, who weren't going to roll over and let people take the piss just because they'd had some family drama. His idiot older brothers were going to get themselves killed, and, if he wasn't careful, him too.

Chapter Thirty-Seven

Siobhan Conlon shook the rain from her umbrella and took a deep breath before ringing the doorbell.

It seemed like an eternity before the door opened, but once it did, Siobhan felt her knees buckle. Finally, she was standing face to face with her mother-in-law. The woman whom she admired more than any other she had ever known, and whose opinion meant more to her than she had previously realised. And now she was also a woman whom Siobhan had betrayed. When she'd lied to Jake, she'd lied to Grace too.

Siobhan swallowed the lump in her throat. 'Hi, Grace,' she said softly. 'Can I come in?'

To say Grace was shocked to see Siobhan standing on her doorstep was an understatement. Despite how close they had been, Siobhan had lied to everyone and Grace was sure she would be keeping her head down, considering the shit-storm she'd helped to create in the past few days. But there she was, as large as life. There was something about the way she stood there, trembling in the rain, but holding her own, and looking Grace in the eye, that reminded Grace of why she had loved her so much. If she had any sense, and she did, Siobhan would be worried about the potential welcome she'd receive from her mother-in-law, but she was standing there anyway, ready to face the music. Siobhan's quiet strength was something that Grace had always admired about her daughter-in-law. She reminded her of herself in her younger days, when she'd had to learn to fend for herself and Jake. That quiet determination, and the unshakable knowledge that you would do whatever it took to protect your child.

Grace opened the door wider. 'Come in.'

Siobhan followed Grace into the kitchen, passing the living room, where Michael was lying on the floor playing with Belle and Oscar. Siobhan caught his eye as she passed and noted the scowl flash across his face.

'Do you want a cup of tea?' Grace asked, already filling the kettle as Siobhan took a seat at the breakfast bar.

'Yes, please,' Siobhan replied and sat patiently while Grace made the two of them a drink. She watched as Grace moved around the kitchen, unable to judge how she was coping with the recent discovery that Jake might not be Isla's father. It was impossible to tell. Grace was impossible to read. Even in situations of extreme stress, she kept a cool head. It was one of the things that must have made her so terrifying to anyone who crossed her. Siobhan felt her heart start to race as she realised she had never been on the receiving end of Grace's ire before.

'There you go,' Grace said coolly, placing the mug of tea on the breakfast bar and snapping Siobhan out of her thoughts.

'Thanks,' Siobhan replied quietly, wrapping her hands around the mug, the warmth offering her some degree of comfort in what was now a decidedly frosty atmosphere.

Grace sat on the stool opposite Siobhan with her own drink and proceeded to stare at her, until Siobhan finally mustered the courage to speak.

'I wanted to explain—'

'I don't think there's any amount of explaining that can dig you, or any of us, out of this mess,' Grace replied curtly.

'I know that,' Siobhan replied. 'But I wanted to try anyway. I feel like I owe that to everyone, but especially you, Grace.'

'Me? Don't you think it's Jake you need to be talking to?'

'Yes. Of course. But he won't speak to me at all. Not that I blame him. But I thought I'd give him a chance to cool off. Especially after…'

'After what?' Grace said, her eyebrows pulled into a frown.

'Nothing.' Siobhan shook her head and absent-mindedly rubbed her neck. She hadn't intended to mention what had happened between her and Jake the other day. She didn't want to be accused of trying to gain sympathy – because she wasn't.

Grace walked around the counter and looked at her closely. 'Did Jake do that?' she asked as she gently touched the bruises on her daughter-in-law's neck, which Siobhan had thought were concealed by the high-necked blouse she was wearing.

'He was upset.'

'Upset? I don't care what he was, there's still no excuse for that. Absolutely none at all,' Grace said before shaking her head and walking back to her seat.

Siobhan watched as Grace appeared lost in thought. 'I really did believe Jake was Isla's father, Grace,' she said. 'I still do.'

Grace stared at her, as though she'd forgotten that Siobhan was in the room for a moment. 'But Connor, Siobhan? Of all people. Why? Why would you even think of going there?'

Siobhan shrugged. 'It was wrong. I know that. But I was so hurt, Grace. When I found out about him and Paul, I thought my heart was going to break. When I slept with Connor, I told myself it was because he was the first person who'd looked at me that way for a long time. But, I suppose a part of me knew that it would hurt Jake as much as he had hurt me.' She stopped talking and looked down at her hands, trying to will herself not to cry.

'So you knew Jake was gay when you agreed to marry him?'

Siobhan felt the flush of heat creeping up her neck. Grace was the smartest woman she knew. There was no hiding anything under the scrutiny of her gaze. 'I knew about him and Paul, yes. But I wanted to believe it was a mistake, Grace. I loved him so much that I thought I could change him. I thought that I could be enough for him,' she sniffed, trying to stop herself from crying but failing to prevent the tears from starting.

Grace simply nodded in response.

_____

Grace had no idea what to think any more. The bruises on Siobhan's neck were shocking, to say the least. It reminded her of the pattern of bruising that she had seen on her own neck so many times before, at the hands of Jake's father, Nathan. Grace knew that her son was no angel. But surely he was better than that? She had raised him better than that – at least she'd thought she had. She tried to put herself in his position. He'd just found out his daughter might not be his child, that his wife had slept with one of his best friends and lied to him, but no matter what Siobhan had done, it didn't warrant that. Nothing did. You didn't do that to people you claimed to love – no matter how much they hurt you.

Grace remembered the disbelief and horror she had felt herself when she'd been told about Jake and Paul's affair. How on earth must Siobhan have felt to find out that the man she loved and had committed her life to was not only gay but had been sleeping with a man who was practically his brother? It didn't excuse what she'd done, not in the slightest, but Grace knew of the pain of loving a man whose very nature meant that he wasn't capable of loving you in return. She had believed the same things of Nathan, hadn't she? That she could change him? That her love would be enough? She knew all about realising that the man you love is not who he claims to be, and finding solace in the arms of someone else. Grace herself had embarked on an affair with Nathan's best friend Ben towards the end of her marriage. Was that any different to what Siobhan had done? And wasn't Connor just as much to blame? Yet Grace hadn't disowned him. She was angry with him for the pain he had caused, but she would never disown him – he was her family, and, like it or not, so was Siobhan.

'So, what are you going to do now?' Grace asked.

Siobhan looked up at her, tears streaming down her pale face. 'I don't know,' she sobbed. 'I've made such a cock-up of everything. I don't know how to even begin to fix it.'

'Well, let's not forget the most important person here is Isla,' Grace said. 'We need to try and keep things as normal as possible for her.'

Siobhan nodded. 'I know. She thinks her dad is working away, but she's been asking for him, Grace, and I don't know how much longer I can keep up the pretence.'

'Do you honestly believe Jake is her dad?'

'Yes. I really do. She has all of his facial expressions and when she frowns, she looks exactly like him. Besides, I just know.'

'But she could be Connor's?'

'I suppose there is a possibility. But a very small one.'

'You know Jake will need proof. One way or another. Not to mention Isla and Connor. It's only fair that they all know the real truth one day.'

'I know. I've got one of those online DNA kits. It came this morning. I've paid for the same-day-results one. But I need a cheek swab from either Jake or Connor. Jake refuses to speak to me, and Connor – well, I'm not sure I'm ready to face him just yet.'

'Well, if you want his DNA, you might have to,' Grace replied.

Siobhan sniffed. 'I doubt he'd even speak to me.'

'Do you have the kit with you?'

'Yes. It's in my bag. That's not why I came here though, Grace,' she said as her cheeks flushed pink.

'Just hand it over and leave it to me.'

'Really?' Siobhan said. 'Thank you, Grace. I know I have no right to ask anything of you, and I really appreciate you helping me out.'

'I'm doing this for my family, Siobhan. For Isla, Jake, and Connor,' Grace said as she took a sip of her tea.

Siobhan wiped away a tear, feeling an acute sense of loss that she was no longer considered to be Grace's family.

'And for you,' Grace added.

Siobhan looked up and saw the faintest glimmer of a smile on Grace's face and fought the urge to run around the breakfast bar and throw her arms around her. Grace Carter was a woman like no other she had ever met. Despite everything that life had thrown at her, she had more compassion and heart than anyone Siobhan had ever known. She was fearless and fierce, and with that simple gesture, she had just ensured Siobhan's continued survival in the Conlon/Carter empire.

Chapter Thirty-Eight

C onnor cursed as he took his mobile phone from his bedside table. Squinting in the dim light of his bedroom, he saw Grace's name flashing on the screen. He swallowed. He wasn't particularly looking forward to this conversation, but he supposed the sooner he had it, the sooner it would be over.

'Hi, Grace?' he said.

'Hi, Connor,' she replied. 'Can you call round this afternoon? I think we need to have a chat.'

'Yeah, of course,' Connor replied. 'What time?'

'Two?'

'Yeah, that's fine. I'll see you then.'

'See you then,' she said and hung up.

Connor slumped back against the pillows. He felt like he'd just been summoned to his own execution. He'd only ever let Grace down once before, when he'd been a stupid eighteen-year-old kid and had tried to impress her with a failed attempt on her ex-husband's life. She had been absolutely furious with him and Paul for it, and they'd been terrified that she'd have someone put a bullet in their heads for the trouble they'd caused her. But instead she had protected them from the fallout and they had been fiercely loyal to her ever since.

Connor had already spoken to his dad, who had given him a bollocking for the whole sorry mess. But his dad was his dad, and nothing would ever come between them. As much as Grace treated him and Paul like family, Jake was her son, and nothing was thicker than blood. He closed his eyes and wondered what his punishment would be. Exile? Thirty lashes? Whatever it was, he would find out soon enough.

Grace watched as Oscar napped in his Moses basket, and Belle sat at her small wooden desk drawing pictures of butterflies and dinosaurs. Michael was in the kitchen cooking, much to Grace's annoyance. She'd told him to go to work, but he'd refused. It was as though he thought she might do a runner while he was out.

The ringing of the doorbell snapped Grace from her thoughts.

'I'll get it,' Michael shouted.

Belle looked up excitedly from her drawing. She loved having visitors.

Grace heard raised voices in the hallway and listened as the footsteps drew closer. Belle was on her feet by this point and heading for the living-room door as it swung open.

'Connor,' Belle shouted as she saw her older brother walking towards her.

'Hey, my little Bella.' He smiled as he picked her up for a hug.

'Can we do cowboys and princesses?' Belle asked excitedly, referring to the game her older brothers often indulged her in, which involved her riding around on their shoulders for hours at a time.

'Not today, Bella.' He sighed as put her back down onto the soft carpet. 'I can't stay for long.'

'Aaw,' said Belle, pouting.

'Why don't you draw Connor a lovely dinosaur to take home with him?' Grace suggested.

It had the desired effect and Belle nodded happily and sat back down at her desk.

Connor came further into the room with Michael close behind him and sat on the armchair.

'Thanks for coming, Connor,' Grace said.

'You invited him?' Michael asked her.

'Yes. I forgot to mention it,' she said.

'I'm really sorry, Grace,' Connor said with a sigh. 'I've really fucked up, I know I have.

I'll do anything to fix this.'

Grace stared at him. 'As much as I'd like to, I'm not going to lecture you, Connor. I can see you're beating yourself up enough, but I want you to know that you and Siobhan, and your lies, have torn this family apart.'

'I know,' Connor said solemnly. 'I can't say I'm sorry enough. And I'm sorry I caused any shit between you and my dad. I'm sorry if I've got you two falling out as well. I should never have put you in that position, Dad.' He turned his attention to Michael, who simply shook his head and cleared his throat.

'You did put your dad in an impossible position. But never mind us,' Grace said. 'What are you going to do about Isla, and Siobhan? And Jake?'

'I don't know. How can I even begin to fix it, Grace?'

Grace stared at him. 'Well, I can think of one thing. That's why I asked you to call round.'

'What? I'll do anything.'

'Siobhan has ordered one of those DNA kits, and she just needs yours or Jake's DNA to send off. So, as Jake is currently wallowing at the bottom of a whisky bottle, it looks like it's on you.'

'I'd really rather not see her. But if I have to—'

'You won't,' Grace interrupted him. 'It's in the kitchen. You can do it here.'

'Let's do it then,' Connor said standing up and walking out of the room.

Grace stood up to follow him.

'Thank you,' Michael said as she walked past him.

She shrugged. 'What choice do I have?'

Chapter Thirty-Nine

Opening the door to his flat, Paul hoped to see that it was Jake incessantly ringing the doorbell. He sighed inwardly when he saw it was his brother, Connor.

'All right, Bro?' he said as he opened the door wider to allow Connor inside.

'Not really,' Connor said with a sigh as he followed his twin into the kitchen.

'Beer?' Paul asked as he opened the fridge to get himself one.

Connor nodded and Paul handed him a cold bottle of Budweiser. Twisting off the cap, Connor took a long swig before leaning against the doorframe.

'Have you seen Grace or me da today?' Paul asked.

Connor rolled his eyes. 'Yes. Grace phoned me up and asked me to call round.'

'Really?'

'Yeah. But to be honest, I was going to go and see them anyway, just to get it all out in the open. I couldn't stand the fucking tension any longer.'

'How was it?'

'What do you think? It was fucking brutal, mate.'

Paul sighed. 'I went to see Jake yesterday.'

'How did that go?'

'Probably even worse than your visit to me da and Grace.'

'Fucking hell!'

'What are we gonna do, lad? Jake's barred us from The Blue Rooms. He's our business partner but he won't be in the same fucking room as us. We've got a shipment coming in next week.'

'I think we need to let him cool off for a bit. Let him handle the shipment. It's not like we need the money.'

'But—'

'There is no but. I banged his missus, Paul. The kid he's been raising as his own is probably mine. And you knew about it and didn't tell him. I think he's entitled to hold a grudge for a bit. He'll calm down eventually.'

'You think?' Paul snorted, wishing that he shared Connor's confidence.

'He's got to. We're family.'

Paul started to shake his head. 'You're a fucking case, Con.'

'What?' Connor said.

'You've asked Grace to sort it, haven't you?'

'No,' Connor replied, defensively. 'But she will. It's what she does.'

Paul watched as his twin downed his bottle of lager

before helping himself to another one. Connor seemed to have a lot of faith that Grace could fix this whole mess they'd got themselves into. And whilst Paul accepted that she could fix most things, he wondered whether this current disaster was beyond even her considerable skills.

'You fancy doing some work tonight?' Connor asked, snapping him from his train of thought. 'An old friend of ours has asked us to take care of a problem for him. He's prepared to pay a lot of money to get it sorted quickly too.'

Paul shrugged. 'Why not? Nothing better to do, have I?'

'You'll feel better once you've done some hard graft, Bro. I'll nip home and get changed and meet you back here in an hour.'

'Okay, see you in a bit.'

As Connor left the kitchen, Paul contemplated the fact that not only might he never work with Jake again, but there was a possibility that they might end up in opposition to each other. There wasn't enough room in Liverpool for all of them to be on top. He hoped that Connor was right and Grace would sort everything out, for all of their sakes.

Chapter Forty

Grace closed the gate behind her and walked up the familiar path of her son's house.

Ringing the bell, she waited for an answer. A few seconds later, Siobhan opened the door.

'Grace?' she said. 'I wasn't expecting you so soon.'

'Well, you know me. Why put off to tomorrow what you can do today? Can I come in?'

'Of course,' Siobhan replied as she took the chain off the latch and opened the door wider.

'Is Isla still up?' Grace asked expectantly, hoping to see her granddaughter for a few minutes.

'No, she went up about fifteen minutes ago and is flat out already. I'd have kept her up if I'd known you were calling tonight. Sorry.'

'Never mind. I suspected she'd be in bed. Just thought I'd ask.'

'You can go up and see her though if you like? She's a deep sleeper.'

Grace nodded. 'Jake was too. He could sleep through an earthquake,' she said with a smile, before realising the implication of that statement.

Siobhan cleared her throat and fidgeted with her cardigan.

'I won't stay long,' Grace went on. 'I just wanted to bring you this,' she said as she took the sealed swab sample from her handbag.

'Oh, that's great. Thanks, Grace. I'll send it off first thing.'

'Will you let me know as soon as you hear the results? Whatever they are?'

'Yes. Of course I will. Thanks again for doing this.'

'It was the only way to get the truth,' Grace said with a shrug. 'Actually, I will pop in and see Isla before I go, if that's okay?'

'Yes. Of course, you can. She'll be so disappointed she missed you.'

Grace put her handbag down and walked up the stairs and into Isla's bedroom. She looked at her sleeping granddaughter and felt a rush of love for her. No matter who was her father, Grace was still her nana, and nothing would change that. Bending over Isla's cot, she reached into her pocket and took out the swab from the testing kit she'd had delivered herself earlier that morning. Grace had already thought about a DNA testing kit herself before Siobhan had even shown up on her doorstep. Gently placing the swab inside Isla's mouth, she retrieved the desired sample. Isla stirred slightly but, to Grace's relief, didn't wake. Placing the sample in its sterile container, Grace put it back in her pocket.

'Goodnight, darling,' she whispered as she stepped out of the room.

Siobhan was waiting when Grace reached the bottom of the staircase.

'She's still fast asleep,' Grace said.

Siobhan smiled. 'She's been asking for her nana and ganga all day today.'

'She must be wondering what the hell's going on. Maybe you could drop her off for a few hours at the weekend? Belle will be missing her too. And Michael.'

'Yes. That would be great. Are you sure?'

'Yes. How about Sunday at twelve?'

Grace saw Siobhan blink back the tears. That was the time everyone would usually arrive for their weekly family gathering. This week, though, there would be no such affair and it made Grace feel like crying too.

'Yes. That would be fine,' Siobhan said.

'Good. But I'll speak to you before then?'

'Yes. I'll let you know as soon as they email me the results.'

'Great. Night, Siobhan,' Grace said as she picked up her bag and opened the front door.

'Night, Grace,' Siobhan replied.

Grace was safely in her car when she took the DNA sample from her coat pocket and placed it carefully in her handbag. She would send hers off first thing in the morning too. With Connor's sample, all Siobhan could prove was whether Connor was Isla's father or not. If the results showed that Isla wasn't Connor's child, then Grace couldn't be sure that meant that she was Jake's either. Given the revelations of the past few days, Grace wasn't confident about who she could trust any more, and she also knew that Jake would demand undeniable proof. Sending off her own sample would ensure that she could provide both of them with that.

Chapter Forty-One

G race glanced anxiously at her mobile phone while she stirred the pasta sauce on the stove for dinner. Siobhan had told Grace that she'd sent the test off first thing the previous morning, and Grace had done the same. They were each paying for the same-day-result service and both tests should have been delivered to the lab earlier today. Grace hadn't had her results yet either, but surely one of them should have heard by now, she thought to herself as she picked up her phone and opened her messages, just in case she hadn't seen the notification. She frowned when she saw there was no message. She checked her inbox for the millionth time too, but there was no email waiting for her.

The call Grace had been waiting for came twenty minutes later as she was serving out helpings of spaghetti carbonara to her expectant family.

'I need to take this,' she said to Michael as she handed him the pan.

He continued dishing up while she walked over to the corner of the kitchen.

'Siobhan,' she snapped. 'I've been driving myself mad waiting to hear from you.'

'The results have only just come back, Grace,' Siobhan said apologetically. 'I've been driving myself mad too.'

'Of course you have. Sorry,' Grace replied. 'Well?'

'She's Jake's,' Siobhan said with a gasp. 'Isla is Jake's daughter.'

'Are you sure?'

'Yes. The test was conclusive that she's not Connor's, so that means Jake is her father. I can forward you the email. Then you can show it to him.'

Grace felt like the some of the weight that had been sitting in the pit of her stomach all day had lifted. Despite the concerns that had driven her to send a sample of her own, she hoped that Siobhan wouldn't have blatantly lied to her face.

'That's great news, Siobhan,' she said as she heard the familiar ping of an email notification against her ear. 'Hang on a second, I just need to check something.' She opened the notification, confirming that she was a match for Isla's DNA, which meant that she was her grandmother, and Jake was her father. Jake being Isla's father was the best possible outcome for everyone. It meant that Jake could go on loving his daughter as he always had. He and Connor could get over their differences, she was sure of it.

'Grace?' Siobhan said on the other end of the line.

'Sorry,' Grace replied, holding the phone back to her ear.

'I was just thinking. Like I said, this is great news. Thank you for letting me know so quickly.'

'Will you tell Jake for me?' Siobhan asked.

'Of course.' Grace replied, wondering about the reception she would get from him, but knowing it would be a damn sight better than any Siobhan would.

'For what it's worth, Grace, I'm really happy that he's her dad,' Siobhan sniffed.

'I know. So am I,' Grace said softly. 'Bye, Siobhan.'

Grace walked over to the kitchen table where Michael and Belle were now eating.

'So?' Michael asked. 'What's great news?'

Grace sat down. She still hadn't forgiven him, and she wasn't sure if she ever could. But he deserved to know the truth too.

'Siobhan did a DNA test,' she said coolly. 'Jake is Isla's dad.'

Michael sighed and put his knife and fork down. 'So all this was for nothing? There was no need for Siobhan to tell anyone about her and Connor after all?'

Although she couldn't help but want to agree with him, the fact was that she would still be in the dark while almost everyone around was keeping secrets. 'No, not for nothing, Michael! At least now everyone knows the truth. At least we all know where we stand, and who we can trust,' she said quietly, conscious that Belle was present and watching her.

'You can trust me, Grace. You know that,' he said.

Grace stared at him. 'But I don't know that. Not any more.'

Chapter Forty-Two

G race walked down the corridor of The Blue Rooms. She hated this place. It held so many painful memories for her – of her ex-husband, Nathan, and also from when she was kidnapped while walking through the car park outside. She'd phoned Jake and asked him to come to the house to talk, but he'd refused to go anywhere near Michael, whom he seemed to hold as responsible for keeping the truth about Isla from him as she did. Grace could have asked Michael to make himself scarce for a few hours, but that would have probably started another argument that ended with him pleading with her to forgive him, and she didn't have the energy. She felt like she was living in some trashy soap opera. If only she was, at least then she could skip ahead twelve months, and hope that by that time this whole awful mess would be behind the lot of them.

Walking into Jake's office, Grace saw that he was drunk again. He'd never been much of a drinker in the past, but whenever he had troubles, he seemed to turn to the bottle for an answer, or for some comfort – just like his father had before him.

'What do you want, Mum?' Jake asked.

'I wanted to give you the DNA test results. They came back yesterday.'

Jake shrugged. 'I don't give a fuck, to be honest.'

'Yes, you do. And you should. Isla is your daughter.'

Jake stared at her. 'What?'

'It's true. I have the results here.' She handed him the printed piece of paper she'd brought with her.

He snatched it from her and glanced at the paper. Then he threw it back onto the desk. 'All this says is that Connor isn't the father,' he spat. 'She could be anyone's. Siobhan could have been fucking half of Liverpool for all I know.'

'I thought you might say that. So I did a test of my own and the results came back today too.'

'What test? You can't test if she's mine without me, only that she's not his.'

'Oh, but I can. Did you know you can do a test with a grandparent?'

Jake glared at her.

'I sent off my own sample with Isla's, and we're a match. I am most definitely her biological grandmother, and that means you, my son, are most definitely her father.'

Grace handed him a second piece of paper from her handbag and watched as Jake read it. 'So she's mine then?' he asked. 'Really?'

'Yes.' Grace smiled at him.

Jake ran a hand through his thick dark hair. 'I need to see her then.'

'Not stinking like an old brewery, you don't,' Grace snapped. 'Why don't you go sleep this off, freshen up, and you can see her tomorrow.'

'And where am I supposed to go? I can't go to my own house. My best mates turned out to be a pair of lying cunts, and your husband isn't much better,' he spat.

Grace stood up. 'Go to a bloody hotel then. Just fucking sober up, Jake. And then you go and get your daughter back.'

He nodded at her and she was suddenly reminded of him as a small child, when there had just been the two of them against the world.

'I know you're hurting, Son,' she said softly. 'But this will all work out in the end, I promise you.'

'And if it doesn't?' he asked.

'Then it's not the end,' she said with a smile before crossing the room and kissing the top of his head. Over the stench of whisky, she could still smell the faint aroma of his favourite expensive shampoo, the one he'd used since he was a teenager, and it broke her heart. If only she could protect him now the way she could back then. The truth was that she didn't know when things would be okay again, but she was sure in her heart that they would be. One day they would all be a family again. She would make sure of it.

Chapter Forty-Three

Arriving home, Grace walked into the kitchen where Michael was washing some of Oscar's bottles. She watched him carefully packing the steriliser and was reminded of what a good father he was to their children.

'He seems to be okay with the powdered stuff,' Grace said.

'Yeah. He seems to like it. He guzzled the last one and fell fast asleep.'

'Well, now that's he's settled and we know he's okay with the formula, I think I'm going to go back to work.'

'Oh? When?' Michael said as he placed the clean bottles in the cupboard.

'Tomorrow.'

'Tomorrow?'

'Yes. I've already spoken to your dad and Sue and they're going to watch the kids for us. I thought I'd just do two days a week for now.'

'Well, you've been thinking about going back to work

194

for a few weeks, so if that's what you want to do then you should.'

'I'm going to base myself at the restaurant so I won't be in your way.'

'You wouldn't be in my way,' Michael said with a sigh.

'It makes sense for me to work from there. It will give Sean a break too. Saves him having to be there seven days a week.'

'You've spoken to Sean about this?' Michael asked.

'I mentioned it to him earlier today.'

'Oh,' Michael said as he closed the cupboard door, a little louder than he'd intended. 'He never mentioned it.'

'Well, I only spoke to him a couple of hours ago. He probably hasn't had time. Anyway, I just wanted to let you know. I'm going to head to bed and watch a film,' Grace said.

'Okay. I'll see you in the morning.'

Grace walked out of the kitchen. She was looking forward to going back to work and having something to distract her from this awful situation with Michael. He'd moved into the spare bedroom the same day she'd told him she'd needed some space, and although she missed waking up next to him, at the same time, she couldn't bear to be in the same room as him. She knew she was being unfair on some level. He'd been in an awful position and she didn't know what she would have done had it been the other way around. But she couldn't get past the fact that he'd kept such a huge secret from her, and she wasn't sure if she ever would.

Chapter Forty-Four

'Thanks, Dad. We'll be home in an hour,' Michael said before ending the call to his father, Pat, who was looking after the kids for the day. Michael had been neglecting work for the past week, ever since the whole Jake and Connor thing had exploded and he'd spent the afternoon trying to regain some sort of order.

Grace had just gone back to work two days a week. She'd been thinking about it anyway, but Michael was sure that recent events, as well as her desire not to be in the same room as him for very long, had expedited her return. They'd always looked after different aspects of the business, so while they'd worked together for a long time, they weren't always in the same place. It wasn't unusual for him not to see his wife during the course of their working day, but nevertheless it still felt like she was deliberately avoiding him.

Michael walked into the office at the back of Sophia's Kitchen and saw Grace sitting behind the large oak desk, with the hulking figure of John Brennan leaning over her shoulder as she showed him something on her laptop. Grace and John had known each other for a long time. He'd once worked for her ex-husband, Nathan Conlon, but now he worked for her. The two of them had also become good friends since John had helped her out with a scumbag named Reuben McBride a few years earlier. But there was something about their familiarity, the closeness between them, as he walked into the room that rankled with Michael. Perhaps it was because Grace was barely acknowledging his existence lately. He wondered whether they would ever share any kind of intimacy again. He felt the anger bubbling under the surface of his skin and admonished himself for thinking there was anything untoward going on.

John leaned in closer to Grace and said something, which Michael didn't hear, making her laugh. Fucking hell! He frowned. They hadn't even noticed him come into the room. The anger surged in his chest and he cleared his throat, causing the pair of them to look up from the screen on the desk.

'Michael?' Grace said as her head snapped up, and the smile disappeared from her face. 'Is everything okay?'

'Sean told me the garage had kept your car to sort the brakes, so I thought you'd need a lift.'

'Well, John was going to drop me off. But seeing as you're here,' she said with a shrug as she closed her laptop. 'I just need to nip to the ladies before we go.'

She stood up and walked out of the office. 'I'll phone you later with the details of that job, John.'

Once she had left, Michael watched John as he started to put on his coat. 'You two looked very fucking cosy when I walked in. So, what are you up to?' Michael asked.

John shrugged. 'This and that.'

'This and that? And just what exactly does "this and that" entail?'

John walked over to him. He was a few inches taller than Michael, who had to crane his neck slightly to look up at him, something he wasn't used to and which only pissed him off more.

'Just work, Michael. Nothing cosy. Grace is my boss.'

Michael brought his face closer to John's. 'Yeah? And she's my fucking wife,' he snarled. 'Don't ever forget that.'

John shook his head. 'You're barking up the wrong tree, mate.'

After a few seconds facing off, Michael stepped aside to allow John out of the office. 'I better fucking had be, John,' he said as John walked past him.

A moment later, Grace popped her head through the office door. 'Ready?' she said.

Michael nodded and followed her out, trying not to think about how good she looked in her pencil skirt and blouse as she sashayed through the busy restaurant.

John Brennan shuddered as he walked along the Albert Dock to his parked car. The last thing he needed was to come between Grace and Michael Carter. He and Grace were good friends. He enjoyed working for her. She was a beautiful woman, and he could see why men looked at her when she walked by, but she was also married to Michael fucking Carter. John had a lot of respect for Michael. He had always been a reasonable man. He wasn't a man who would fuck you over for nothing. But if he thought John was carrying on with his missus, he would cut him into tiny pieces and feed him to some pigs. There was obviously something going on between the pair of them, which was odd, because they'd always seemed like the perfect couple. Whatever it was, John hoped they sorted it out, and fast. He couldn't stand to be caught in the middle – it wasn't good for his health.

Sitting in the car on the way home, Michael tried to concentrate on the road but he couldn't get the image of Grace and John out of his mind.

'What job have you got John on?' he asked her.

She turned her head to look at him, probably deciding whether to answer him or not. She had barely said more than a dozen words to him since the previous night.

'He's looking into a new security contract for us. The previous firm have made an absolute balls-up of the job but despite that, they're refusing to roll over.'

'I could have the lads handle it?' Michael offered.

'No need. John will sort it out.'

'Oh, will he?'

'Yes,' she snapped and turned her head back to looking out of the window.

'How long are you going to punish me for, Grace?' he asked.

'I'm not punishing you,' she said with a sigh.

'It certainly fucking feels like it.'

'I knew I should have just let John drive me home.'

'Really? You'd rather be with him rather than your own husband?' he shouted.

'I'd rather not have to go through this again, Michael,' she shouted back. 'I told you I need some space to think.'

'Think about what, Grace? You either want to be with me, or you don't.'

'It's not that fucking simple, is it?'

'It is from where I'm sitting.'

Grace shook her head in frustration. 'Everything is just so black and white for you.'

He pulled the car over to the side of the road and turned in his seat. 'How do you not see that it is? You either love me and you want us to work this out, or you don't, Grace. Which is it?'

Grace shook her head. 'I honestly don't know. Of course I love you, Michael, but I don't know if I can get past this.'

Turning back to the wheel, Michael restarted the engine and pulled the car away from the kerb. He swallowed the lump in his throat and focused on the brake lights of the car in front of him. His world felt like it was crumbling around him and there wasn't a single fucking thing he could do.

Chapter Forty-Five

Bradley Johnson walked into The Kings Arms with his brothers Ged and Craig as though he owned the place. It was a dive bar near Bootle's Dock Road, but it was frequented by cousins, Neil and Davey Parkes, who operated their lucrative business from the corner near the toilets.

'All right, Neil? Davey?' Bradley said as he and his brother approached and took a seat at the table.

'All right, lads,' Neil replied. 'Don't usually see your ugly mugs round these parts.'

'Well, we have a unique business opportunity for you,' Craig said with a grin.

Neil and Davey shook their heads. 'We work for Jake Conlon and the Carters,' Davey said. 'There's no business to be had with us.'

'Haven't you heard?' Bradley laughed. 'They've had a falling-out. They're no longer in business together.'

'Yeah, they've gone into liquidation.' Ged joined in with Bradley's laughter.

Neil shrugged. 'I've heard rumours. But until I hear directly from the horse's mouth, we'll be sticking with what we know. Thanks though, lads,' he said as he took a mouthful of his pint.

'They're not going to be able to get you any gear any time soon from what I hear,' Bradley went on. 'It will disrupt your supply chains no end. We can get you some of the finest quality marching powder money can buy, and we can get you it today. Shouldn't you be trying to keep your customers happy?'

'I'd rather keep my knob attached to my body,' Davey said with a shudder.

Neil put his pint down on the table. 'Like I said, Bradley, I appreciate your offer, but we work for Jake, Paul and Connor.'

Bradley gave the nod and before Neil or Davey knew what had had him them, Craig and Ged had the two of them by their throats with a knife pressed against their ribs. 'Now, listen to me, you pair of fuckwits. This is the perfect opportunity for you two to branch out on your own a bit, isn't it? Fuck Jake Conlon and the twins! They're too busy fighting with each other to give a shit about anyone else now. You'll start selling our gear from today. Okay?'

Despite their threats, Neil and Davey didn't respond and Bradley knew they would take more convincing.

'I saw those lovely birds of yours on their market stall at the weekend, lads,' Bradley added. 'Some nice gear they're flogging there. I hope they're careful driving home with all that money?'

Bradley noted the anger and terror flash across Neil and Davey's face before Neil spoke. 'Okay. We'll sell your gear.'

'Brilliant,' Bradley exclaimed as Ged and Craig released their grips and Neil and Davey rubbed at their necks. 'Drinks all round, Ged,' Bradley said, indicating for his brother to go to the bar. 'And then we can agree terms.'

'What did I tell ya? Like taking candy from a baby, lads,' Bradley said with a laugh as he drove him and his brothers to his house in Kirkby.

'Fucking result,' Craig added. 'If we can get Jimmy Kelly and his lot onside as well, we'll be fucking quids in.'

'Too right.' Bradley laughed.

'Jimmy won't be as easy to persuade as Neil and Davey,' Ged warned them.

'Jimmy's a fucking quilt,' Bradley snorted. 'He should have given up the ghost years ago.'

'That may be so, but his nephews are as hard as nails, Brad. And they're all loyal to the Carters. They've worked for them for years.'

'Everybody's loyalty has a price, Ged,' Bradley replied. 'We just need to find out what theirs is, that's all.'

'Is that so?' Ged replied with a sneer. 'So, you think everyone can be bought then, do you, Brad?'

Bradley turned in his seat to glare at his brother. 'I just said so, didn't I?'

'That include you?' Ged replied.

'What the fuck's that supposed to mean?' Bradley snarled.

Ged shrugged and sat back in his seat with a grin on his face. He loved to push his brother's buttons. 'You said it. I was just wondering what your price is, that's all?'

'Shut the fuck up, Ged,' Craig said. 'Can we just celebrate for five minutes without you acting like a knob?'

'Yeah. We're supposed to be fucking celebrating,' Bradley chipped in.

'We're going to rule the fucking Pool soon, lads,' Craig said with a grin.

Chapter Forty-Six

Scott Johnson held on tightly to the baseball bat in his hand as he sat in the back of the Peugeot Boxer van with three of his older brothers. He listened to their excited chattering and their boasts of what they were about to do, but all Scott wanted to do was throw up, and then after that he'd like to jump out of the van and run as far away from his crazy brothers as he possibly could. If he was honest, he wouldn't miss any of them except Billy, who was the only one of them who even tried to understand him.

Scott was nothing like any of them and they seemed to resent him for it. It wasn't his fault that he'd been born so long after they had and had been their mum's favourite. He closed his eyes and rested his head back against the cool metal of the van. Suddenly he felt a hand giving his shoulder a gentle squeeze. Opening his eyes, he saw it was Billy.

'You'll be all right, kid. We won't let anything happen to you,' he said with a grin.

Scott tried his best to return the smile.

Bradley Johnson watched as his four brothers jumped out of the back of the van armed with baseball bats and machetes. He climbed out of the driver's seat, putting the handgun he'd brought with him safely inside his coat pocket, and followed them into the Lady Muck beauty salon. The salon was in the process of being renovated, ready for its grand reopening, so there were no customers – not that the Johnson brothers were there to purchase any services themselves.

'We're not open for a few weeks,' the young woman inside said, barely looking up from the catalogue she was flicking through.

'That's all right, love,' Ged said with a laugh. 'I'm not after a back, sack and crack today.'

She looked up and, noticing the five men armed with an array of weapons, began to scream. 'Jay! Alan!'

Jay Marshall and Alan Kelly ran out of the back room and into the front of the shop wearing paint-covered overalls and brandishing large wooden mallets.

'What the fuck?' Jay shouted.

'Hello, lads,' Bradley said. 'No need for any aggro, especially not in front of the lady. We just came to talk.'

'Doesn't look like it,' Alan added, nodding towards the five heavily armed men.

'Just insurance, boys,' Bradley said with a grin. 'To make you more amenable to our offer.'

'Sandy, why don't you go home, babe,' Alan said to the now trembling woman.

'I don't think so,' Bradley said. 'She can stay right here, can't you, love?'

Sandy stared at the men in horror and Alan walked towards her. 'Whatever you want to discuss has nothing to do with her,' he said. 'Let her go home and we can talk.'

'Or she can sit her fat arse right there,' Bradley said as he took a baseball bat from Craig and pointed it towards one of the salon chairs.

'Now!' Bradley barked when Sandy didn't move quickly enough.

'It's okay, babe. Just do as he says,' Alan said through gritted teeth as he put an arm around Sandy and guided her to the chair.

'Great. Now that you're all paying attention,' Bradley started, 'let's talk some business, shall we?'

'Go on,' Jay growled.

'We hear you and your Uncle Jimmy have got yourselves quite a lucrative business on the go, and we'd like to become your new suppliers, lads, that's all.'

Alan shook his head and Jay started to laugh. 'Are you serious? You do know who our suppliers are, don't you?'

Bradley nodded. 'Of course, but I hear they're having a bit of trouble at the moment. So, we thought we'd kindly step in and fill the gap, didn't we, lads?'

Bradley's brothers affirmed their agreement.

'There's no way Paul and Connor will let you do this,' Jay said.

'Well, it's not really up to them, is it? If you two agree to supply our gear instead of theirs, there wouldn't be very much they could do about it, would there?'

Alan stared at him as though he'd grown an extra head. 'Are you for fucking real, mate? You have met the Carter twins, haven't you? There's a lot they can fucking do.'

'Such as pulling our teeth out with some pliers, or detaching our limbs from our bodies,' Alan added.

Bradley shook his head. 'I think the Carter twins are going to have their hands full for a while. They're too busy fighting with Jake Conlon to worry about you pair of wankers and your old fart of an uncle. Trust me.'

Alan and Jay both shook their heads at the same time. 'Thanks for the offer, mate. But we'll stick with the Carters.'

'You must have misunderstood me. This isn't a request. You will start selling our gear from now on.'

Alan and Jay walked towards them. 'It's not happening,' Jay snapped.

Bradley shrugged. 'Let's show them we mean business, lads.'

Craig, Ged and Billy lunged for the two men while Bradley and Scott began trashing the shop. Breaking every mirror and piece of furniture they could see, amidst Sandy's screams.

Alan and Jay were putting up a good fight, and poor Billy in particular had taken a bit of a kicking. Bradley watched the carnage unfolding around him and decided enough was enough. Taking the handgun from his pocket, he pulled Sandy to him and held it to her head.

'Stop,' he shouted.

He could feel Sandy trembling beside him and smiled

when he noticed the trickle of pale yellow liquid pooling beneath her feet.

'Do we have a deal?' Bradley said.

Alan and Jay stared at him. Bloody and breathless.

'Yes,' Alan said finally. 'Just let her go.'

'Good. That wasn't so hard, was it?' he said as he pushed Sandy into Alan's arms. 'We'll be in touch in the next day or two to organise a drop.'

Jay and Alan nodded while Sandy sobbed quietly.

Chapter Forty-Seven

B radley Johnson signalled to his brothers Ged and
Craig as they walked into The Grapes. They sauntered
over to him and sat down. He'd bought the first round
while his brothers had taken the van home.

'Why didn't Scott and Billy come?' he asked.

'Billy wanted to go home and get stoned, and Scott went
to see his mates,' Craig replied with a shrug.

Bradley lifted his pint. 'Ah, well. Sod 'em. Cheers, lads,'
he said with a smile.

The three men lifted their pints and toasted the success
of their earlier confrontation at the Lady Muck salon.

'Did you see the look on Alan and Jay's faces when you
pulled that gun out?' Ged said with a grin. 'I thought they
were going to shit their pants.'

Bradley laughed. 'I know. Pair of tarts.'

'I wouldn't write them off completely, Brad,' Craig
warned. 'They didn't have much choice but to back down

today, did they? Don't take for granted that they'll stay down.'

'What are they gonna do? Run crying to Jake and the Carters? They can't fucking stand each other any more. Remember? Too busy fighting amongst themselves.'

'I hope you're right,' Craig replied.

'I fucking enjoyed myself today, lads. I haven't had a scrap like that for years,' Ged said with a smile on his face.

'You were scrapping almost every day inside, if I remember correctly?' Craig reminded him.

'Yeah, but that was different. Today was full-on carnage. Just how I like it.'

Craig shook his head. 'You're a fucking nutter, Ged. Do you know he spent most of his time in seg when we were inside, Brad?'

Bradley nodded. 'I'm not surprised. You've never played well with others, have you, Ged?'

Ged frowned at his older brother, obviously sensing his observation as a dig. 'I'd like to see how you'd have handled yourself in prison,' he spat. 'You've never done a day in your life though. How is that?'

Bradley tapped the side of his temple. 'Because I'm too fucking smart, that's why.'

Ged snorted. 'Is that so?'

'Lucky, more like,' Craig said with a laugh, trying to lighten the mood. He was used to the constant tension between his two older brothers.

'Hmm, very lucky,' Ged replied before taking a swig of his pint.

'What the fuck are you getting at, Ged?' Bradley snapped at him.

'Yeah, just fucking leave it, Ged,' Craig added. 'We're supposed to be fucking celebrating.

'I was only asking a fucking question,' Ged snarled. 'A perfectly reasonable question. Why is it that our dearest big brother has never had his collar felt, when he's always been as up to his neck in shit as we have?'

Bradley slammed his pint glass down on the table. 'I've fucking had enough of this. I'm getting off,' he said as he stood up.

'Brad, just sit down and I'll get us another round in,' Craig pleaded. 'Ged will keep his gob shut now, won't you?'

Ged shrugged and continued to drink his pint.

'Nah. Fuck this. I'm off,' Bradley said as he zipped up his favourite Hugo Boss tracksuit top. 'I'll phone you later, Craig.'

Craig watched his oldest brother leaving the pub and shook his head. 'Why do you always have to pick a fight with him?' he snapped at Ged.

Ged smiled at him. 'I can't help it, he's so fucking easy to wind up.'

'You don't really think there's anything dodgy going on though, do you? Like Bradley said, he's just lucky.'

Ged started to laugh. 'Whatever you say, little brother.'

'Oh, fuck off. I'm going the bar,' Craig said as he eyed up the blonde barmaid who'd been staring in his direction since he walked in.

'Get us another one then, will ya?' Ged said with a belch.

'Get one your fucking self,' Craig replied. 'I think my luck's in.'

Craig sauntered over to the bar. 'Another pint of Stella, please, gorgeous,' he said with a wink.

'Coming right up,' she replied with a smile as she took a pint glass from behind the bar and began to pour.

Craig watched her and thought about Bradley and Ged's most recent row. Although he was used to their constant needling of each other, things seemed to be ramping up lately. Ged took the piss out of everyone, it was a given, but he wouldn't let go of this thing about Bradley never being arrested. Now Craig was starting to wonder too. Was his brother just an incredibly lucky bastard, or was there something else going on?

Chapter Forty-Eight

G race was home alone when she heard the sound of the doorbell ringing. She made her way to answer it and saw the unmistakeable outline of one of the twins through the glass. It was difficult to tell which one when she couldn't see their features. It had been over a week since the whole Isla bombshell had been dropped, and despite it being proved that Jake was Isla's biological father, there had been no improvement in family relations. She could still barely stand to look at Michael, who had taken Belle and Oscar to his dad's for the afternoon. While she'd seen Jake, Connor and Siobhan during that time, it suddenly dawned on her that she hadn't seen Paul at all.

Opening the door, Grace suppressed a smile when she saw it was Paul standing there. As angry as she still was with everyone, him included, it was good to see he was okay. It made her remember how much she missed having the three boys around. 'I was just thinking about you,' she said.

'Oh fuck!' he replied with a grin. 'Am I in trouble?'

'You *are* trouble,' she replied. 'Come through.'

He followed her into the kitchen. 'Can I grab a drink?' he said as he walked towards the fridge.

'Of course you can. You know you don't have to ask.'

'Well, I feel like I haven't been here for ages,' he said as he took out a bottle of mineral water.

'That's because you haven't.'

'Well, it hasn't exactly been business as usual, has it? I wasn't even sure if I'd be welcome.'

'Whatever's gone on, Paul, this is still your home.'

'So, where is everyone?' Paul asked as he sat at the breakfast bar.

'Your dad's taken the kids to see your grandad and Sue for the afternoon.'

'Getting under your feet, was he?'

'Yeah, something like that. Did you want to see him?' she asked as she sat down opposite.

'Yeah and no. I came to see you really.'

'Okay.'

'I wanted to say sorry for everything that's gone on, Grace,' he started.

'I appreciate your apology, Paul. And I won't pretend I'm not bloody furious at you all for lying to me. But, having said that, I understand why you of all people felt like you had to keep Connor's secret for him.'

'And Jake's?' Paul added with a sigh.

'Yeah, well, I won't say that wasn't a shock,' Grace replied with a shake of her head. 'I feel like I'm only just getting my head around it now. You and him?'

Paul nodded. 'We weren't just fucking about, you know, Grace? It means something. Or at least it did. He won't give me the fucking time of day at the minute.'

'Well, he's not really giving anyone the time of day right now, Paul,' Grace replied with a sigh of her own. 'I wish I knew what to do to snap him out of it.'

'And will he? Snap out of it, I mean?'

'God, I bloody hope so. Because this is torturous. Everyone walking around on eggshells and no one really speaking to each other. I can't bear much more of it.'

'Me neither,' Paul said and took a swig of his water.

'Is there something else on your mind?' Grace asked.

'You and my dad. I know it's none of my business, Grace, but I could kill Connor for putting him in that position.'

'Well, your dad's a grown man—'

'I know. And I know what goes on between the two of you is between you and him alone, but he loves you, Grace. I have never seen him as happy as he's been these past few years. It would kill him if he lost you.'

'No pressure then?' Grace said.

'I'm not trying to make you feel bad. But remember when those nutters took you a couple of years ago, my dad told me that he wasn't sure he could live without you, Grace, and I think he meant it. And a few days afterwards, when I came to see you, and you made me watch that fucking awful film with you—'

'You mean *Dirty Dancing*?' she interrupted. 'That is a classic film. Jake used to watch that with me all the time.'

'Is it any wonder he turned out gay then, being forced to

sit through that shit?' he said with a laugh. 'Anyway, forget the shite film. You told me that life was too short not to forgive the people you love. So I just hope the two of you work something out. Because, to be honest, you look pretty fucking miserable too,' he finished with a grin.

Grace gave him a playful shove. 'You always were a cheeky sod, Paul. But I can see why my son loves you so much.' Grace remembered their conversation well, and she had meant every word of it. So why couldn't she apply that principle now? Why couldn't she forgive Michael?

Paul looked down at the breakfast bar. Grace heard him sniff and sensed he was trying to hold back his emotions. She stood up and put an arm around him, kissing the top of his head.

'He'll come round, you know. I promise.'

'You think?' Paul said quietly.

'Yep. It'll be all be all right in the end.'

'Yeah, I know,' Paul said.

Grace made Paul a cup of tea and they talked for a further half hour before she noticed the time. 'I'm really sorry, I've got a meeting at two, Paul,' she said as she drained her mug.

'No worries, Grace,' he replied. 'I need to go and see Connor anyway. I'd better get off.'

'It was good to see you,' Grace said as she gave him a final hug. 'Don't stay away for so long again. The kids really miss you. And that goes for Connor too.'

'I'll tell him,' Paul said. 'Maybe we could pop round for scouse tomorrow?'

'Yeah, okay. I'll ask your dad to put a pan on tonight when he gets home. It's always better the next day.'

'Sound,' Paul replied. 'We'll see you both tomorrow then?'

Grace nodded and watched as Paul let himself out. It would be good for them all to sit down together and have a meal. It had been weeks since they'd done so. It would be good for all of the kids, the little ones and the grown-ups – if only she could convince Jake to come too. Grace smiled as she picked up her handbag from the kitchen table. It would be good for her and Michael too. Perhaps Paul was right, and it was time for her to start forgiving the people she loved. Why was it always the ones we loved the most that were the hardest to forgive?

Chapter Forty-Nine

Paul scrolled through his mobile phone as he sat at the kitchen table of Connor's flat looking for any sign that Jake had been on social media in the past few days.

'Are you listening to me?' Connor said to him.

Paul's head snapped up. 'Yes! As much as I'm trying not to. You've been looking at a place. So what?'

'I just think we need a base of operations, Paul. Now that we can't use The Blue Rooms, we need somewhere to go. We can't keep having all and sundry coming here or to your flat. The concierge is already asking questions.'

Paul shook his head in annoyance. It was true that eyebrows were already being raised about the number, and calibre, of visitors they'd been receiving in recent weeks. Previously they'd conducted all of their business out of Jake's club, but now they weren't allowed to set a foot inside the place. But getting their own gaff wasn't an option he'd even considered. It all made their partnership dissolving too real – too final.

'Jake will come round eventually, Con. Even Grace said so.'

'I know he will. And I'll keep trying to talk to him until he does, but in the meantime, we need to look elsewhere. I've been in touch with some contacts and we have some big deals in the pipeline. We need somewhere to work out of that's not here.'

'What deals?' Paul snapped.

Connor shrugged. 'Nothing new. Just what we were doing, but on our own.'

'So you mean we'll be in direct competition with Jake?' Paul spat. 'Well, that will go down fucking well, won't it? That's really gonna make him more amenable to talking to us again.'

'Paul!' Connor snapped. 'I know you and him are, were … well, whatever you were, but this is fucking business. We can't just sit back and wait for Jake to decide to play nice again. Besides, do you know how many people would rather work with us than Jake? He can be a bit of a loose cannon at the best of times. And I hear he's been permanently off his face for the past week. No one will want to work with him at all if he keeps on as he is.'

'So we just take everything from right under his nose?' Paul said as he shook his head. 'It's not right, Con.'

'We're not taking anything that isn't already ours.'

Paul snorted in response.

'Well, look at it this way, we're keeping everything going. Once Jake comes to his senses, he can have back in. Equal partners. Just like we've always been.'

Paul considered his brother. Connor was always the one

thinking about the business. He was better at accounts and book-keeping and all that boring stuff, while Jake and Paul had preferred the more exciting and hands-on side of the business. If Connor thought it was good business, he didn't feel equipped enough to argue against him. Connor would have his best interests at heart, Paul knew that, and Paul would make sure that Jake's interests were protected too.

'Where's this place you've seen then?' Paul asked.

Connor smiled at him. 'It's the space above Eric's gym. It has its own entrance. There's a couple of rooms we can use as an office or whatever we need. It's perfect.'

'Is Eric okay with this?'

'Of course he is. He's renting the place for a good rate too. I told him I'd drop the first six months' rent off today if you were up for it. His daughter's twenty-one next week and I think he could use the extra cash.'

'All right then. I'll come with you and have a look at the place myself. We could have a spar?' Paul, suddenly feeling brighter.

Connor smiled. 'Sound,' he said as his phone rang.

He answered it and Paul listened to the one-sided conversation.

'Hi, babe...

Now?...

I'm not sure...' he said as he looked at Paul.

Paul, realising that it was Connor's girlfriend, shook his head. 'Just go,' he mouthed. 'I'll take Eric's money.'

'Yeah. I'll meet you there in half an hour,' he said as he hung up the phone, a smile plastered across his face.

'Thanks, Bro,' Connor said.

'No problem. Who am I to stand in the way of true love?' Paul mocked him.

Connor handed over a wad of fifty pound notes. 'Ere. Give this to Eric for me then. I said I'd be there about two.'

'No problem,' Paul said as he put the money into the pocket of his jeans. 'I'll just nip to mine and get my gym gear. Enjoy your date, *babe*,' he said as he stood up to leave.

'Fuck off,' Connor replied good-naturedly.

Chapter Fifty

P aul stepped into Eric's gym and walked through the back to the small room that Eric used as an office.

'All right, Eric,' Paul said as he tapped on the open door. 'Our Connor said to give you this.' He tossed the money onto the desk. 'We're going to take the rooms upstairs.'

Eric smiled at him. 'Fantastic. That'll save them sitting empty. What are you doing here anyway? I thought Connor was coming in?'

'He was, but he had a better offer,' Paul said with a wink. 'I'm off for a spar. Anyone decent in?'

'That young Carl lad is in. He was hoping to have a spar with Connor. So he'll be gutted you're here instead,' Eric said with a laugh. 'He thinks you're a fucking animal.'

Paul wiped the sweat from his head with his towel before throwing it, along with his boxing gloves and mobile phone, into his gym bag and zipping it up. He'd shower and change at home because the showers in Eric's gym were filthy. He always felt great after a sparring session or some time on the pads. And lately, he'd needed the pick-me-up more than ever. Before Siobhan and Connor had dropped their bombshell the week before, he'd been as happy as a pig in the proverbial shit. He and Jake had been on the verge of becoming something, and now Jake was refusing to even speak to him. Paul had gone to The Blue Rooms a few times to see him, only to be met with a mouthful of abuse or a bouncer telling him Mr Conlon wasn't receiving visitors.

Paul sighed as he closed his locker. He'd never been one for relationships or feelings, but Jake was the one person who had changed all that. Paul could understand Jake's anger about the whole Isla situation. He'd found out that the daughter he'd idolised since the day she was born might have fathered by one of his best mates. Now it seemed like Jake was Isla's father after all, and Siobhan had caused all of that shit for nothing. But sides had had to be taken, and obviously Paul would always stand by his twin. Nothing would ever come between them – not even Jake.

Picking up his gym bag, Paul headed towards the door. Jake would come round eventually. He had to. He couldn't freeze Paul out for ever. He'd tried that before, numerous times, but with little success. Jake loved him. That hadn't changed in just over a week. Connor and Jake would sort out their differences, and Paul would be waiting with open arms. It was only a matter of time before Jake was back at their side where he belonged. It was the only way really.

Smiling to himself, Paul stepped out of Eric's gym and out into the bright sunshine. Things were looking up already.

Grace frowned at the screen on her phone. She'd charged it that morning and the battery had just died on her. She'd have to plug it into her car to charge on the way home. 'Piece of crap,' she mumbled before remembering that she'd given it to Belle to play with to keep her occupied while she was getting a shower earlier that morning. She could have shouted to Michael to take her downstairs with him and Oscar but she still wasn't speaking to him, and she hadn't wanted to give him the satisfaction of thinking she needed his help. It was childish and she knew it, but she was still so angry with him. Deep down, she understood he'd been in an impossible position, but that still didn't make being lied to by the people she most loved any easier to swallow. She couldn't take it out on Jake, he needed her too much right now, so Michael was taking the brunt of it. But maybe, after her conversation with Paul earlier, that was something that had to change. When the possibility of premises for a new restaurant and wine bar in Lytham came up, Grace had jumped at the chance to check it out. It would give her something to do and something to focus on other than the whole sorry mess her family had dragged her into.

As she walked down one of the side streets back to her car, she smiled as she considered the offer she was going to put in in a couple of days. The place had been perfect, but she knew it was a buyers' market and the owner was desperate to sell. This was going to be a lucrative venture for their family, she knew it.

Zak Miller edged the motorbike along the pavement. He took slow, deep breaths and listened to the steady thumping of his heart. He'd done this kind of job dozens of times before, but he'd never had to take out someone quite as high profile. This was the kind of job that paid money that would set you up for life. Because after this, he would have to disappear – and fast. He'd already sold his apartment in Manchester. Now he just had to wait for the sale of his cottage in Wales to go through and he'd be gone. Off to Ibiza to live out the rest of his days in a villa by the beach. He'd already put the deposit down. It was a four-bedroom house with a pool, Jacuzzi and a bar – a party palace. In a few weeks' time he'd be soaking up the sunshine and the constant stream of bikini-clad women. God, his life was going to be fucking awesome. Just one more job and then he could retire.

His target was approaching. Smiling to themselves with no idea of what was to come. Not long now and he'd have the perfect shot. He reached inside his jacket pocket. His breathing slow and steady. Lifting his arm, he squeezed the trigger and his target dropped to the floor like a sack of bricks.

Chapter Fifty-One

Propping himself up on one elbow, Connor lay on the bed in the dingy hotel room and smiled as he watched his naked girlfriend Jazz sashay across the hotel room.

'Come back to bed, babe,' he said, grinning as he patted the empty space beside him.

Jazz smiled at him. 'You know I'd love to, but I can't. I have to get back home before anyone notices I'm missing.'

'But you said he's away for a few days.'

'He is. So, that means he'll have one of his goons *popping* round later just to make sure I'm where I'm supposed to be. I can't risk it, Con.'

Sighing, Connor flopped back against the pillow. 'For fuck's sake,' he mumbled.

'Hey,' Jazz said as she walked over to the bed and sat beside him. 'You knew I was married when we met. You knew what you were getting into.'

He took hold of her hand. 'I know, babe. I just hate that we can't spend the night together. I want to wake up in the morning and see your gorgeous face. I want to have lazy morning sex, instead of a few hours' fucking here and there.'

Connor watched as a look of hurt flashed across her face and she snatched her hand away. 'Well, I'm sorry but that's all I can offer you. Maybe we should end it now before things get even more complicated?'

Connor sighed as he reached for her hand and laced his fingers through hers. 'I'm sorry, Jazz. I didn't mean to make you feel bad. I love spending time with you. I just wish we could do more of it, that's all.'

Her face softening, she lay on the bed beside him and snuggled into him. 'So do I, Con,' she said softly. 'I love being with you too. But my husband would kill us both if he ever found out.' She sniffed and he could tell she was holding back tears.

'I would never let him hurt you, Jazz,' he said as he tilted her chin to look at him.

'I know.' She blinked at him, her long lashes wet with tears.

Oblivious to the incessant calls to his mobile phone which was on silent, Connor rolled on top of Jazz and kissed her. He groaned in pleasure as she raked her long fingernails down the length of his back.

'I suppose another half hour wouldn't hurt,' she whispered in his ear.

Chapter Fifty-Two

G lancing at his mobile phone, Connor felt his stomach lurch as he noticed over twenty missed calls. His fingers trembled as he unlocked the home screen and returned the most recent call, which was from his dad. It was his Uncle Sean who answered on the second ring.

'Connor. Where the fuck are you?'

Before he could answer, Sean went on. 'You need to come to your dad's. Now.'

'Why? What's happened?' Connor stammered as he felt his heart start to pound in his chest. 'Is my dad okay?'

'Look, just get home as soon as you can, mate,' Sean said quietly.

'Is it Paul?'

'Just come home, Connor.'

The phone went dead and Connor scrambled around the room for his shoes and clothes. He dialled Paul's number as he did, leaving the phone on loudspeaker, only to be repeatedly met with his voicemail. The adrenaline thundered around his body. Why wouldn't Sean tell him what was going on? He phoned Grace and her phone went straight to voicemail too. What the fuck was going on? Why couldn't he speak to his dad or get hold of Paul or Grace? The feeling in the pit of his stomach told him that something terrible had happened.

Connor Carter drove home from Crewe to Liverpool in record time, flooring the accelerator and breaking every speed limit on the way.

Chapter Fifty-Three

With the exception of Paul and Grace, the whole of the Carter family were in the kitchen of Grace and Michael's house. All of them huddled and talking in hushed tones. Even Bella and Oscar, usually in full voice, were quiet. It was his father's face that Connor saw first. He saw the pain there and knew that his world would never be the same. His dad – his rock – was a broken man and Connor knew that only one thing could have caused it.

Suddenly his dad looked up and their eyes locked. Pushing through the huddle of people in front of him, Michael Carter rushed towards his son and pulled him into his arms. At that moment, Connor knew that his father wasn't just dealing with his own anguish, but was also trying to offer him some comfort, squeezing him so hard that Connor felt like he was starting to struggle for air.

'I'm sorry,' Michael breathed into the collar of Connor's jacket. 'I'm so sorry, Son. Paul's been shot. He's gone.'

Connor felt his knees buckle, as though he had been hit

from behind with a sledgehammer. If his dad hadn't been holding him up he'd have dropped to the floor like a sack of spanners. He sobbed like a child while his father stroked his hair and told him everything was going to be okay. But it wouldn't be. It would never be okay again. Paul was gone. He'd been too busy banging some bird when his brother had needed him. And now his twin, his other half, was dead. Gone for ever. Connor wanted to scream. To rage at the whole world. But now wasn't the time. Things would have to be dealt with first.

Straightening up, he wiped the tears from his eyes. 'What happened?'

His dad closed his eyes and took a deep breath. 'He was shot outside Eric's gym. He didn't stand a chance. He was dead by the time the ambulance arrived.'

'Do we know who did it?'

Michael shook his head. 'Not yet. There's time for that later.'

'No, Dad. Now is the time. We need to know who did this before they come after anyone else.'

Just as his dad was about to argue with him, Jake Conlon burst through the kitchen door. Connor bristled instinctively. The last time he'd seen Jake the pair of them had sworn they would kill each other if their paths ever crossed again. It had all been bravado – but still. Jake's eyes searched the room until he saw Connor. Then wordlessly he crossed the room and the two men embraced like long-lost brothers, clinging onto each other as though their lives depended on it.

Connor started to sob as Jake leaned into his ear. 'We're

going to find the bastards, Con. Anyone who had a hand in it. And we're going to fucking end them. Every last one of them,' he growled.

This was exactly what Connor needed to hear. Jake had loved Paul too. He was the only one who understood how he felt right now.

When he finally looked up, Connor saw the tears in Jake's eyes and knew that he was desperately trying to hold it together, with his jaw clenched shut and his body vibrating with anger. Connor supposed that anger was easier to feel right now than the unimaginable pain of losing Paul.

'I can't believe he's gone,' Connor said.

'I know, mate,' Jake replied as a solitary tear escaped. 'We'll get whoever did this. I promise you.'

Connor nodded. They had to find out who did this as fast as possible and let them know that taking out Paul Carter was the biggest mistake that anyone had ever made since time began. It was what Paul would have wanted. It was exactly what he would have done for either of them.

Chapter Fifty-Four

Grace cursed the red traffic light as she raced for home. As soon as she'd plugged her phone into her in car charger she'd seen the missed calls from Michael and Sean. She'd tried to stay calm, telling herself that they were just worried about not being able to get hold of her. Michael's phone had been engaged when she'd tried to call him back so she'd phoned Sean instead. Her heart had almost broken in two when he'd told her the news. All she could think of was getting home to Michael – her wonderful husband who had just lost a son. She'd almost lost Jake once and it had nearly killed her. She knew something of the pain he was in but she wanted nothing more than to wrap her arms around him and tell him how much she loved him.

Grace burst through the front door of her house and

followed the sound of hushed voices into the kitchen. She'd phoned Jake on her way home and told him the news. He'd been speechless and had hung up the phone, so she was relieved to see he was already there, standing with a protective arm around Connor. But it was Michael she was looking for. He was standing alone, looking out of the kitchen window at his father and Sue playing with Belle and Oscar. She put a hand on his shoulder as she reached him. Turning to look at her, his eyes locked onto hers. No words were needed. She had none to give. None that would offer him any comfort, at least. He laid his head on her shoulder and started to sob as she wrapped her arms around his neck. She had no idea how long they stayed together like that, hugging and crying at their kitchen sink, but when she looked up, the room was empty except for the two of them.

Grace had so many questions, as she was sure Michael did, but now wasn't the time.

'I have to go and formally identify his body,' he said when he finally lifted his head from her shoulder. 'I was waiting for you. Will you come with me?'

'Of course. I can do it if you'd rather not see him like that.'

'No, it has to be me. I have to see him.'

'Okay. Let's go.'

———

Michael sat in Grace's car in silence as she drove them to the police station. She searched for words of comfort that might soothe him but realised there were none. She had loved Paul too. He had been a part of her life for as long as she'd known Michael, but in recent years she had come to love him like a son. She wondered how his mother Cheryl must be feeling. Grace had never had a lot of time for Michael's first wife, but she felt nothing but sympathy for her right now. And Connor. God, how we would her ever get through this? He and Paul were inseparable. She couldn't even begin to imagine how he was feeling.

'Have you spoken to Cheryl?' Grace asked him.

'Yeah. She's coming back as soon as she can.'

'Oh, good,' Grace replied. Cheryl had been in Turkey for the past three months with her new boyfriend.

'I had to tell her,' he said as he choked back a sob. 'The police couldn't get hold of her, so I told them I'd do it.' He shook his head. 'It was the hardest thing I've ever had to do, Grace. Telling her our son was dead.'

Grace gave his arm a gentle squeeze. 'I can't even imagine. I'm so sorry, Michael,' she said, because there was nothing else to say.

'I know.'

Chapter Fifty-Five

G race had held tightly onto Michael's arm as he formally identified Paul's body. He had simply stood there and nodded. Anyone who didn't know him well would no doubt have thought him cold and emotionless. But Grace could feel the tension in his arms and shoulders. His jaw was clenched so tightly, he could barely speak. Suddenly, he no longer felt like flesh and blood, but solid iron.

Aware of a figure approaching them, Grace turned, while Michael continued staring at his son.

'I'm DI Moss,' the intruder said softly. 'My team will be leading the investigation.'

At this, Michael turned around too and stared at the woman who had interrupted them.

'I'd like to offer my deepest condolences to you both,' she said as she pushed a stray strand of dark hair from her face.

Michael nodded in response.

'Thank you,' Grace replied.

DI Moss gave a nod to the Sergeant who had accompanied them to identify Paul's body.

'Mr Carter,' the Sergeant said. 'If you follow me, you can pick up some of your son's belongings.'

Grace let go of Michael's arm. 'I'll wait just outside for you,' she said with a faint smile. Michael silently followed the Sergeant out of the room and along the corridor. Grace turned her attention to the Inspector. 'It's been a long time, Leigh,' she said.

DI Moss bristled at the familiarity before taking a furtive glance around the corridor.

'Do you have any idea who was responsible for this?' Grace asked.

Leigh paused before shaking her head. 'Not yet.'

'But you wouldn't tell me, even if you did?'

'Of course I wouldn't. I really am sorry for your loss, Grace. But I have a job to do here. So, stay out of my way.'

Grace glared at her. 'Don't forget who you're talking to, Leigh,' she warned. 'But, you don't need to worry about me. I'll stay out of your way.' Catching sight of Michael coming further down the corridor, she brushed past the Inspector.

'We'll find whoever did this,' Leigh said as a parting shot.

Grace turned on her heel. 'Not if I find him first,' she replied.

Grace caught up with Michael, who was now holding Paul's gym bag in his hand. She linked her arm through his and they walked out of the station.

'Did that Inspector have anything to say?' Michael asked.

'Nothing important,' Grace replied. 'Just said she'd be doing her best to catch whoever did this.'

'Well, I won't hold my breath. Half of that lot couldn't find their arse with both hands,' he replied, the words catching in his throat.

Grace gave his arm a squeeze. 'Come on. Let's get home.'

Together they walked to the car and Grace thought about Leigh Moss. They had been friends, of a sort, once. But that felt like a lifetime ago now. Certainly, they had been leading very different lives back then. It had been almost six years since they'd last seen each other, but Grace had followed Leigh's career and already knew about her temporary promotion to the Organised Crime Task Force. Nobody knew about their connection, not even Michael, and Grace was determined it would stay that way. Despite their differences now, Grace had a lot of admiration and respect for Leigh. She had turned her life around and become someone – just as she'd promised she would. Grace would never betray Leigh's trust. But, as true as that was, Grace's loyalty came at a price, and both women knew it was only a matter of time before that debt was called in.

Chapter Fifty-Six

G race dialled the number of DI Tony Webster. He was a bent copper whom Grace had had on her payroll for years, since he was a lowly sergeant. She paid him a substantial retainer, although she felt increasingly as though he did little to earn it.

'Grace?' he said when he answered.

'I assume you've heard what happened?' she replied. They never bothered with formalities.

'Yeah. My condolences to you and Michael.'

'Thanks. I need to know everything that the police do on this, Webster.'

'Well, we don't know much of anything yet. And the Senior Investigating Officer is a new Acting DI, and she isn't exactly my biggest fan,' he said sarcastically.

'I don't give a shit,' Grace snapped. 'I'll expect you here tomorrow to give us an update.'

She heard him sigh. He never came to their house ordinarily. It wouldn't do his reputation any good to be seen there. But there was no way Grace was asking Michael to leave the house if he didn't have to.

'Okay?' Grace said.

'Yeah,' Webster agreed. 'See you tomorrow.'

———

Walking into the bedroom, Grace saw Michael sitting on the edge of their bed with his head in his hands. Sitting beside him, she placed her hand on his shoulder.

'How are you doing?' she asked, realising what a stupid question that was as soon as the words were out of her mouth.

He shrugged.

'Everyone has gone. Sean and Sophia have taken the kids for the night. I hope that's okay?'

Michael nodded and then he started to cry. Deep, gulping sobs that shook the whole bed beneath them. Putting her arms around him, Grace kissed the top of his head, the smell of the shampoo he always used filling her nostrils and reminding her how much she had missed him over the past few weeks.

'I'm so sorry,' she said, although her words felt hollow and meaningless in the face of his unimaginable loss – of their loss.

'I can't believe he's gone,' Michael said as he straightened up and wiped the tears from his face. 'He still had his whole life to live. What will we do without him, Grace?'

'I don't know,' she answered honestly.

'I'm worried about Connor and Jake. Did you see them tonight? Huddled in the corner. They're going to go off and do something stupid.'

'I'll take care of that. Don't worry,' she soothed, although she was worried about the two of them herself. She had seen them talking animatedly in hushed tones, slipping into silence when anyone approached.

'I'll sort this out,' he assured her. 'I'll find whoever did this and make sure they regret they were ever born. But now is not the time.'

'I know that,' she said as she continued stroking his hair. 'I'll have a word with them, I promise.'

He nodded.

'I've asked Tony Webster to come round tomorrow if you're up to it. He can fill us in on what the police know so far. It's about time the lazy bastard actually did something to earn his money.'

Michael looked at her. 'Yeah, okay,' he said and Grace noticed the lines on his face. Had they been there that morning? Would she have even noticed if they had? She felt a rush of remorse for everything she'd put him through over the past few weeks. It all seemed so meaningless now.

'Why don't you try and get some sleep? You look exhausted,' she said as she brushed his hair back from his face.

He attempted a smile. 'I'm not sure I'll ever sleep again,' he said before standing up to leave.

'Where are you going?' Grace asked as she took hold of his arm.

'I'll let you get to bed.'

'Michael. You don't have to go anywhere,' she said. Her heart almost broke at the thought of him going and the fact that he thought that she would turn him away when his son had just been murdered.

She was relieved when he sat back down on the bed, and when she lay down, he lay beside her, putting his head on her chest. She stroked his hair and thought about her next move. She had to be smart, and careful. Because of who Paul was, the police would be all over his murder and she couldn't afford to draw too much attention to them all. Grace closed her eyes. It was no use trying to think straight right now. Her head was all over the place. She was heartbroken about Paul, not only for her but for Michael and the rest of their children. And she felt guilty too. If she hadn't been so angry with them all for the past week and a half, maybe she would have seen this coming? But mostly she just thought about Paul, and how none of their lives would ever be the same again.

Chapter Fifty-Seven

Jake sat on Paul's bed, in Paul's apartment, and scanned the room, looking at the pieces of himself that Paul had left behind. The pair of unwashed jeans hanging over the open wardrobe door; the trainers hastily discarded next to the bed; the half packet of chewing gum and the bottle of Creed aftershave on the dresser. Jake hadn't allowed himself to cry while he'd been at his mum and Michael's house. Not only had he felt the need to hold it together for everyone else's benefit, he still wasn't ready for everyone to know the depth of feeling he had for his step-brother. As he'd driven Connor home, they'd talked about what their next moves would be. They had made plans to avenge Paul's murder in any way they could. Connor had cried and talked about how much he would miss his twin, but Jake had focused on his anger instead, fearing that if he started to think about the pain of losing Paul he might never recover. But, here in Paul's apartment, his grief was inescapable.

Jake still hadn't sorted himself anywhere to stay, so Connor had given him the key to Paul's place. As soon as he'd unlocked the door and stepped inside, Jake's senses had been overwhelmed. The flat smelled like Paul. Everywhere Jake looked, Paul was there. The place was just as he'd left it earlier that day, just waiting for him to walk back inside and carry on with his life as normal.

And now Jake was alone. Alone with every memory he had of the man he loved. He started to cry. Deep, gut-wrenching sobs that shook the breath from his body. He thought at first of all the happy times they had shared together, of how much they had loved each other. How they never seemed to be able to spend more than a day apart. Until recently, that was. Jake felt a searing physical pain deep inside his chest as he remembered the last time they'd spoken. He remembered it as clearly as if it had happened only seconds ago – when he'd told Paul that he never wanted to see him again. The memory was agony to him, but soon it was all he could think of, until the guilt felt like it was going to swallow him whole. Did Paul die thinking that Jake hated him?

Jake knew now that he forgave Paul for everything. It didn't even matter any more that he had lied to him. Only it was too late. He would never get the chance to tell him. Never see his cheeky smile, or kiss him, or feel the warmth of one of his hugs. Lying back on the bed, he could still smell Paul on the pillows and sheets and he breathed in the scent. It was all he had left of him now. Tomorrow he would wake up in this bed without Paul. Every day for the rest of his life he would wake up without him, and the realisation of that made him feel like his heart had been ripped from his chest, leaving a gaping black hole in its place.

The only thing Jake had left to give the man he loved was the promise he would find whoever had killed him, and make him feel pain like he had never experienced before.

Chapter Fifty-Eight

G race showed DI Tony Webster into the sitting room where Michael was waiting for them both. Michael looked up as Webster entered the room but didn't offer him any greeting. As far as Michael was concerned Webster was the lowest of the low. All he was interested in was money. Grace and Michael had paid him a lot of money over the years, which he did very little to earn in Michael's opinion. But Grace had had him on her payroll for as long as Michael had known her and whilst everything Michael believed about him was true, he did have his uses.

Grace didn't bother offering Webster a drink. He wouldn't be staying long.

'So?' she said as she sat down next to her husband on the sofa. 'What do you have for us?'

Webster cleared his throat and looked anxiously at Michael, who continued to glare at him. 'Well,' he started. 'We don't have much to go on.' He sucked air through his teeth – a habit which had always grated on Grace.

'Just tell us what you fucking do have,' Michael barked.

Webster flinched. 'We have no CCTV of the incident, but we do have CCTV footage of a motorbike turning into Harkness Street from Stanley Road, and out onto Westminster Road fifteen minutes later before speeding off towards Southport Road. That same motorbike was found abandoned in a ditch on a country lane in Lymm later that evening. It had been stolen a few days prior but it had plates from another bike that was registered to a fifty-year-old pastry chef named Harvey who lives in Bristol.'

'The plates were cloned?' Grace asked.

Tony nodded. 'As for the shooter. He was a pro. One clean shot straight through the carotid artery. Paul would have been walking towards him. It wasn't a point, pray and shoot, like we usually see. It was a calculated and professional hit.'

'Anything else? Any leads?' Grace asked.

'From the bullet's trajectory, and the skid marks left by the bike driving away at high speed, we believe the shooter was right-handed. But as for any leads, we have nothing tangible yet. You probably know more than us on that score.'

'What?' Michael growled.

Webster flinched every time Michael spoke. 'I said you'd probably know more than us,' he mumbled.

'I heard what you said, fuckwit! But what the fuck do you mean by it?'

Grace placed her hand on Michael's leg, sensing that another wrong word from Webster, and her husband would start using his face as a boot scraper.

'I don't mean any offence, Michael,' Webster said as he held his hands up in defence. 'I just mean that you would know more than we do about Paul's associates. Anyone who might have reason to … well, you know what I mean,' he said quickly as he stood up. 'I need to get back to the station.'

'Thanks, Tony,' Grace said as she stood up to show him out. 'Let us know if you get any more information.'

'I will do.'

Walking back into the living room, Grace saw Michael was pouring himself a drink.

'Are you okay?' she asked, realising what a ridiculous question it was as soon as the words had left her mouth.

'He's a fucking cretin,' said Michael. 'So basically they've got fuck all to go on. My son gets shot in the middle of the street in broad daylight and all he can tell us is that the shooter stole a motorbike and was right-handed? He's a waste of fucking space.' He downed the glass of brandy in one.

'It's still early days,' she said as she approached him. 'Besides, we don't want the police finding him, do we? We can handle that ourselves. And then when we do…'

'I know,' he said with a sigh before wrapping his arms around her and burying his face in her hair. 'I know.'

Chapter Fifty-Nine

The doorbell rang for what felt like the hundredth time that day. The seemingly never-ending stream of visitors had stopped only half an hour earlier. Grace had finally managed to settle Belle and Oscar and was about to make herself and Michael something to eat when it rang again.

Swearing under her breath, Grace headed for the door, leaving Michael sitting in their kitchen. Opening the door of their house, Grace saw Michael's ex-wife Cheryl standing in the rain. There had never been any love lost between the two women. Cheryl had made no secret of the fact that she despised Grace and resented the fact that Michael and she were married. Despite that, Cheryl had just lost her son, and Grace knew that in the face of that, none of that mattered any more.

'Cheryl, come in,' Grace said as she opened the door.

Cheryl walked straight past her towards Michael who was now standing in the hallway. Upon reaching him she wrapped her arms around him and started to sob uncontrollably. Michael held her until the tears subsided a little.

'I'm sorry, Cheryl,' Michael said to her. 'I'm so sorry.' He stroked her hair and gave her a brief kiss on the top of her head and Grace saw a glimpse of the tenderness and love that must have once existed between them. Cheryl had been Michael's first wife. They were married young and had the twins shortly after. Michael had thought she was the love of his life at one time, and had been devastated to learn that she had cheated on him throughout their twelve-year marriage, including with Grace's ex-husband, Nathan. After their divorce Cheryl had never recovered financially or in terms of her status and lifestyle. Once upon a time, she was manicured, buffed and coiffed to within an inch of her life. But since their divorce she hadn't been afforded the same lifestyle she'd enjoyed as the first Mrs Carter even though Michael had given her a generous monthly allowance until the twins turned eighteen. Once they were adults, the twins had supported their mother's frequent trips to Turkey and her false nails and sunbed addiction, but she'd never quite regained the polished facade of her twenties and early thirties.

Feeling like a voyeur intruding on their grief, Grace slipped past them both. Michael caught her eye as she did and gave her a look that reminded her of a rabbit trapped in headlights. 'I'll make you two a drink,' she mouthed.

Putting the kettle on, Grace took three mugs from the cupboard and then leaned against the kitchen counter. She was heartbroken by Paul's death. She had loved him like a son and had no idea how they would all cope without him. But she could only imagine what Michael and Cheryl were going through. Paul was their child, whom they had raised and loved from the moment he was born, and now he was gone.

As she carried a tray of hot tea out of the kitchen, Grace noticed that the hallway was empty and could hear voices coming from the living room. She walked in and placed the tray on the table in front of Michael and Cheryl who were both sitting on the sofa.

'Haven't you got anything stronger?' Cheryl sniffed as she looked at the mugs of tea with open disdain.

'I'll get you a brandy,' Michael replied before Grace could. He walked over to the drinks cabinet and poured two large measures of brandy. 'Want one, love?' he asked Grace.

'No, thanks,' she said with a shake of her head.

Returning to sit on the sofa, Michael handed Cheryl her drink. She took it without a word of thanks and turned her attention to Grace. 'Don't you have somewhere to be?' she said as she shot Grace a withering look.

'Yes she does. Right here,' Michael snapped as he glared at his ex-wife.

Grace groaned inwardly. Cheryl would never change. Even in her grief she couldn't see Grace as anything other than a threat.

'I should check on the kids, to be honest,' Grace lied as she picked up her mug of tea from the table. 'I'll let you two talk.' She smiled at Michael and gave his shoulder a squeeze as she walked past him.

'Goodnight, Cheryl,' she added on her way out. 'And for what it's worth, I'm truly sorry.'

Before Cheryl could offer a snarky comeback, Grace left the room.

'I still can't believe you married that stuck-up bitch,' Cheryl said as she downed her brandy after Grace had left the room.

Michael glared at her. 'I thought you came here to talk about Paul?'

Cheryl shrugged. 'I did. I'm just saying. I don't know what you see in her. She's not your type at all.'

'I don't think you have any idea what my type is, Cheryl. And you have no fucking business coming into my house and insulting my wife.'

'Okay, keep your hair on. I'm sorry,' she said. She smiled at him and fluttered her eyelashes and he realised he'd never been able to tell whether she was being genuine or not.

'Any chance of a refill?' she asked as she held up her empty glass.

Grace was putting some laundry away when Michael came into their bedroom.

'Has Cheryl gone?' she asked.

'Just. I thought she was going to stay the night at one point. She kept hinting at it, but I put her off.'

'She could have stayed if she needed to,' Grace said as she closed the dressing-table drawer and walked over to him.

'Are you joking? We'd never get rid of her. Can you imagine her flouncing round the place demanding to be fed and watered?' he said as he pulled Grace into a hug.

'She probably wants to be close to you,' Grace said. 'It must be hard for her going home to an empty house. Maybe being with you makes her feel close to Paul?'

'Or she just wants to cause aggro as usual,' he said with a sigh. 'I'm sorry about what she said to you.'

'Don't worry about it,' Grace reassured him. 'She's grieving. Besides, it would take more than a dig from Cheryl to bother me.'

'You're an angel, do you know that?' he said as he brushed her hair behind her ear.

She smiled. 'I don't think your ex-wife would agree with you.'

'Well, no, she thinks you're the devil incarnate. But who gives a shit what she thinks?' he said with the faintest of smiles.

'Do you think she'll be okay?' Grace asked in all seriousness.

Michael shrugged. 'I don't know. She's a survivor though, I know that much.'

'I hope she's got someone she can ring for company. Maybe you should have asked her to stay?'

Michael shook his head. 'I think we've got enough on our plates, don't you?'

Grace nodded and rested her head on his chest. 'How are you?' she asked softly.

Michael rested his chin on her head and sighed. 'I don't know, Grace. I feel kind of numb today. Maybe that's a good thing though?'

Grace squeezed her arms tighter around him. 'Just know I'm here for whatever you need.'

'I know,' he replied before planting a kiss on her forehead.

Chapter Sixty

J ake stopped his car outside the terraced house in Kensington and turned off the engine.

'You think these fuckwits will know anything?' Connor asked.

'Who knows? They can't know any less than the other four dozen fuckwits we've spoken to today, can they?'

Connor nodded and absent-mindedly rubbed the knuckles on his right hand, which were already bruised. 'Seems as good a place as any then.'

The occupants of the house were a pair of nut-jobs who'd moved down from Glasgow a few months earlier, and occasionally operated as armed robbers. Not knowing the local area, they had burst into The Blue Rooms one quiet Sunday morning when only the cleaners were in, and tried to rob the safe. They hadn't been able to get into it, and had escaped with a few crates of spirits instead. Jake and the twins had paid the pair of them a visit and had ensured they learned exactly who they had fucked with by putting them in hospital for a few nights. The only reason they'd escaped a more severe punishment was because they hadn't harmed either of the cleaners who'd been unfortunate enough to be on duty that morning. Both women had been shaken up, but otherwise unharmed, and Jake and the twins had given them some credit for that.

Since then, Jake had heard that the pair had made it their business to get to know every villain in the city and had quickly learned who they could take on and win, and who to leave well alone. Neither Jake or Connor seriously believed that either of them had anything to do with Paul's murder, but they might just know who did.

Getting out of the car, Jake and Connor put on the leather driving gloves they always carried in their pockets. Then they scanned the street before opening the boot and taking out a baseball bat each. Jake also had a blade tucked away inside his long coat, while Connor had brought a Baikal handgun. If things went south, they always had a back-up plan.

'You do the honours, mate,' Jake said to Connor as they approached the front door. With one swift kick, Connor booted through the rotten wood and the door sprang open, ricocheting against the interior wall. They ran inside and almost collided with the occupants, who had obviously heard the noise of the door almost coming off its hinges, and had decided to make a run for it.

'Woah. Where the fuck do you think you're off to?' Jake said as he pushed one of the cousins through the open doorway to the living room. He fell onto his cousin behind him as well as a third man whom Jake and Connor had never seen before, causing them to fall like a row of dominoes.

The three men scrabbled over each other to get up.

'Sit the fuck down!' Connor barked at them as he walked into the room behind Jake.

The three men scurried to the sofa and sat on it, staring up at Jake and Connor who stood in front of them, each of them holding a baseball bat over their shoulder.

'We've come looking for some answers, lads. And if you don't start talking, we'll start breaking some bones,' Jake said.

The three men nodded. 'What do you want to know?' one asked in a thick Scottish accent.

'Anything that you know about my brother's murder,' Connor replied.

They sat in silence with pale faces staring at Jake and Connor. Fed up with the silence, Jake swung his bat and cracked one of them on the kneecap. He howled in pain, causing the other two to start talking.

'Nothin'. We don't know nothin',' they said, shaking their heads furiously.

'Don't believe you,' Connor snapped as he swung the bat and popped another kneecap.

Jake pulled the knife from his coat. 'I think it's about time we stopped pissing about, don't you?'

Ten minutes later, Connor and Jake walked out of the house to a chorus of wailing and sobbing.

'Don't think they knew anything?' Jake said with a shrug.

'Nope,' Connor agreed. 'So, where to now'

'How about we pay all of our dealers a visit? Maybe one of them decided to try a takeover?' Jake replied. He didn't believe that was the case, but he was out of ideas.

'Why not?' Connor replied. 'I've got fuck all else to do.'

Connor climbed into Jake's car and sat in silence as Jake drove. 'Shall we start with that prick Stu Poynter?' Jake said.

'If you like,' Connor replied with a nod. Jake didn't like Stu. He didn't like that Paul and Stu were mates – or at least they had been. That was why he wanted to visit Stu really. He just wanted an excuse to beat the shit out of him, and why not? Connor felt like beating the shit out of someone too. He'd lost his best mate in the whole world – someone who was quite literally his other half, and if he even thought about Paul for more than a second, he felt so much anger and grief that he worried his heart would burst out of his chest and he would spontaneously combust. To make matters worse, Jazz had started avoiding his calls too. Just when he really needed her, she was ghosting him.

Chapter Sixty-One

Acting DI Leigh Moss groaned inwardly as she noticed DI Webster walking across the busy office towards her. He grinned as he finally reached her and perched himself on the edge of her desk. Leigh rolled her chair back a few inches in order to put as much distance between her and her former boss as possible. She'd worked for Tony Webster in CID until six months earlier when she'd secured her acting up promotion to the Organised Crime Task Force, and she hated him. To Leigh, Webster was the embodiment of everything she despised in a police officer – his arrogance, his sense of absolute entitlement, his conviction that he was invincible, and his belief that he was irresistible to women. If all of that wasn't bad enough, Leigh knew without a doubt that Webster was bent. But he'd been her boss and he had the ear of the Chief Super, so there was no way she was going to be the one to try and expose him, no matter how much she wanted to.

'How are things?' Webster said with a flash of his eyebrows. 'Missing me yet?'

'Not yet, Tony,' Leigh responded quickly, grateful that she no longer had to call him Sir. She was only an acting DI, for now, but that still meant that for the time being, at least, she no longer had to address him as her superior officer.

'How are things in organised crime?' he asked.

'Same old, same old. You know how it is,' Leigh replied. She knew he was fishing for intel from her. Any little titbit could be useful to him in order to keep his benefactors happy.

'What? I'd heard the whole city's going to shit. Four shootings in the last two days alone, not to mention a surge in violent crime,' he said as he picked up one of the case files from her desk and started to flick through it.

Leigh snatched the file from his hands. 'Don't believe everything you hear.'

Webster frowned at her. 'Don't forget where you come from, Leigh,' he said with a snarl. 'At a time like this, you should remember who your friends are.' Then he stood up and gave her a patronising pat on the shoulder. 'Keep up the good work, Detective,' he said before walking away.

Leigh scowled after him. What the hell did he mean by all that 'remember where you come from' crap? He acted like he was her mentor or something – like she had ever learned anything remotely useful from him! As she was thinking that, a cold trickle of fear ran down her throat and into her chest. Surely he didn't actually know anything about her past? Almost nobody did. She had worked hard to erase any trace of her former identity and become the woman she was today. But there was one person who knew the truth, and that person just happened to be the queen of the bloody underworld. The same woman who kept Webster, and no doubt a few of his colleagues, in her vast pockets. Leigh shook her head and admonished herself. She was being paranoid. There was no way Grace Carter would betray her, Leigh was sure – least of all to a scumbag like Tony Webster.

'What did he want?' The familiar voice of DS Nick Bryce interrupted Leigh's thoughts and she realised he had made her way over to her desk while she'd been glaring at Webster's retreating figure.

Leigh shook her head and gave him a faint smile. 'Nothing really. You know what he's like. Thinks I'm his mate or something,' she said dismissively.

Nick frowned. 'He's a dick. I've never liked him. Hated working for him in CID.'

'Me too,' Leigh agreed. 'Do you have something for me?' she said, indicating the manila folder in his hand.

'A stabbing early hours this morning,' he said with a sigh. 'But we think it's connected to our case.'

'A stabbing? For God's sake,' she muttered in response.

'Well, not so much a stabbing as a slashing really,' Nick corrected himself. 'Victim has two slices across his face and four on his forearms.'

'Defensive wounds?' Leigh queried.

Nick shook his head and passed her the folder, which included photographs of the injuries. 'He had the shit kicked out of him first. I doubt he could have defended himself even if he'd tried. Besides, the knife wounds appear deliberate. They're carved into the victim's flesh rather than random slices. The doc thinks so too.'

'Who is our victim and where is he now?'

'Stu Poynter. He lives in Heswall, but he was at his girlfriend's in Gateacre last night. She drove him to A and E. He's not been one of our big players up to now. Has a few assault PCs on his record and a couple of possessions. Not someone who's been massively on our radar anyway. He's in The Royal being stitched up. Refuses to give a statement or co-operate in any way.'

'And the girlfriend?'

'She didn't see a thing. Obviously.'

Leigh shook her head. 'Of course not.'

'He claims he was mugged on the way home from town.'

'How many muggings on the way home from the pub has it been this week then?' she said with a raised eyebrow.

'He's our fourth so far,' Nick replied.

'And those are just the ones we know about,' Leigh said as she absent-mindedly rubbed the bridge of her nose.

'We knew Paul Carter's murder was going to cause problems,' Nick reminded her.

'I know that, but in the meantime, Jake Conlon and Connor Carter are making this unit look bloody incompetent. What's happening with the surveillance?'

'Still not approved, Ma'am. DCI James is still saying we don't have enough to go on. It's not like the pair of them have ever even been arrested or anything. And no one is willing to give us their names. They've got the criminal community running scared.'

'I'll bloody follow them myself if I have to,' Leigh snapped.

'It's at times like this I almost wish Grace Carter was back at the helm,' Nick said quietly. 'At least she kept the rest of them in line.'

'Well, she's not at the helm any more, is she? Or if she is, she's lost control. There's no way she'd have sanctioned this kind of mayhem.'

'You sound like you speak from experience,' Nick said.

Leigh nodded. 'I was only a beat copper when Grace Carter, or Conlon as she was then, rose through the ranks. Before she took control, there had been a few years of carnage and chaos as the factions battled for the top. Then Grace stepped in, and everything calmed down. Stayed like that for years. She has a way of doing things that doesn't involve shooting or maiming every scumbag in the city.'

'If I didn't know you better, Ma'am, I'd almost think you admired her.'

Leigh stared at him. 'Don't be so bloody soft,' she snapped. 'Why don't you make yourself useful and make me a coffee while I have a look at this.' She turned away from him and opened the folder.

'Whatever you say, Ma'am,' Nick replied with a shrug.

Leigh leafed through the photographs in the folder, paying little attention to Stu Poynter's wounds. Instead, she thought about her conversation with Nick. The truth was, not only did she admire Grace Carter, or Grace Conlon as Leigh had first known her so many years ago, but she also had a great deal of respect for her. Not that she would ever admit that to anyone, including Grace. No matter how much respect Leigh had for the other woman, it didn't change the fact that everything Grace stood for was the complete antithesis of everything Leigh believed in. They were two very different people on two very different paths, and even their shared past would never change that. Now Grace's son and her stepson were running unchecked across the city, causing untold damage, and Leigh was determined to bring them down, even if she had to bring Grace down too.

Chapter Sixty-Two

B radley, Craig, Billy and Ged Johnson waited in the deserted car park for Jimmy Kelly and his nephews to turn up.

'They're fuckin' late,' Craig griped as he looked at his watch.

'They'll be 'ere soon,' Bradley said with a sigh. 'Trust me.'

A few minutes later, Jimmy's bright blue BMW X5 rolled into the car park.

'Does he know the meaning of the word discreet?' Ged said with a roll of his eyes.

Jimmy Kelly hadn't taken kindly to the Johnsons beating up his nephews, destroying their latest money-laundering front, and extorting them into buying their gear, but he'd swallowed it because he'd had to. What choice did he have against the growing might of the Johnson empire?

'You got the gear?' Jimmy asked as he sauntered over, accompanied by just one of his nephews, Alan.

'Of course. You got the money?'

Jimmy nodded and Alan threw a holdall full of money onto the ground at Bradley's feet.

'I take it it's all there?' Bradley asked.

'Of course,' Alan said with a growl.

'Good. Get the gear out of the car, Ged.'

Ged took another large holdall out of the boot of Craig's old Sierra before passing it to Alan.

'You driving it back to your gaff in that thing?' Bradley said with a raised eyebrow.

Jimmy smiled at him. 'Not really any of your fucking business once I've paid you for it, is it?'

'S'pose not,' Bradley said with a shrug. 'But if the plod pull you, don't mention our names.'

'Do you think I'm fucking soft, lad?' Jimmy snapped. 'I was in this business when you were still shitting in your nappies.'

'All right, Jim. Touchy today, aren't we? You on your period or something?'

As Bradley finished speaking, a grey Fiesta drove into the car park and came to a stop near Jimmy and Alan. A few seconds later, Jimmy's second nephew, Jay, stepped out of the vehicle. Picking up the holdall full of cocaine, he placed it in the boot of the Fiesta before joining his uncle and cousin.

Jimmy stared at Bradley. 'We done then?'

Bradley nodded. 'Until the next time.'

'Next time? Do you honestly think there'll be a next time? I'm sure our former suppliers won't be very forgiving once they've found out what you've been up to,' Jimmy said.

Bradley laughed loudly. 'You not heard about Paul Carter's unfortunate accident then? I told you they'd be kept busy, didn't I?

Jimmy stared at him open-mouthed, while his two nephews fidgeted nervously beside him. 'You're telling me that you took out Paul Carter?'

Bradley shrugged. 'I never said that. But would I tell you if I had, Jimmy?'

'You've just signed your own death warrant, mate. Connor Carter and Jake Conlon are gonna skin you alive.'

Bradley shook his head. 'Whatever you say, Jim. You just fucking behave yourselves, eh? And let me know when you need some more gear.'

'Fucking dickheads,' Jimmy mumbled, then he and his nephews got back into their cars and drove away. Bradley watched them and felt a sickening feeling building in the pit of his stomach. What the hell had he just done?

As soon as the cars were out of sight, Billy turned to his older brother and shoved him hard in the chest, causing Bradley to stagger backwards. 'What the fuck are you playing at, even mentioning Paul Carter's name, Brad?' Billy shouted. 'Are you completely fucking soft, or what?'

Bradley regained his footing and pushed him back. 'No one is gonna think we had anything to do with it,' he snarled. 'Jimmy's an old has-been, and no one will pay a blind bit of notice to him.'

Ged snorted at this remark and Bradley glared at him. 'Don't you fucking start,' he warned.

Ged took a step towards him and Craig moved to stand in the middle of the three of them.

'Shall we all just calm down and get the fuck out of here before someone sees us scrapping and calls the plod?' Craig interrupted.

There were mumbles of reluctant agreement and Bradley was relieved when his brothers starting making their way to the car. As he was about to open the driver's door, Craig stepped up behind him.

'I hope you know what you're doing, Bro,' he said quietly in his ear.

Bradley studied Craig's face as he walked past and climbed into the back seat, but it was impassive, and he couldn't quite tell whether Craig had just delivered a friendly warning or a threat.

Chapter Sixty-Three

Craig Johnson sat next to his brother Billy while he played on his smartphone, and watched as his two older brothers stood at the bar of their local, The Grapes. The two of them had always had a difficult relationship, as though they always had a score to settle with each other. They behaved themselves when they had to, and always made sure their beef never interfered with business, but they could never put their differences aside for very long. Ged provoking Bradley was becoming increasingly frequent, and annoying, and Craig had decided to have a quiet word with Ged as soon as he got the chance. There was no doubt that Bradley had crossed a line last night, even mentioning Paul's name. The last thing they needed was anyone thinking they were taking credit for Paul's murder. But it was done now. Bradley knew what he was doing. He'd been out getting the true feel of all that had been going on these past few years, while they'd all been stuck inside. Craig trusted his older brother's judgement, even if he didn't always agree with his decisions. Bradley was the boss. That was how it always had been and always would be. It wasn't his fault that he was born first and got to be the head of the family, and it was about time Ged fell in line like the rest of them had had to.

Craig smiled as his brothers walked over to his table carrying four pints and four whisky chasers.

'Feel like celebrating, did ya's?' Craig asked as they sat down.

'Well, we have good reason to, don't we?' Bradley answered with a grin. 'Jake Conlon and the Carters are too busy mourning the loss of their beloved Paul to give a shit what we're up to. They're in fucking pieces, mate. I doubt they'll be doing anything for a while. Not to mention, the plod will be all over them waiting for them to make a move. They'll be on their best behaviour.'

Ged rolled his eyes, downed his whisky and slammed his glass on the table.

'What the fuck was that about?' Bradley asked.

Ged glared at him. 'What?'

'The eye roll? I'm getting fucking sick of you questioning every single thing I say.'

'Well, I'm getting sick of you poncing around pretending you're John fucking Gotti,' Ged snapped.

'Who the fuck do you think you're talking to?' Bradley fumed, slamming his fist onto the table.

'Fucking pack it in lads, will ya?' Craig said with a sigh. 'You're like the fucking Hecklers lately. Give it a rest!'

Bradley was about to respond when Billy interrupted. 'Can we forget about your petty squabbling for minute, and remind ourselves just exactly who we're dealing with here, Brad?'

Bradley turned his attention to Billy while Ged sat back and sipped his pint.

'Of course I know who we're dealing with, Bill. Don't you fucking start an' all.'

'But I don't think you do,' Billy said with a shake of his head. 'You think that Jake Conlon and Connor Carter are just going to sit back and let Paul's murder go unpunished? They don't exactly have reputations as reasonable men, do they?'

'I told you—'

'Never mind what you told me,' Billy interrupted him. 'I'm telling you that there isn't a chance in hell that those two are going to sit back and wait for the plod to solve this. They will go to great lengths to find out who was behind the hit on Paul, and you're fucking going around blabbing about being involved. Are you fucking soft, or what?'

'If we don't take the credit, someone else will,' Craig said while Bradley sat glaring at Billy, his face becoming redder by the second. Craig knew that his older brother could take a lot of Ged's shit before he blew his top, and he sensed that boiling point was imminent, now that Billy was weighing in too.

'Well, fucking let them,' Billy snapped. 'I'd rather remain attached to all of my limbs and appendages if you don't mind. Even if they don't come looking. What about Grace Carter? That woman has more contacts than MI5. And don't even get me started on Michael and Sean. Do you know there's a story about them two that goes around the nicks – about what they used to do to people who crossed them?'

'That's an urban legend,' Craig interrupted.

'No, it's fucking not. Mark my words, it's absolutely fucking true.'

'Well, our Brad would never have heard that particular story, Bill,' Ged said with a grin. 'Coz he's never been in prison, has he?'

At this slight against him, Bradley launched himself across the table at Ged, sending the glasses toppling and spilling the remaining drinks over the table. Ged ducked and landed a punch on Bradley's jaw before Craig pulled him away. 'What the fuck are you doing, Ged?' he growled.

'Me?' Ged shouted. 'He fucking attacked me.'

Billy helped Bradley up off the floor. He dusted himself down before trying to launch himself at Ged again, but Billy held him back. 'Will you two fucking pack it in?' Billy said. 'I think we have enough to worry about without you two at each other's fucking throats every five minutes.'

'I've had enough of your shit, Ged,' Bradley growled.

'Oh, I'm only fucking messing, you big quilt,' Ged said with a laugh. 'It really pushes your buttons when I mention you not being in the nick though, doesn't it?' He raised his eyebrow at Bradley. 'Anyone fancy another pint then?' he added before Bradley had a chance to answer.

'Not me. I'm off,' Billy said as he stood up.

'Tell Scott I want to see him at the pub after our next job,' Bradley insisted. 'It doesn't look good that he's never here. He should be celebrating with us.'

'Oh yeah, because this has been a fucking barrel of

laughs, hasn't it? I'll see you tomorrow,' Billy snapped before walking out of the pub.

'Oh, fuck him. I'll have another pint and a chaser,' Craig said.

'Same,' Bradley growled.

'Sound,' Ged said, rubbing his hands together and walking over to the bar.

'You shouldn't let him get to you so much, Bro,' Craig said to Bradley once Ged was out of earshot. 'You know he lives to wind you up.'

'He's a cheeky fucking cunt, Craig,' Bradley snapped.

Craig shook his head. One of these days the pair of them were going to kill each other.

Chapter Sixty-Four

G race closed the bedroom door behind her. Pulling her mobile from the pocket of her jeans, she dialled John Brennan's number.

He answered on the fourth ring. 'Hiya, Boss.'

'Hi, John. Are you busy today?'

'Only with the usual. I always have time for you though. What do you need?'

'Can you meet me? I need your help with something.'

'Of course. Where and when?'

'Sophia's Kitchen? About four?'

'That's fine. I'll see you there.'

Grace hung up the phone as Michael walked into the room holding Oscar. 'Who was that?' he asked.

'John Brennan. I've got a few things I need him to look into for me.'

Grace saw the flicker of a scowl cross his face but he didn't say anything. She recalled the argument they'd had in the car a few days before Paul had died and wondered if

Michael suspected her and John of anything. Not that he had cause to. John was a good friend. Nothing more.

'I'm going to nip out for an hour this afternoon. Will you be okay with the kids, or do you want me to ask your dad to call in?'

'He's calling round anyway in a bit,' he replied. 'I think he was hoping to see you too?'

'I won't be long. I'll see him when I get back,' she assured him.

Grace was sitting at her desk in Sophia's Kitchen when John Brennan tapped on the open door.

She looked up and smiled at him. 'Come in, John.'

He walked over to her and they hugged. 'How are you doing?' he asked her when he released from his embrace.

'I honestly don't know. One minute I'm sad, the next I'm angry. Mostly, I'm just worried though,' she replied as she sat down.

John down opposite her and waited for her to continue.

'I'm worried about Michael and how he's coping. Belle has been asking where Paul is and I'm trying my best to explain – but how do you explain death to a three-year-old? But mostly I'm worried about Jake and Connor.'

John nodded.

'Have you heard what they've been up to?'

'It's hard not to,' he replied. 'Last night's antics have certainly caused a stir.'

'They've roped in some of our bouncers too. They've

been running around shooting anything that moves, did you know that? You know some of them lunatics only need half an excuse to have a go.'

'Murf has seen his arse, but he's handling it. He'll bring the lads back in line.'

'But not Jake and Connor! They seem to think they're invincible, John, and it's terrifying me. They're either going to get arrested, or bloody killed themselves. You'd have thought Paul's murder might have made them lie low for a bit – make them see they're not as untouchable as they thought. But it seems to have had the opposite effect.'

'You know that's not how this game works, Grace. Lying low would be seen as a sign of weakness. Besides, they're angry. And they're still just kids. This is all they know how to do.'

'I know,' she replied with a sigh. 'I think I forget sometimes how young and naïve they still are. I was bloody stupid to think I could take a back seat and let them run things. I should have known, John. I took my eye off the ball. And if I hadn't, maybe I could have stopped it?' she said, the words catching in her throat.

'You can't blame yourself for this, Grace. You've always done everything you could to protect those boys. Nobody saw this coming.'

Grace shook her head and wiped a tear from her cheek. 'But I *should* have seen it coming.'

John shook his head. 'You have to stop thinking like that, or you'll drive yourself crazy.'

Grace took a few seconds to compose herself. Although she knew it was well-intentioned, John's sympathy was only making her feel worse. 'Anyway, that's partly why I've asked you here. I want you to keep an eye on Jake and Connor for me. Clean up their messes if you have to. Pay whoever needs paying to keep their mouths shut. Speak to our contacts in the police and encourage them to look the other way as much as possible.'

'Okay.'

'And I know this goes without saying, but keep your ear to the ground, John. Any information you get, no matter how seemingly insignificant, about who ordered the hit on Paul, or if you suspect Jake and Connor are in immediate danger, then you come straight to me.'

'Of course, Grace.'

'I need this kept between you and me.'

'It will. Believe me, I have no desire for the two of them to find out I'm keeping an eye on them for you.'

Grace nodded in appreciation. She'd known she'd be able to count on him. 'I know what I'm asking you is not easy.'

'It's not a problem. Anything else I can help you with?'

'I think that will keep you busy enough, don't you?' she replied.

'I reckon so. If there's nothing else, it seems I've got a lot to be getting on with,' he said as he stood up. 'I'll keep you posted.'

'Great. Thanks, John.'

Grace watched him walk out of her office and wondered whether she was doing enough to protect Jake and Connor from the effects of the violent rampage they were currently on. She was used to them doing things their own way and it had always been different to hers – much less subtle. But currently they were letting their emotions rule their heads, and in her experience, that was when mistakes were made. She sat back in her chair with a sigh. She was doing all she could for now. Her efforts were needed elsewhere, and the best thing she could do for everyone was find Paul's killer as soon as possible.

Chapter Sixty-Five

G race was still in her office at Sophia's Kitchen looking for some paperwork when Jimmy Kelly knocked on the open door.

'Grace? Could I have a word?'

Grace put the papers on the desk and brushed her hair back from her face with her hand. 'Jimmy? I haven't see you for years.'

'I know,' Jimmy said with a faint smile. 'Not since you helped me and our Alan out. It's been a while.'

'I was only popping in to sort something out. I'm heading home shortly. So, I can only spare you a few minutes. But come in.'

'I appreciate you've got a lot going on,' Jimmy said apologetically. 'And I'm truly sorry about what happened to Paul. Please pass on my condolences to Michael and the rest of the family, won't you?'

'Of course.'

'But that's sort of what I wanted to talk to you about, to be honest.'

'Oh?'

'Me and the lads – you know our Alan's lads, Jay and young Alan, don't you? – well, as you know, we've done business with your Jake and the twins for years. But a couple of days ago Bradley Johnson and his idiot brothers turned up at our Alan's bird's beauty salon with a load of machetes and baseball bats and smashed the place up. Beat the lads up too, and threatened poor Sandy. They wouldn't leave until the lads agreed to start working for them instead.'

'Oh?' Grace said. 'Why didn't you mention this to Jake, or the twins?'

'Well, I'd heard they had a falling out, to be honest, Grace and I didn't know who to speak to. But I'd decided to speak to the twins about it, but then the next day, Paul was…'

'And you want me to sort this now?' Grace said as she stared at him.

Jimmy shook his head frantically. 'God, no! Of course not. But that's not all. When my lads told them the twins wouldn't stand for their threats, Bradley laughed and said they'd have bigger things to worry about, like they knew something was going to happen. Then we had a meeting with the Johnsons yesterday, and that fucking slimy bastard Bradley as much as admitted he was the one responsible for Paul's murder.'

'What? He actually admitted it?'

'He didn't deny it. And he looked very pleased with

himself when I accused him of it, Grace,' Jimmy said as he stood across the desk from her, wringing his hands. 'I spoke to the Parkes brothers from Bootle, and Bradley has pulled the same stunt with them too. When they asked him about Paul, he didn't deny it either.'

Lost for words, Grace shook her head in disbelief.

'I thought you'd want to know,' Jimmy went on.

'Of course. Thank you, Jimmy. I appreciate you coming to me.'

'I thought you'd know the best way to handle it,' he said.

Grace nodded. 'I appreciate that, Jimmy. And you'll have no more bother with the Johnson brothers from now on.'

'Well, that's good news, Grace, but that's really not why I came here,' he assured her.

'I know that,' she said with a smile.

'I'll let you get back to it then,' Jimmy said as he backed out of the office. 'Bye, Grace.'

'Bye, Jimmy.'

Grace watched Jimmy disappear through the crowded restaurant and sank onto her office chair. Jimmy knew the Carter family well and had worked for them long before she'd even known them. He was loyal, and she appreciated that he had trusted her with the information, rather than going straight to Michael. Mostly because she didn't believe for a second that the Johnson brothers were responsible for Paul's murder. They were a load of brainless idiots who couldn't organise a piss-up in a brewery. Bradley, the oldest, was the leader, and he was as bent as a nine bob note. He relied on the muscle of three of his younger brothers to throw his weight around, but he was an idiot who, though most people didn't know it, had a gambling habit as big as his ego, which meant his money disappeared faster than he could earn it. Grace knew these things because her old friend Nudge Richards was a gambler too and he also kept company with most of the criminals in Liverpool and beyond. Whilst his job as the best fence in Merseyside meant that he was usually the embodiment of discretion, he told Grace everything. She had helped him out years earlier when no one else would, and he had never forgotten it. He'd been loyal to her ever since and was a prime source of information.

It was because she knew Bradley so well that she knew he couldn't afford the services of the kind of professional that had shot Paul. He was too much of a coward to try and take out one of the Carters, and even if he wasn't, he'd have ordered one of his brothers to do the job, not pay someone else. It just didn't add up to her.

Grace took her phone out of her handbag and dialled Sean Carter's number. While she waited for him to answer, she wondered if she had it all wrong. Had Bradley and his brothers organised themselves into a professional outfit without her noticing? Was she that out of touch? They had to have someone backing them to think they could take over some of Jake and the twins' business with no repercussions.

'Hi, Grace,' Sean answered the phone.

'Hey. Are you free tomorrow morning?'

'Yes. Sophia's taking the girls to the Trafford Centre, and

I was planning on coming to see you and Michael. Is everything okay?'

'I'm not sure. I might have a lead, but it could be nothing. Fancy making a quick visit to Bradley Johnson with me?'

'Tomorrow?

'Yes. He's probably out on the pull looking for some strange tonight. Let's catch him at home reading the Sunday papers in his slippers.'

'Of course. What shall I bring?'

'Nothing too heavy. His wife and kids will be there. I'll pick you up at half ten.'

'I'll see you tomorrow then.'

'Bye, Sean.'

Chapter Sixty-Six

The following morning, Grace walked into the kitchen holding Oscar and saw Michael staring out of the kitchen window. Belle was drawing quietly at the kitchen table and didn't look up when Grace entered. Walking over to him, Grace placed a hand on Michael's shoulder making him jump.

'Sorry,' she said. 'I didn't mean to startle you.'

'It's okay,' he replied. 'I was in a world of my own.'

Oscar gurgled and made a grab for his dad's beard, something which would have ordinarily made Michael smile and take him from Grace's arms, but he did neither. Instead he stared blankly across the kitchen, as though he was waiting for someone to walk through the door.

'I need to pop out,' Grace said. 'I'll ask your dad and Sue to watch the kids for a few hours, okay?'

'Yeah, if you want.'

'Will you be okay if I go out? Do you need me to stay here?'

Michael looked at her but his expression didn't change. 'Yeah, I'll be fine.'

Grace put a hand on his cheek. 'I won't be long,' she said.

'I'm fine,' he repeated.

Grace walked over to Belle. 'Want to go see grandad and nanny Sue?' she asked.

'Yes,' Belle said excitedly.

'Come on then. Let's go and ring them,' she said as she took her daughter's hand. Leading her out of the kitchen, Grace glanced back at Michael who had gone back to staring out of the window at the rain.

An hour later Grace had dropped Belle and Oscar off with Michael's dad, Patrick, and was pulling up outside Sean Carter's house.

'Thanks for doing this with me,' Grace said with a faint smile as Sean climbed into her car.

'No problem at all. But does Michael know what you're up to?' he asked.

Grace shook her head. 'I doubt it. I'm not sure Michael even knows what day it is at the moment.'

'I'm worried about him, Grace.'

'Me too,' Grace said with a sigh. 'Which is why we need to find out who was responsible for the hit on Paul sooner rather than later.'

'Let's get going then,' Sean said as he fastened his seatbelt.

Twenty minutes later, Grace pulled her car up outside Bradley Johnson's house.

'Are you sure about this? You said his wife and kids would be in there too,' Sean said to her as she turned off the ignition.

'We're only going to talk to him. Remember?' she reminded him.

'We'll see about that,' Sean responded gruffly as he climbed out of the car.

Arriving at the front door to Bradley's house, Grace turned the handle and was unsurprised to find the door unlocked. It was eleven o'clock on a Sunday morning. The kids were probably in and out with their mates. Bradley Johnson considered himself untouchable in his neighbourhood. No one would ever dare confront him at his family seat. So why wouldn't he leave his door open?

Stepping inside with Sean close behind, Grace motioned him to lock the door after them. They didn't want any interruptions.

Bradley Johnson was sitting on the sofa in his boxer shorts with a plate of bacon and eggs on his lap when Sean and Grace walked into his living room and gave him the shock of his life.

He stared at them open-mouthed. 'What the fuck ' he started.

'Shut the fuck up and listen, Bradley,' Sean interrupted him. 'And if you're lucky, no one will get hurt.'

'What's going on?' a female voice shrieked behind them.

Sean turned to glare at Bradley's wife Tina and then back to Bradley as Grace took a seat on the armchair.

Understanding the look Sean had given him, Bradley spoke. 'Nothing, love. But get the kids from upstairs and take them over to your mum's for half an hour.'

'Nope.' Sean shook his head. 'The kids can stay upstairs. And you can have a seat next to him,' Sean said to Tina, indicating the empty space on the sofa next to Bradley. Sensing the tension in the air, Tina did as she was told.

'Good,' Sean said as he walked over to Grace's chair and stood behind her.

'So, Bradley,' Grace said as she stared at him. 'Tell me everything you know about the murder of Paul Carter.'

Chapter Sixty-Seven

Bradley Johnson sat on his sofa and stared at the two people who had just marched into his living room unannounced. Grace and Sean Carter. He had met the two of them briefly many years earlier, not that he thought they'd remember that encounter, but despite that he knew exactly who they were and what they were capable of. He hadn't realised that the pair of them still got their hands dirty, but here they were in his fucking house. He looked at Sean in his expensive Barbour jacket and wondered what manner of weapons he might have hidden in there. Then there was Grace, sitting on his armchair with her legs crossed, staring at him with that ice-cold exterior she was well known for. They were a pair of ruthless fuckers, and Bradley had never been so terrified in all of his life. He prayed that Tina would keep her big gob shut as she perched next to him, and that the kids kept to form and stayed in their bedrooms playing on their various gadgets. If he played his cards right, he might get out of this alive.

His throat felt as though it was about to close over, and he swallowed in an attempt to relieve the sensation. The blood thundered in his ears and he closed his eyes, willing for quiet so he could think straight.

'I know fuck all about it,' he said eventually as he opened his eyes and looked at Grace.

'Really?' Grace raised an eyebrow at him. 'I thought you and your brothers were taking the credit. That's what we'd heard, wasn't it, Sean?'

Sean nodded. 'Yep.'

'What?' Tina snapped as she turned to look at her husband.

Bradley shrugged. 'We never told anyone it was us. Not one of us took any credit for the hit on Paul. But people talk, and well…'

'And you didn't deny the rumours?' Grace asked.

Bradley shook his head. 'No. And I won't insult your intelligence by pretending that it hasn't been good for our business, but we had nothing to do with it. Not a single thing.'

'Hmm,' Grace said. 'What do you think, Sean?' she asked as she looked up at her accomplice, six feet of pure muscle and hatred.

'Me? I wouldn't trust this piece of shit as far as I could throw him. But you're the boss.'

Grace sat back in the chair. 'Why should I believe a lying waste of oxygen like you, Bradley?'

'Because it's the truth,' Tina answered for him. 'He didn't have anything to do with it.'

'And how would you know?' Grace asked her.

'Because he tells me everything. Don't you, Brad?' she whined.

Sean gave a snort of derision and Bradley glared at him in defiance, which prompted Sean to take a step towards him, opening his coat as he did so and revealing a glint of the machete blade he had tucked inside there.

'Okay,' Bradley said, raising his hands in surrender. 'I get it. You're both pissed off. Understandably. You want to know who did this, but it wasn't me. It wasn't my brothers. And to be honest, I haven't got a fucking clue who it was.'

'Still not convinced though, Bradley, to be honest. Maybe your kids might know something?' Grace said as started to rise from her chair.

'No,' Bradley shouted. 'I swear we had nothing to do with it. Please. You have to believe me,' he pleaded. He could hear the change of tone in his voice and he despised himself for it. But there was the truth, as plain as day. For all his talk, Bradley Johnson was a coward. He had always known it and now they did too. He'd relied on his brothers to fight his battles, always happy to be the one giving the orders and pulling the strings, but never really in the thick of it.

Grace Carter stood up and walked over to the sofa where Bradley and his wife were sitting. She'd known the threat to his kids would be his breaking point. She would never act on it. She'd never hurt a child, no matter what the circumstances, but Bradley didn't need to know that. Desperate times and all that.

'I think Bradley here has said all he's going to say today, Sean,' she said. 'But be careful,' she warned as she turned her attention to the quivering man on the sofa. 'I'll be watching you, and your brothers. If any of you take one step out of line, I will end the fucking lot of you,' she snapped before walking out.

Sean followed behind her in silence. They were driving away in Grace's car before either of them spoke another word.

'Do you think he was telling the truth then?' Sean asked.

'Do you think he'd still be sitting at home in his undies if I didn't?' Grace replied.

'But how do you know it was nothing to do with him? He wasn't exactly going to fess up to you, was he?'

'No. But I already suspected it was nothing to do with him or his idiot brothers. Do you think any of them have the money or the clout to pull it off? Whoever did this was a bloody pro. Probably one of the most expensive hitmen money can buy. They won't work for just any old Tom, Dick or Harry. So, why on earth would they work for that shower of bell-ends?'

'So, what was today's visit about then?'

'I just wanted to look him in the eye and ask him the question and I think he was telling the truth. I also wanted to put a stop to him taking any credit for Paul's murder. Not only is it incredibly distasteful, but it might just stop my son and your nephew wiping out the whole Johnson clan in an epic rampage.'

'Good luck with that,' Sean said with a sigh. 'Have you seen either of them lately?'

'Not for a few days.' Grace shook her head. 'They're planning something big. I know it. I just hope I can find out what really happened before they go off and get themselves killed or locked up for life.'

Chapter Sixty-Eight

B illy Johnson heard the vibration of his mobile phone as it continued to ring incessantly and sighed. He was getting head off a woman he'd picked up in The Grapes the night before and he'd rather she finished the job before he sent her home.

'Sorry, girl, but I'll have to answer that,' he said with a groan as he pushed her away from him and leaned over to pick up his phone from the bedside table. As he suspected, it was one of his brothers.

'What, Ged?' he snapped.

'Grace and Sean Carter paid our Bradley a visit this morning.'

This news sent all the blood rushing from Billy's dick to his head and he felt suddenly faint. 'What?'

'You heard me. Grace and Sean paid him a visit.'

'Hang on a minute,' Billy said.

Covering the mouthpiece of the phone, he turned to face the woman, whose name he couldn't remember. 'You'll have to get off, girl. I need to get to work.'

She pouted at him. 'Billy—' she started.

'Look, I said fuck off. There's a tenner in my jeans. Go downstairs and phone yourself a taxi.'

She glared at him before retrieving her clothes from his bedroom floor and storming out of his bedroom naked, clutching her clothes in her hand.

'Sorry about that, just throwing some bird out,' he said to Ged who was waiting impatiently on the other end of the phone.

'Like, I've not got all fucking day, Bill,' he snapped. 'Anyway, just be on your guard. Who knows where they'll turn up next?'

'But what happened at Brad's? Is he okay? Are Tina and the kids okay?'

'Everyone's fine. Brad told them he had nothing to do with it, and they believed him – apparently!'

'Hmm. Not sure I buy that. Do you reckon they're planning something?'

'Possibly, Bill. But listen, that's not all we've got to worry about.'

'Oh?'

'It seems our beloved big brother – our illustrious leader – has also gone and done a bunk, with all of Alastair McGrath's money.'

'What the fuck?' Billy shouted.

'Yep. I told you he was a fucking lying weasel.'

'No. He must be planning something, Ged. He wouldn't just get off and leave us all like that.'

'Wouldn't he?' Ged snorted. 'It wouldn't be the first time

he fucked off and left us all in the shit, would it?'

'Nah,' Billy said. 'He'll be back. He wouldn't just leave Tina and the kids.'

'Well, he has. She phoned me wondering where he was. She's fucking livid with him.'

'Shit,' Billy said as his heart started to pound in his chest.

'Yep. So, if the Carters don't come looking for us, Alastair McGrath will.'

'Well, Alastair won't need to know about his money for a week or so. That buys us some time at least.'

'For what?'

'To find our dickhead brother,' Billy snapped.

'If Sean and Michael Carter don't string us up by our balls first!'

Billy put the phone down on his brother and sank back against the pillows. To think five minutes earlier he'd been thinking about how good his life was. Ged and Bradley had never got on. Billy liked to stay out of their drama and keep to himself as much as he could, although that was hard, being a Johnson brother. For as long as he could remember, his older brothers had caused him nothing but trouble. He'd wanted to go into engineering, or mechanics, but that wasn't possible for a Johnson. Eventually, he'd been sucked into their world and now he couldn't get out. Now he saw the same thing happening to Scott, and he felt sorry for the kid.

No matter what he thought of his brothers, though, Billy had been, and always would be, loyal to them. Despite Ged's constant sniping at Bradley, Billy had never actually taken it seriously, and he hadn't thought that Ged did either. He'd always assumed it was just part of their sibling rivalry, set up at birth and encouraged by their violent bully of a father. He'd tried to encourage a similar rivalry between Billy and Craig, but had been missing a vital ingredient – neither he nor Craig gave two shits about what their dad thought about them. When he'd died, it had been a relief to everyone except Bradley and Ged, who had mourned him as though he was some sort of saint.

But now it looked like Bradley had disappeared with Alastair's money and Billy wondered if Ged's dislike of their oldest brother was born of something else. Did Ged really believe that Bradley had used nefarious means to escape a prison sentence when three other brothers had been sent down for their part in a massive conspiracy-to-supply operation? Money had gone missing then too. Solomon Shepherd's money – and Solomon was just as ruthless as Alastair McGrath. How the hell did Bradley walk away from the whole thing unscathed? He was either the luckiest man alive – or a dirty, lying cunt! Only time would tell which.

Chapter Sixty-Nine

J ay Marshall and Alan Kelly walked through to the office at the back of The Blue Rooms. They knocked out of respect for the two men on the other side of the door.

'Come in,' one of them bellowed.

Jay pushed open the door and the two of them walked inside to see Jake Conlon sitting behind his desk and Connor Carter pacing the room.

'What do you two want?' Connor snapped. 'I've been hearing all kinds of rumours about you two and your fucking uncle Jimmy. If it wasn't for the fact I used to like you, and I've had my hands full, I'd have been paying you two a fucking visit.'

'We know. We were going to come and see you. But then we heard about Paul, so we thought we'd leave it until things calmed down. But we've got some information for you,' Jay said.

At this, Jake sat up and Connor walked over to them. 'Oh? And what's that?' he asked.

'Bradley Johnson and his brothers are the ones who've been trying to take over your turf. They came to us. The five of them all tooled up. Smashed up the shop and everything.'

Connor shook his head. 'I thought you two could handle yourselves?'

'We can, Con,' Alan replied. 'But there were five of them. Bradley had a shooter. And Sandy was there! They threatened her too.'

Connor nodded, seeming to understand they were in an untenable position.

'We were going to come and let you know. Go over there and do them over. But…'

'But?' Connor snapped.

'It was the day before Paul was shot.'

Both Connor and Jake bristled at the mention of Paul's murder.

'So, why are you telling us this now?' Jake barked. 'In case you hadn't noticed, we're kind of busy looking for the fucker who murdered my best mate and his brother.'

'Well, that's what we wanted to talk to you about. We think the Johnson brothers were behind it.'

'What?' Connor said. 'You think that shower of pathetic no-marks murdered my brother?'

Jay and Alan nodded. 'I know they've always been beyond useless, Con,' said Alan, 'but the other week they looked like a proper professional outfit. I told you, Bradley had a gun. The five of them were well up for it. They said that you and Paul would have your hands full for a while. We thought they just meant with you sorting out your business after...' Jay stopped speaking when he realised he was approaching the delicate subject of the rift between Jake and the Carter twins, and he didn't know what that was about, or whether it was still an issue. 'Well, after you all seemed to have a falling out.' He looked between the pair of them and they said nothing, so he went on. 'Then we saw them again yesterday, and Bradley as much as admitted being behind Paul's murder.'

'What?' Jake and Connor shouted at the same time.

'If this happened yesterday, why are you only telling us about it now?' Jake shouted.

'We came here yesterday, but neither of you were about. We didn't want to speak to anyone else about it.'

'Of course not,' Connor said. 'Thanks, lads.'

Alan and Jay continued to stare at Jake and Connor until they realised they had been unceremoniously dismissed.

Chapter Seventy

'Ready?' Jake asked as he looked at Connor.

Connor nodded and the two of them used the battering ram they'd acquired to break down the door to Bradley Johnson's house.

The sound of screaming filled the house as Bradley's wife Tina came flying down the stairs. 'He's not here,' she screeched at them.

Jake pushed her aside.

'Please. My kids are up there,' she pleaded with them.

'We won't hurt any kids,' Connor snapped at her. 'But I'm going to search every fucking inch of this house until I find your gob-shite husband.'

'I swear he's not here,' she continued, crying and shouting as she followed them around the house.

Jake ran upstairs while Connor concentrated on the ground floor. He searched every room, including all of the cupboards, despite the fact Bradley would have had to be a contortionist to fit into any of them. He stood in the hallway glaring at Tina. 'Tell me where he is and you and your kids can go back to your beds,' he snarled.

'He's not here. He left after your uncle and Grace Carter came today. I swear I don't know where he is,' she cried, snot and tears streaming down her face.

'Grace and Sean were here today?' Connor snapped at her.

'Yes. This morning. Bradley told them he had nothing to do with Paul and I thought they believed him.'

'So they just left?'

She nodded.

'So why did he do a runner then? If he didn't do it?'

'Probably because he knew it was only a matter of time before you showed up,' she snivelled.

'So, he left you and his kids here to deal with that on your own? He's a real fucking charmer, isn't he?'

Tina was about to respond when a breathless Jake came running down the stairs. 'He's not up there,' he said. 'Just a load of terrified kids.'

Connor glared at Tina. 'When you hear from him again, tell him we won't stop looking for him. So if he really had nothing to do with my brother's murder, he'd be doing himself and his fuckwit brothers a favour to come and find us instead.'

With that ringing in her ears, Jake and Connor walked out of Bradley's house and climbed into Connor's car.

'What now?' Jake asked.

Connor shook his head. 'Fucked if I know. Did you know your mum and our Sean went there today?'

Jake blinked at him in surprise. 'No! Why?'

'Probably the same reason we did. Only they found Bradley there, and left him unscathed apparently.'

'Really? That doesn't sound like my mum, and certainly not like Sean.'

'I know, mate. Maybe they know something we don't? Maybe we're barking up the wrong tree with the Johnson brothers?'

'For now, they're the best leads we've got, Con. I say we find at least one of the fuckers and find out what he knows.'

'You're right. How about we go looking for one of the others instead then?'

'Sounds like a plan,' Jake replied.

———————

Billy Johnson had been on edge all day. Ever since his phone call with Ged. He'd been thinking about Grace and Sean Carter's visit to Bradley's house earlier, and while they had left seemingly believing that Bradley was telling the truth about not being involved in Paul Carter's murder, he wasn't sure there still wouldn't be any repercussions. When he saw the headlights of a car stop in the street beneath his bedroom window in the small terraced house he shared with Scott, he jumped up to look outside. Billy almost shit his pants when he saw the unmistakable figures of Jake Conlon and Connor Carter getting out of a car and walking towards his door.

Billy ran into his brother's bedroom. 'Scott,' he shouted as shook him awake. 'Scott. Get up, and get out now.'

'What?' Scott said as he rubbed his eyes.

'I said get up and get the fuck out, kid,' Billy shouted. 'Quick! Out the back way. Jake Conlon and Connor Carter are outside, and I don't think they're calling round for a brew.'

As soon as Billy had finished speaking, they both heard the hammering on the front door.

'Shit!' Scott jumped up and started scrabbling for his clothes.

'You've got no time to get dressed,' Billy snapped. 'Just get the fuck out.'

'What about you?' Scott stared at him.

Billy shook his head. 'I'll try and stall them. You get away. Go to Craig's and get him and Ged round here.'

'But Billy…' He stared at his older brother in horror.

'Just go, Scott,' Billy said as he pushed his baby brother out of the bedroom and down the stairs.

The banging on the door continued and Billy couldn't help but feel it was like a death knell. He prayed that Scott got out in time. Scott had never wanted to be part of the family firm. He had brains and he could have been so much more, but Bradley wouldn't have it. Billy would be fucked if he'd let his baby brother pay for his oldest brother's ego.

'We should have brought the ram with us,' Jake sighed to Connor. 'We'd be in there by now.'

'Calm down. He's probably in bed. I've just seen a light go on. He'll be here in a minute.'

Sure enough, a few seconds later the front door opened and Billy Johnson stood before them in boxer shorts.

'Billy?' Connor said before pushing his way into the house, with Jake close behind.

Connor bundled Billy into the back room of the house. Billy remained quiet and unusually compliant, which suggested to Connor that he'd had an idea they'd be paying a visit.

Connor pushed Billy onto the old leather sofa.

'Where's your brother?' Jake snapped.

'Which one?' Billy asked.

'Bradley,' Connor shouted.

Billy shrugged. 'I don't know. He fucked off this afternoon after he was paid a visit by your mum and your uncle.'

Jake punched Billy in the back of the head. 'We don't fucking believe you.'

'I know you don't,' Billy replied. 'But it's the truth. I don't know where he is. I swear.'

Connor delivered a swift kick to Billy's balls that made him double over in agony. Lifting his head up by his hair, Connor looked into his eyes. 'Did you have anything to do with my brother's murder, Billy?'

Billy shook his head. 'No,' he groaned, earning him a punch in the face which broke his nose.

'We can keep going like this all night, Billy boy,' Jake said to him. 'Tell us what you know and we'll go easy on you.'

Billy shook his head and spat the blood from his mouth. 'I don't know anything.'

'He's a tough one, isn't he?' Jake said to Connor. 'I'm going to enjoy making him talk.'

'Me too,' Connor agreed.

When Craig, Scott and Ged Johnson arrived at their brother's house thirty minutes later, all they found was the broken and battered body of Billy Johnson. Scott broke down in tears and cried like a baby while Craig phoned an ambulance, which could do nothing other than carry his brother's dead body to the police morgue.

'This is all fucking Bradley's fault,' Ged hissed. 'What the fuck was he thinking taking credit for Paul Carter?'

Craig shook his head. Even he didn't know. It seemed Bradley had disappeared and left them all in the shit.

Chapter Seventy-One

B radley Johnson peered out of the door of his dad's old caravan and cursed the incoming rain clouds. The caravan had a leaky roof, and it was fucking freezing in there as it was. Nobody else knew that he'd kept the old rust-bucket on a tiny campsite in North Wales. Not even Tina or Craig. No one would know he was here. His initial plan had been to hide out until things calmed down back home and the Carters had stopped their bloody rampage.

He looked at the bag of money on the small Formica-topped coffee table and wondered whether he should just do a runner somewhere hot and sunny instead. That was Alastair McGrath's money, and he suspected that the old Scot wouldn't take too kindly to someone stealing even a fiver from him, never mind two hundred grand. He could get himself settled somewhere, and then send for Tina and the kids. He would miss his brothers, but they would never forgive him for abandoning them when the going got tough.

Besides, he'd suspected that Ged was getting increasingly sceptical about why Bradley was the only brother who hadn't been sent down after they'd all been arrested in a massive drugs operation years earlier. The official reason had been that there just hadn't been enough evidence to pin on him. He'd been referred to as the luckiest bastard who ever lived, but the truth was Bradley was a grass. He'd sold out his own brothers to save his own skin and had turned informant for the police in return for no charges being brought against him. With a death threat from Solomon Shepherd hanging over his head as well, he'd also pegged Ged and Craig as the brains of the whole operation, swearing that Sol Shepherd had nothing to do with any of it. It was why Ged and Craig had been handed much heftier sentences than Billy. Bradley wasn't cut out for prison. His brothers had done their time with ease, but there was no way he would have survived inside. It had killed him to turn on his brothers, especially Craig, but it had had to be done. It was simply a matter of survival. And that's what he was doing now. Surviving. His brothers could look after themselves in a way he'd never been able to.

Sitting down on the threadbare sofa, Bradley picked up the Pot Noodle he'd heated up for his dinner and stuck a fork into it. He slurped down the hot noodles and sat back in the chair. He felt no guilt at all for leaving everyone in the shit. Instead, he focused on his relief that he was still alive and with all of his limbs and bones intact.

Chapter Seventy-Two

G race had been surprised to see Connor and Jake standing on their doorstep earlier that evening. Surprised and relieved. She had barely seen them since the day Paul had been killed, and was living in a state of constant worry about where they were and what they were doing. The fact that Billy Johnson had been found beaten to death in his home late the previous night hadn't escaped her attention, and she was sure that Jake and Connor must have had a hand in it. Right now, though, she didn't want to think about that. The boys had turned up and suggested getting a takeaway and watching a film, and she wanted to have just one night of normality again. It would be good for all of them. However, Billy's death had only strengthened her resolve to find Paul's killer as soon as possible. The sooner she put an end to all of this madness, the better.

Belle and Oscar were tucked up in bed, and Jake and Michael had gone out to pick up the food, leaving Connor and Grace alone in the kitchen. Grace poured him a mug of coffee and placed it on the table in front of him.

'How are you feeling?' she asked.

He shrugged. 'I don't even know, to be honest, Grace. I feel like I'm missing a limb. I keep turning around expecting him to be there, or looking at my phone waiting for him to phone me, but...'

'I can't even imagine, Connor,' she said softly.

'I can't believe I'm never going to see him again. The thought of my whole life without him is just mind-numbing. How can I do anything without him when he's always been a part of everything I do?'

Grace shook her head. 'I don't know.'

'It hurts so much, Grace, and I don't know how to start to make it better.' He sniffed as a fat tear rolled down his cheek.

Grace put an arm around him and kissed the top of his head. 'Grief is the price we pay for love, Son,' she said.

'You know it should have been me,' Connor said as he wiped his face with the back of his hand.

'Don't say that.'

'No. You don't understand. It should have been me. I was the one who was supposed to be at the gym that day, not Paul.'

The hairs on the back of Grace's neck stood up. Connor and Jake had gone off and done their own thing after Paul's murder. They hadn't had put any stock in getting intel from the police or finding out the detail of what went on. They'd been too busy trying to avenge Paul's murder in as bloody and violent way as possible.

'What do you mean?' Grace asked, her voice calm and steady, despite her heart starting to race.

'I was supposed to go there and give Eric some money so we could rent the place, but I went to meet my bird instead. If I hadn't, then it would have been me who took that bullet, not Paul.'

Grace pulled his head to her shoulder and stroked his hair. 'You can't think like that, Connor.'

After a moment, Connor lifted his head and nodded. He took his mug of coffee and took a big swig of it. 'Where's my dad and Jake with that pizza?' he said, in an obvious attempt to change the subject as he looked at his watch.

'Probably stopped at the off licence for a few bottles of Bud on the way back. We haven't got any beer in.'

'Probably. Can't have pizza without a beer.'

Grace smiled at him, but her brain was spinning and she wanted to have some time to herself to think things through. What if Paul hadn't been the intended target? And who knew that Connor was supposed to be going to the gym that day? Obviously Eric did. She couldn't believe she hadn't thought to speak to him before now. But then she'd had no idea about Connor's planned meeting with Eric, she'd just assumed Paul had been followed, as had the police. It was still a possibility, but she wanted to speak to Eric as soon as she got the chance. Glancing at the clock, she saw it was after nine o'clock. Eric's gym closed at eight. She'd have to wait to speak to him tomorrow.

Chapter Seventy-Three

Not wanting to spoil the first evening she and Michael had spent with the boys since Paul's death, Grace had put thoughts about Connor's revelation to the back of her mind, promising herself she'd follow it up as soon as she could. It was the following lunchtime before she decided what she was going to do about it. She picked up her mobile phone and dialled Sean's number. 'Sean, it's me. I have another possible lead. Fancy a little trip with me later?'

'Of course. Want to pick me up from the restaurant? Sophia is starting to asking questions about where I'm disappearing to all the time.'

'I can ask John to come with me. I don't want to cause you any drama at home.'

'You're not. Sophia worries about me. You know what she's like.'

'But I can—'

'No,' Sean interrupted her. 'Paul was my nephew, Grace.

Michael is my brother. I'm doing this with you.'

'Okay,' Grace said, relieved that he hadn't taken her up on her offer. The truth was, with the exception of Michael, Sean was the only person she wanted at her side. 'I'll pick you up just before eight?'

'Where are we going?'

'Eric's gym.'

'Oh?'

It was growing dark when Grace and Sean pulled up outside Eric's gym. Walking inside, they saw Eric in the ring, training with a young lad.

'Can we have a word, Eric?' Sean asked.

'Of course,' Eric said as he took off his pads and climbed through the ropes.

'I think it might be a good idea if you told everyone to call it a day,' Sean suggested.

Grace saw the fear in Eric's face as his skin turned a peculiar shade of grey. He swallowed and then started ushering the few people who were using the gym out of the door. There were some grumbles, but mostly people looked at Sean and realised they were better off out of the way.

When everyone was gone, Eric pulled out a couple of foldable chairs and unfolded them before beckoning Sean and Grace to sit down. They did so and Eric followed suit.

'So, what's this about?' Eric asked, with a slight tremor in his voice.

'We want to speak to you about the day Paul was killed,' Grace said.

'Okay,' he replied as he looked back and forth between Grace and the imposing figure of Sean. Even sitting in a chair he looked like a giant.

'Were you expecting Paul at the gym the day he was shot?'

'No,' Eric said confidently, with a shake of his head. 'Connor was supposed to be coming here to give me some money. But Paul came instead. He said Connor had something more interesting to do. I assumed it was a bird. Sorry, woman,' he said with a cough as he looked at Grace.

'What was the money for?' Grace asked.

'I was renting them the rooms upstairs to use as their new base. They were paying six months upfront.'

'So, until Paul arrived, you were expecting Connor to be here?

'Yeah. That's right.' Eric licked his lips.

'Who else knew that Connor was supposed to be coming here?' Grace asked.

'No one that I know of,' Eric replied.

'You didn't tell anyone?'

'No.' He shook his head again.

'Are you sure?' Grace asked.

'One hundred per cent, Grace. I never talk about the lads and their business to anyone. They look after me and I keep my gob shut. That's how it's always worked between us.'

Grace didn't know Eric particularly well, but she knew that he was one of the few people the twins trusted. They'd trained in his gym since they were thirteen years old. Michael had a lot of time for Eric too, and Grace didn't want to believe that he would betray them. He didn't look like he had it in him, if she was honest, and she considered herself a good judge of character – although Paul's murder had changed everything and she wasn't entirely sure she trusted her judgement as much as she once had.

'Why were you renting the rooms out?' Sean asked. 'As long as I've known you, you've never done that.'

'The boys wanted somewhere to make a temporary base. They're here a few days a week anyway, and, like I said, they look after me. I thought it would be nice to have them around more often. Those Johnson brothers are back out and they used to give me a load of aggro back in the day. I thought it would be a win-win for me and the lads. I didn't charge them much, you know?'

'You been having any money problems lately Eric?' Sean asked.

'No.' He shook his head vehemently. 'Never have. I won't lie and say the money didn't come in handy, Sean, it was my Lisa's twenty-first last week, but I didn't need it, no.'

Grace and Sean watched Eric closely. Sean reached inside his jacket and Eric flinched.

'Just checking my phone, Eric,' Sean said. 'What are you so edgy for?'

Eric looked at him and raised his eyebrows. 'Because you told me to clear everyone out, Sean, and in case you hadn't noticed, you two make a pretty fucking terrifying pair. I'm surprised my heart hasn't packed in by now,' he said as he took a towel from a nearby bench and mopped his brow.

Grace smiled. 'Are you sure no one knew that Connor or Paul were supposed to be coming here, Eric?' she asked again.

'I certainly didn't tell anyone, Grace. But that doesn't mean the lads didn't. And like I said, they're here a few times a week so anyone who wanted to find them could come looking here.'

'I suppose so,' Grace said with a frown.

'Actually, Carl knew Connor was coming,' Eric said as he rubbed his chin. 'I remember because he told me about it. He'd been looking forward to a sparring session with him. You know how he loves a good scrap.'

'Carl Young?' Grace asked.

Eric nodded.

'Who's he?' Sean asked.

'He works for us,' Grace replied. 'The twins recommended him to your dad.'

'So he thought Connor was supposed to be here?' Sean asked.

'Yes. He ended up sparring with Paul instead, who, as you can imagine, wiped the floor with him,' Eric said with an unmistakable look of pride on his face.

'Where can we find Carl?' Sean asked.

'At home, I imagine. Or on his way to work?' Eric said as he looked at his watch.

'We've got his address on file,' Grace said as she put a hand on Sean's arm. She stood up and Sean did the same while Eric breathed a visible and audible sigh of relief.

'I just want you to know, I love those boys,' Eric said as his eyes brimmed with tears. 'And I would rather take a good kicking myself than see anything happen to either of them.'

'Thanks for the information, Eric,' said Grace.

'If we find out you're lying to us, we'll be back,' Sean said as they left.

'What do you think?' Sean asked as they climbed into Grace's car.

'I don't know. It's still possible that someone followed Paul, or waited until he showed up here. But let's speak to Carl and see what he knows.'

'Okay, but if I don't at least punch someone soon, Grace, I think I'll fucking explode!'

She nodded. She was keeping him on a tight leash, and she knew he hated it, but they couldn't afford to draw any attention to themselves and alert Paul's killer that they were onto him, or piss off the police.

Chapter Seventy-Four

'Mind if I handle this one?' Sean asked as he pushed open the gate leading to Carl's house.

Grace considered him. He was spoiling for a fight with someone, that much she knew. And he was as frustrated as she was that their leads continued to bring nothing but dead ends, but she trusted him to get the job done.

'Okay. If that's what you want.'

Sean banged repeatedly on the front door of Carl's terraced house in Anfield until Carl answered the door. 'All right,' he said as he did. 'What's the fucking—'

Before he could finish his sentence, Sean had put a large hand on his chest and pushed him inside the house, sending him flying backwards onto the floor. Grace followed Sean into the house and closed the door behind them.

'What the fuck? Grace?' Carl said as he got up from the floor, dusting himself off.

'We need to talk to you, Carl,' Grace said.

'Okay,' he said with a puzzled look on his face. 'Come through.'

Grace and Sean followed Carl into his living room.

'What's this about?' Carl asked.

'Why were you in the gym the day Paul was shot?' Sean barked.

Carl stared at him. 'What?'

'Are you fucking deaf? Why were you in the gym when Paul was shot?'

Carl blinked at him. 'I was training. The same reason I'm there nearly every day.'

'Did you know he was going to be there?'

Carl shook his head. 'No. Maybe. I don't know.'

'So, which is it? No? Maybe? Or you don't know?' Sean shouted as he took a step towards Carl, who stepped back and bumped into the armchair.

'I mean, he's there most days, like me. But I didn't know he'd definitely be there.'

'And what about Connor?'

'What about him?'

Sean slapped Carl around the back of the head, causing him to stumble backwards onto the chair. 'Are you fucking stupid or something? Did you think Connor was going to be there?'

Carl closed his eyes as though he was deep in thought. 'Yes,' he finally said with a nod. 'Connor had arranged to have a spar with me. But then he didn't turn up.'

'Who else knew Connor was going to be there?' Sean barked.

'I don't fucking know,' Carl said and Sean punched him in the face, breaking his nose in the process.

'Ow. What the fuck?' Carl howled as he clutched his nose.

At this point, Grace stepped forward and placed a hand on Sean's arm. He looked at her and she gave him a slight shake of her head, indicating a change of tactics was in order.

'Carl,' she said softly as she sat on the coffee table opposite him. 'Did you tell anyone you were meeting Connor in the gym?'

He stared at her as the blood poured from his nose.

'This is really important. Did you talk to anyone at all about it?'

Carl sat up straight, his hand still over his nose. 'I think I mentioned it to a few of the lads at work. But it wasn't a secret or anything, Grace. I always spar with the lads. Everyone knows it.'

'Did you mention it to anyone unusual? Anyone you'd never usually talk to? Maybe someone asked you about it?'

Carl shook his head. 'No. I was just talking about it at work, that's all.'

'Someone could have overheard then?'

'I suppose so,' Carl said with a shrug. 'But it's not like I would have been talking specifics. Do you think this has something to do with Paul being shot?' he asked, his eyes wide with fear as Sean glared at him from the other side of the room.

'Maybe,' Grace replied, then turned to Sean. 'Come on, I don't think we're going to find out anything here.'

Sean nodded at her, his face set in a grimace. Grace knew he'd feel better if he could give Carl a good kicking, but it would be unwarranted in her opinion. Instead, he followed her silently out of Carl's house.

Grace sighed as she started the engine of her car. Yet another dead end. It was beyond frustrating.

'This is getting fucking ridiculous,' Sean said as if reading her mind. 'I don't understand how nobody seems to fucking know a thing. Maybe we need to try a change of tactics?'

Grace shook her head. 'You know we can't afford to draw too much attention to ourselves with this one. Besides, Jake and Connor are trying the different approach and, apart from a marked increase in A and E admissions, they haven't had any results either.'

'So, what now then?'

'Maybe it's time to cast our nets further afield,' she said as she pulled the car away from the kerb. 'Leave it with me.'

Chapter Seventy-Five

Grace slipped out of the house, closing the door softly beside her so as not to wake Michael. Not being able to arrange Paul's funeral was getting to him, preventing the closure he so desperately needed and leaving him in some awful purgatory where he didn't seem to know whether he was coming or going. Belle and Oscar were staying with their grandparents and Grace was fed up with chasing leads that went nowhere. She had to find out some useful information soon or she would go crazy. Every time she thought about Paul, and Michael in his grief, she felt like her heart was going to break. It didn't help that she had the added worry of wondering what Connor and Jake were up to. They had been on a violent rampage across Liverpool since the day Paul had been murdered. Not only were they putting themselves at risk, but they were drawing far too much attention to the whole family.

Grace sighed as she reached her car. She supposed she couldn't blame the boys reacting the way they had. They both loved Paul – adored him, in fact. He had left a gaping hole in their lives, one that she wasn't sure could ever be filled. Violence seemed to be their preferred outlet, and the only way they knew to solve their problems They obviously had no tangible leads. She would have to rein them in before too long, before they caused irreparable damage. She just hoped that she'd be able to.

In the meantime, while her son and stepson went around breaking bones and smashing heads together, she would do what she did best and tap every source of information she could think of. Someone, somewhere must know something. Paul's murder was a professional hit carried out by someone with considerable skill and that limited her suspect pool considerably. Grace had never had cause to use the services of a hitman herself, but an old acquaintance of hers, Solomon Shepherd, had. Grace was intending to pay him a visit and see if he had any names for her.

Grace pulled up her car at the gates of Sol's huge detached house in Didsbury. Buzzing the intercom, she waited until Sol's thick Mancunian accent filled the speaker.

'Grace,' he said, obviously able to see her on his security camera. 'What the hell are you doing here?' he asked.

'I was hoping you could help me out, Sol,' she replied.

'I'm off out with the wife soon. It's not exactly a good time. You should have called me first.'

'I know, Sol.' She smiled at the camera. 'But I've driven

all the way here. Just ten minutes of your time is all I'm after. For old times' sake?'

He took a few seconds to reply. 'All right. Ten minutes,' he said as the electric gates started to open.

———————

Grace walked into Sol's lavish house and followed him into one of his many rooms. She noticed a young woman with dark skin and long black hair slipping down the hallway and into the back of the house. She assumed it was his wife, Jasmine.

Sol sat down on a leather wingback chair in what appeared to be his sitting room and indicated for Grace to do the same. She sat in the chair opposite him.

'I am sorry to disturb you so early in the morning, Sol, but I wondered if you might be able to help me out.'

Sol nodded at her with a concerned expression on his face. 'I assume this is about Michael's lad being shot?'

Grace nodded back.

'It was a damn shame what happened to him, Gracie. Do pass on my regards to Michael, won't you?'

'Of course I will, Sol. Thanks.'

'So, what makes you think I could help you? I haven't got a clue what happens over there in la-la land any more.'

'It was a professional hit, Sol,' Grace told him.

'Oh?' He sat up straighter in his chair. 'What makes you think that?'

'It was clean and quick. One shot through the neck. From the angle and the direction the motorbike rode off in, the shooter was right-handed. The police inspector told us it was a perfect hit, tearing straight through his carotid artery and ensuring he died instantly. It was either an extreme stroke of luck, or someone who knew exactly what he was doing.'

Sol nodded in agreement as she spoke.

'And there was the getaway. The motorbike was stolen and then dumped on a country lane in Lymm. No prints. No DNA. Nothing to identify the shooter in any way.'

'How do you know all this?' Sol queried.

'Same way you know everything that happens in Manchester, Sol. I have people in very high places on my payroll.'

'But not high enough?' he replied with a grin.

Grace bristled. She'd assumed that recent events might have afforded her the liberty of forgoing Sol's usual arrogance and pissing contests – but he just couldn't help himself. 'Nope. Just not dirty enough,' she countered. 'Even bent coppers draw the line at hiring professional hitmen.'

'Only because they can't afford them,' Sol scoffed.

'Well, it seems there's not many who could. Not the decent ones anyway. Not the type who murdered Paul.'

'But I can?' Sol said, realising what information she wanted from him.

'Exactly.'

Sol shook his head. 'I can't be giving you the names of my contacts, Grace.'

'Why not?'

'Because I don't even know their real names, and besides that, I intend to use their services again some day, and I'd rather they weren't all at the bottom of the Mersey in concrete boots.'

'Come on, Sol. This is Michael's son we're talking about.'

'Why have you come to me, Grace? You could get this information, no problem, with your contacts. Why me?' he said as he stood up and started to pace the room.

'Because I need the information fast. And I also wanted your opinion on who it might be. Does it fit with the MO of anyone you've used before?'

'No. But that doesn't mean anything. They're experts. They try not to have an MO.'

'So you won't help me then?'

'I can't, Grace. I don't know who the shooter was. I'm not giving you the name of every hitman in the North West in the hopes you might not torture them all to death before you find the killer.'

'Fine.' Grace said as she stood up. Sol had always been a monumental arsehole, but she hadn't expected him to turn her down flat the one and only time she had come asking for his help. Fortunately, she had one last weapon in her arsenal. 'I thought you could help, Sol. I would have thought you'd jump at the chance for me to owe you a favour.'

That seemed to recapture his attention and he started to walk towards her. 'You'd owe me?'

'Of course I would. If you gave me information that helped me find Paul's killer.'

'I suppose Michael would owe me too?' he said with a glint in his eye.

Grace groaned inwardly. A long time ago, in a previous

life, Michael had worked for Sol. He'd been his best and most feared enforcer, and Sol had never quite forgiven him for leaving.

'I can't speak for my husband, and I know you wouldn't capitalise on his grief, Sol,' she said pointedly. 'But I will certainly owe you one.'

He rubbed a hand across the stubble on his chin. 'Leave it with me and I'll see what I can do. But understand this, even if I give you a name, it doesn't mean they'll know who you're looking for. It's not like they all belong to some club, you know. They don't get together for dinner a few times a year and swap hints and tips,' he sneered.

'Thanks, Sol,' she said as she resisted the urge to slap the smug grin off his face.

Sol walked Grace to the door and showed her out. 'I'll be in touch in the next few days. I really hope you find the bastard who did it.'

Grace nodded. 'I will.'

Chapter Seventy-Six

Grace had returned home and had just finished dressing a wriggling Oscar when she looked up to see Michael walking into their bedroom with his mobile to his ear.

'Okay, thanks,' he said before letting his hand fall to his side.

He closed his eyes and took a deep breath and Grace knew he'd just had the phone call he'd been waiting for all week.

'Was that the police?' she asked as she picked Oscar up and crossed the room to her husband.

Michael nodded. 'His body is being released to the Coroner this afternoon.'

Grace put her free arm around him and pulled him into a hug and he rested his head on her shoulder. 'At least that means we can lay him to rest,' she said softly.

He didn't answer, but she felt his hot tears on her bare

shoulder. He hadn't cried since he'd found out Paul had been killed, seven days earlier. Since that time it had been as though he'd been in a state of non-existence, unable to see his son or make any preparations for his funeral. It was almost as though their grieving had been on pause. She pulled him tighter to her as he started to sob. Stroking the back of his neck, while their youngest son gurgled happily on her other shoulder, her heart felt like it might break for him.

Grace was feeding Oscar when she felt the vibration of her phone in the pocket of her jeans. Being careful not to disturb her son, who was happily suckling and nodding off to sleep, she slipped it out and saw that it was Sol calling. It had only been a few hours since she'd visited him at home, and to think she'd been worried that he wouldn't come through for her.

'Hi, Sol,' she said quietly.

'I've got a name for you. I've never used this guy myself, but some contacts of mine from down south use him for all of their jobs. Lee Hanson. I'll text you his address.'

'Thanks, Sol. Like I said, I owe you one,' Grace said before hanging up.

Grace settled her son to sleep in his cot before phoning her brother-in-law.

'Hey, Grace,' Sean said.

'I've got a name and an address. I want to check it out.'

'Now?'

'Seems as good a time as any. I'll ask Michael to keep an eye on the kids for a couple of hours. I'll pick you up in half an hour.'

'See you then,' Sean said and they both hung up.

One hour later, Grace and Sean were pulling up outside Lee Hanson's address in Ainsdale. It was a nice house on the beachfront and was clearly owned by someone with a few quid.

Grace and Sean knocked on the front door and listened to the bolts being drawn back, before a face appeared through the small opening, which was still fastened by a chain.

'Lee? Can we talk?' Grace asked.

The panic on Lee's face was almost instantaneous, but before he could close the door again, Sean had kicked it with such force that it sprang open, and they saw Lee running down his hallway towards the back of his house. Running in after him, Sean only took a few long strides before he caught Lee by his shirt collar.

'And just where the fuck are you running off to?' Sean growled at him.

Lee held his hands up in surrender. 'I don't know who the fuck you two are, but you don't look like you're here to pay me a social visit.'

Sean let go of Lee's shirt and pushed him into the living room. 'Sit,' he barked at him.

Lee dusted himself down and sat on the sofa before taking his vape from the coffee table. 'Mind if I?' he said, before taking a long drag.

Grace sat on the armchair, while Sean stood at the door in case Lee decided to make a run for it again.

'Lee,' Grace started. 'I hear you have some very specific services for hire?'

Lee looked at her, considering her. 'Are you two plod?'

Sean laughed, while Grace shook her head. 'Not exactly. Grace Carter,' she said as she stood up to shake his hand. 'And this is my brother-in-law, Sean.'

Lee shook Grace's offered hand limply and she noted the colour draining from his face. Sitting back in the chair, Grace noticed that Lee held his vape in his left hand. He stretched his long legs out in front of him and rubbed his free hand over his shaved head.

'I hear you two don't need the services of the likes of me?' he said with a wan smile before taking another pull of his vape.

'And you'd be right,' Grace replied. 'But we believe someone who's in your line of work had something to do with the murder of my stepson, and Sean's nephew, Paul.'

Lee nodded sagely. 'I heard about that. Whoever took that job had a death wish!'

Grace sensed Sean shifting his weight from one foot to the other in the background.

'Hang on! You don't think it was me, do you?' Lee said as he pulled his legs back towards him and scooted back onto the sofa.

'Well, we don't know who it was yet,' Grace replied. 'That's why we've come to speak to you.'

Sensing that he was in trouble, Lee continued talking. 'It wasn't me. Do you think I'd be sitting in me living room watching Netflix if I'd shot Paul fucking Carter? I'd have fucked off to the other side of the world. Trust me.'

Grace watched him. He was nervous, who wouldn't be? But she was impressed with how cool he appeared. No fidgeting or babbling, like most would in his situation. He continued looking between her and Sean, in between taking drags of his vape.

'Do you have any idea who might have done it?' Grace asked him.

Lee stared at her as though he was thinking. 'Weapon?'

'A Beretta.'

'How did the shooter get away?'

'Stolen motorbike.'

'How many shots?'

'One. Straight through his carotid artery.'

'Left- or right-handed?'

'Right,' Grace confirmed.

Lee sucked air through his teeth. 'As much as we don't like to have an MO – it's not good for business – I like to think I can identify some of my counterparts if I have enough information.'

'And can you?' Grace asked.

'I don't do this lightly. Discretion is part of what makes me good at what I do, you know,' he said as he shook his head. 'But I have heard the urban myths about what you and your brother used to do to people who crossed you.' He nodded at Sean. 'And I have absolutely no desire to find out if they're true. I happen to be very attached to my bollocks – both physically and emotionally.'

'So you're going to tell us then?' Sean growled from the corner of the room.

Lee nodded. 'I met Paul once. At a party.' The memory of their encounter seemed to make him smile.

'Lee?' Grace snapped.

'Zak Miller,' he said with a shrug. 'If I had to put money on it, I'd say it was Zak's work.'

Grace had never heard the name, but that was no surprise to her, having never needed the services of a professional hitman. 'Any idea where we could find him?' she asked.

Lee shook his head. 'Nah. Sorry. Used to live in Manchester, on the waterfront. But he sold that place months ago. Don't know where he is now.'

Grace stood up. 'Thanks for your help, Lee.'

'How can you be sure it wasn't him?' Sean said. 'Why did he run if he had nothing to hide?'

'Have you ever looked in the mirror, mate?' Lee shouted from what he obviously assumed was now the relative safety of the sofa.

Grace turned on her heel and took her car key from her coat. 'Catch,' she said as she threw it towards Lee, who ducked slightly but caught the key easily with one hand.

'Left-handed,' Grace said as she held out her hand, indicating for Lee to throw the key back to her, which he did, with a smile on his face.

Grace took her mobile phone from her pocket as Sean climbed into the driver's seat of her Audi A8 and dialled Tony Webster's number.

'Yeah,' he said when he answered.

'Webster. I need you to do something, and quickly.'

'Okay,' he replied.

'I need anything you can find me on a man named Zak Miller. He was living in Manchester up until recently in the Dockside apartments. I need to know where he is – and fast. I suspect he might try and flee the country, if he hasn't already.'

'I can check with my airport contacts to see if he's left the country, but finding out where he's living isn't easy, Grace,' he said with a sigh. 'I don't just have a magic database of criminals, you know?'

'That's exactly what you have, you arrogant prick. And if you don't use it to get me the information I need, I'd be more than happy to let all of your colleagues know just who you really work for.'

'Now, hang on, Grace, we have a mutually beneficial arrangement—'

'Mutually beneficial? I have put each of your three kids through private school and uni with the money I've paid you over the years, as well as funded that nice little place you've got yourself in the Costa Del Sol. Did you think I didn't know about that? And apart from occasionally looking the other way, or giving me a bit of information I could just as easily get from the *Liverpool Echo*, you've done fuck all. So, get me the information I need, or our *arrangement* will come to an abrupt end.'

'Okay. Give me a few days,' he said. 'I'll do my best.'

'You better fucking had,' Grace snapped before ending the call.

Chapter Seventy-Seven

Grace was impressed, when, less than twenty-four hours after phoning him, DI Tony Webster came through for her with an address for Zak Miller.

Grace dialled Sean's number and waited for him to answer. 'I have Zak's address.'

'Already? Did Webster get it for you?'

'Yeah. I have a feeling Miller is well known to the plod, but they've never been able to pin anything on him.'

'Makes sense,' Sean agreed.

'But we need to act fast. He's already sold his flat in Manchester and is hiding out in his cottage in Abersoch. That's on the market too, and priced for a quick sale. Lovely little place on the Welsh coast, it is. He's obviously planning on going somewhere very soon. Can you get there today?'

'Of course. Are you not coming?' Sean asked.

'I can't. We're meeting with the funeral directors today and I can't let Michael do that on his own.'

'Okay. Do you want me to deal with him straightaway?'

'No. We need to find out who paid him, and Michael might want to be involved in that himself.'

'Right. I'll bring him in,' Sean replied. 'I'll let you know as soon as I have him.'

'Great. I'll text you the address.'

'Sound. Good luck with the funeral people,' he said softly.

'Thanks, mate,' she replied. 'I'll speak to you later.'

Grace had just shown the funeral director out when her phone started to ring. Glancing at the screen she saw it was Sean calling.

'Who's that?' Michael nodded towards her phone as he spooned some baby rice into Oscar's mouth.

'It's work,' she replied, not entirely lying. 'I'll take it in the living room.'

'Okay,' Michael said as he went back to feeding their son.

Grace slipped out of the kitchen before answering the call. 'Hey,' she said as she pressed the phone to her ear. 'How did it go?'

She heard Sean sigh before he answered and realised he wasn't about to give her any good news. 'He was dead by the time I got there, Grace.'

'What? Dead? How?'

'Bullet to the head. Looks like he was asleep in bed. Looked like a professional hit, and he hadn't been dead long.'

'So one hitman has taken out another?' she asked incredulously.

'Whoever paid Miller must have been trying to cover his tracks. Miller must have known something.'

'So, whoever ordered the hit on Paul must have had Miller killed too?' she whispered, conscious that Michael might overhear.

'Yep. Miller was one of the best. He was well known for his discretion, but if it was a choice between dying or giving up whoever paid him to kill Paul, I'm sure he would have talked.'

'Fuck,' Grace seethed. 'So we're back to square one?'

'Seems like it.'

'For fuck's sake.'

'What do we do now?'

'Leave it with me, Sean. I'll be in touch.'

'I'll see you later anyway. I've persuaded Michael to come out for a drink with me and my dad for his birthday. No one feels like celebrating, but it would be good for him to get out, I think.'

Grace nodded even though Sean couldn't see her. 'Yes, I think it would. What time will you be here?'

'About five. We'll grab something to eat as well.'

'Good. I'll see you later then.'

Chapter Seventy-Eight

After settling Oscar, Grace popped her head into Belle's bedroom and smiled as she heard her daughter's soft snores. She walked down the stairs and stepped into the living room, only to be stopped in her tracks by the sight of Michael standing near the sofa, a glass of brandy in his hand. The last time she had seen him was earlier that evening when Sean had picked him up to go out for a drink. She'd expected him to be out for the night.

'I didn't hear you come in. Did Sean drop you off?' she asked.

He ignored her question. 'Would you have left me? If Paul was still alive, would you still be here?'

'What?' She frowned at him. 'Where the hell has this come from?'

'It's a simple fucking question,' he snapped.

'Why does it even matter?'

'Well, it might not matter to you, but it does to me. I

need to know if you're only here out of pity, or if you actually want to be with me.'

'Oh, for God's sake. Are you serious?'

He walked towards her, downing his drink as he did and placing his empty glass on the coffee table. He stopped as he reached her, his face only inches from hers. 'Just answer the question.'

'What do you think?' she snapped back at him.

He shrugged. 'I have no idea, to be honest. One minute you couldn't stand to be in the same room as me. You couldn't bear to let me touch you … and then Paul … and well, here we are.'

'Of course I want to be with you.'

'But you still haven't answered my question. Would you have stayed if Paul hadn't been killed?' He glared at her, his eyes burning into hers as though he was trying to read her mind.

'I don't know,' she admitted. 'Probably.'

'Probably? For fuck's sake,' he shouted before walking away and shaking his head.

'Michael.' She walked after him. 'Who knows what would have happened? I was angry and hurt and I took all of that out on you. Who knows what stupid shit I might have done? But does any of that even matter now?'

He turned to face her again, his face full of anger. 'It fucking matters to me. I don't want to be one of your little projects, Grace. I don't want you here out of some sort of obligation, or, even worse, out of pity. There was a time when I thought I'd have taken you any way you'd have me, but not any more. If this isn't real, then I'd rather not be part of it.'

'Real? This is about as real as it gets, Michael! What the hell has got into you? Of course I don't pity you. I love you. You are the only man I want to spend the rest of my life with. Why do you think it hurt me so much when you lied to me?'

'I didn't lie!'

'Okay. When you hid the truth from me then.'

He frowned at her and she wondered whether she could shake him out of this foul mood he'd come home in. It wasn't like him at all and it was a side of him she didn't particularly enjoy seeing.

'Look, I really don't want to go over all of that again. It's in the past now. Can we just leave it there? So much has happened that makes all of that seem so pointless now. If you want me to tell you that things changed between us when Paul died, of course they did. Paul's death changed both of us, fundamentally. How could it not? Neither of us will ever be the same. It would have torn us apart if we'd let it. But we didn't. Here we are – just like you said. I don't know why you've come home spoiling for an argument tonight, but I can think of at least a dozen things I'd rather be doing right now.'

When he didn't answer, she stepped towards him and placed her arms around his waist. 'Do you honestly think I don't want to be with you? Do you think I'm that good of an actress?'

He stared at her, tucking her loose hair behind her ear.

'No,' he finally whispered as he leaned his forehead against hers.

She smiled at him as she pressed her body into his. 'Glad to hear it,' she said as she moved her hands up to his neck and pulled his face close to hers. 'The kids are both fast asleep and I've missed you.'

'Grace,' he sighed as he kissed a trail along her neck. 'I love you so fucking much.'

'I know. I love you too.'

Chapter Seventy-Nine

M ichael woke early, with Grace's warm body pressed against his, and smiled. It had seemed like forever since he had felt anything, as though he'd been walking around in a daze since Paul's death. Now, finally, some of the fog had started to lift and although his grief still threatened to overwhelm him at any time, and his heart felt like it was broken beyond repair, he knew that he would know happiness again, largely thanks to the woman who lay beside him, and their other four children, who, he realised, needed him now more than ever.

Michael knew that Grace had been up to something. She had been doing what she did best – quietly going about her business, with minimum noise and fuss, and silently getting the job done. He hadn't asked her what she'd learned yet, trusting that she would tell him when he needed to know. Sometimes he wondered if she knew him better than he knew himself. She knew exactly what he needed. She was exactly what he needed.

She stirred beside him and opened her eyes.

'Morning, handsome,' she said

'Morning,' he replied before kissing her.

'How are you feeling this morning? You'd had quite a bit to drink.'

'Not that much,' he reminded her with a grin. 'I'm okay. Better than I've felt in a while.'

'Good. I've really missed this,' she said as she wrapped an arm around his neck and snuggled in closer to him.

'So, what have you found out so far?' he asked, matter-of-factly.

'What?' She moved her head to look at him.

'I may have been walking around like a zombie, Grace, but I'm not stupid. I know you've been looking into it. At least I hope you have.'

'Of course I have. But so far all my leads keep coming to a dead end,' she said with a sigh.

'As soon as you find out who's responsible—'

'I'll tell you as soon as I do. It's your call how we handle it,' she said before he could finish his sentence. 'I'll find him. I promise.'

'I know,' he replied, pulling her to him for a kiss.

———————

Grace stepped out of the shower and wrapped a fluffy towel around herself. Michael had taken the kids downstairs for some breakfast and she was relieved to see she was alone in the bedroom. Grace was about to call in a favour that she had promised she never would – but desperate times and all that.

Picking up her phone, she dialled the number and waited for the person at the other end to pick up.

After six rings, there was an answer. 'I can't believe you still have the same number after all these years. Especially in your line of work.'

'I could say the same about you,' Grace replied.

'I can't believe you're calling me.'

'I'm desperate,' Grace said.

'You must be if you think I can help you.'

'But you can help me, and you know it.'

'But I won't, and I can't believe you're even asking me to.'

'Don't make me say it,' Grace warned.

She heard laughter on the other end of the phone. 'I knew you'd call in the favour one day. Despite all of your promises.'

'I saved your life, Leigh,' Grace said.

'Meet me in the Old Bank pub on Stanley Road at six tonight. Don't be late.'

The phone rang off and Grace sat down on the bed. There was no going back now.

Chapter Eighty

G race made her way through to the back of the Old Bank. The place was almost empty apart from a few stragglers at the bar. Old men with red faces, who she guessed were the regulars, but who were far too drunk or engrossed in their newspapers to notice her sliding past them. She suspected her companion had slipped past similarly unnoticed and wondered if this was why Leigh Moss had chosen this particular establishment for their meeting. It was a pub not too far from the station so she could explain nipping in for a quick one after her shift, but one coppers didn't usually frequent. It was dark and quiet – a perfect spot for illicit meetings.

Grace noticed Leigh tucked away in the corner. Two glasses of a dark liquid on ice sat on the table in front of her. Leigh was looking at her smartphone but her head snapped up as she heard Grace's footsteps approaching. She stood up then, smoothing the creases from her navy woollen skirt as she did. Her dark hair was pulled back into a neat chignon, and despite the circumstances of their meeting, she smiled.

'I hope you still like brandy,' she said as she indicated the glasses on the table.

'Yes. Thanks, Leigh.'

The two women sat down and took a sip of their drinks. Both of them sat in silence for a few moments, each waiting for the other to speak first. Finally, Leigh gave in.

'So, why did you want to see me, Grace?'

'I think you know why,' Grace replied.

Leigh shook her head. 'I've already told you I'm sorry about Paul. Despite who he was, if he meant something to you, then I truly am. And I know you have my old boss Weasel Webster in your pocket, Grace. But in case you hadn't noticed, I don't play those sort of games. In fact, I'm insulted you've even come to me.'

'But you're here though, aren't you?'

'I came here out of courtesy to you. I will never forget what you did for me, Grace. Never,' Leigh whispered. 'But I would never jeopardise my career for you. We may have been friends a long time ago, but we have chosen very different paths. I could never condone what you do.'

'I'm not asking you to.'

'Then what are you asking?'

'I honestly don't know, Leigh. But someone high up arranged to have Paul shot. It was a professional job. You know most of the people round here haven't got the clout or the money to pull off a job like that.'

'If that's the case, then your list of suspects must be very short,' Leigh replied.

Grace sighed. 'Try non-existent. I don't know of anyone who would have that kind of backing, who would want Paul dead.'

Leigh snorted in response.

Grace glared at her. 'I know full well the line of work Paul Carter was in, Leigh. I know he has connections up and down the country. But if it were about that, I'd have heard some whispers. And why take him out and not Connor? They each knew as much as the other. This had to be something personal, but for the life of me, I can't figure out what.'

'I still don't get where I fit into all this,' Leigh said.

'I know you're good at your job, Leigh. I know how much you sacrificed for your career and ordinarily I would never ask you to risk any of that for me…'

'But?'

'But I saved your life once, Leigh. I never thought I'd have to use that as a bargaining chip, but I'm out of options.'

Leigh shook her head. 'You don't realise what you're asking of me.'

'I do. But I'm asking you anyway. We both know that Paul's murder has caused mayhem. There is a war going on out there. Every day I hear something new and I know it's connected to the ramifications of Paul's death. I want all that to stop. For the people I love, I need that to stop,' Grace pleaded. She would never expressly admit that Jake or

Connor had anything to do with the spate of shootings and violence that her recently erupted across the city, but Leigh was smart enough to know that was exactly what she meant. 'If I can find out who was really behind all of this, I can stop that.'

'Just like that?' Leigh said as she sipped her drink.

'Yes. You know I can.'

Leigh stared at Grace. 'I never thought you would become one of them, Grace. After everything you went through with Nathan.'

Grace shrugged. 'If you can't beat them.'

'I made myself a promise that I would never get sucked back into this world, Grace. That's why I joined the police. To make a difference. To stop people like you, not to help you get revenge.'

'I know that, Leigh. I know your all about your past. I was there—'

'Is that a threat?' Leigh interrupted.

'Of course not. Your secrets are safe with me. You should know that by now. All I'm asking is for you to keep your ears open for any information that might lead me to who is really behind this. A name is all I'm asking for. Just give me a name and I will never bother you again.'

Leigh shook her head. 'I don't know.'

Grace placed her hand over Leigh's as it rested on the vinyl-topped table. 'Please just think about it, Leigh. For old times' sake?'

Leigh nodded. How could she refuse this woman, to whom she literally owed her life?

DI Leigh Moss climbed into her car and checked her smartphone. She'd missed two calls from one of her sergeants while she'd been chatting to Grace. She dialled his number as she pulled away from the kerb, allowing the call to be picked up by the Bluetooth system in her car.

'Evening, Ma'am,' Nick Bryce said as he answered the phone.

'No need for the ma'am, Nick,' she said. 'I'm in the car. On my own. What is it?' Nick Bryce was her best sergeant, one of her best mates, and a friend with benefits when the mood struck them both.

'There's been another shooting in Everton.'

'Another one? That's the fifth this week.'

'I know. The boss told me you'd want to know asap.'

'Yeah. Text me the location, and tell the team I'm on my way.'

As Leigh drove to the crime scene, she thought about her meeting with Grace. She hadn't seen her for six years. Not since she'd become a sergeant. Before that, they'd maintained sporadic contact. Maybe twice a year they'd go for dinner. But then Grace had seemed to be getting deeper and deeper into a world that Leigh had no right being involved in. It had become too difficult and dangerous to remain on friendly terms with the woman who had become the queen of the Liverpool underworld. Not that Leigh and her colleagues hadn't noticed the calming effect that Grace's reign had had at one time, but now her son and stepson had taken over and all hell was breaking loose. Could Grace really put a stop to it all? Leigh wondered. She had never encountered a woman like her. She was benevolent, yet terrifying. She was loyal and fierce, and for a short while, a lifetime ago, she had been the truest friend Leigh could have ever asked for.

Leigh shuddered at the memory. She had been twenty-one, working as an exotic dancer called Candy after dropping out of uni, when she'd fallen head over heels for Nathan Conlon. He had promised her the world. Then she'd fallen pregnant and he'd talked her into having an abortion, promising her that he'd leave his wife and son if she terminated the pregnancy. Of course he hadn't. He'd laughed in her face and called her a cheap slut. Her cheeks burned with shame as she remembered storming into the Rose and Crown pub one freezing cold Christmas Eve and screaming the place down, demanding that he leave his evil bitch of a wife.

It was Grace who had found them together less than an hour later, in a freezing cold alleyway behind the pub, after Nathan had raped her and was choking the life from her. He'd sworn he would kill her and she could see in his eyes that he was telling the truth. She promised herself that if she made it out alive she'd stop using drugs and do something useful with her life. It was then that Grace appeared. She distracted Nathan long enough for Leigh to make her escape and Leigh had no doubt that Grace suffered the consequences of her actions that night for some time to come. After learning that Nathan had ended up in prison, Leigh summoned the courage to go back to the Rose and Crown to apologise, and also to thank Grace for saving her life.

Leigh had found a different woman from the hollow shell she'd encountered twelve months earlier. Grace had hardly recognised Leigh either. Gone was the bleached blonde hair and false eyelashes – and everything else that had made her Candy. Instead she was Leigh again, working as a support worker for a sexual abuse charity and applying to become a police officer.

She and Grace had developed a kind of friendship afterwards. At first it had been based on their mutual fear and hatred of Nathan, and then it had developed into something more, each of them spurred on by their past to become better versions of themselves. Who would have thought they would take such different paths? Leigh had joined the police force shortly after, and had excelled in everything she did. Recently promoted to Acting Inspector of the newly created Organised Crime Group Task Force, she was one of Merseyside Police Force's brightest stars.

Grace Carter was a shrewd woman. She knew exactly who she was dealing with when she asked Leigh for information. And the truth was, Leigh already had a name. As the OCG Task Force Inspector, she had been one of the first to have been given the intel from the Crimestoppers line. A female. Her voice trembling as she'd whispered the name of the man responsible for Paul Carter's death and the reason why. This wasn't a name that she'd heard bandied about before. For all their big talk about loyalty and respect, half of the criminals she knew couldn't wait to grass each other up, given the first opportunity. Not that they'd ever be obvious about it: it was always whispers and hearsay – nothing they could hang a case on. Names were always thrown into the frame when someone was murdered – especially someone like Paul Carter. But this particular name had only been given once. By one solitary woman who had sounded terrified. But Leigh knew that a frightened woman was capable of bringing down an empire. Suddenly, Leigh realised that it all made sense. It was a pity she didn't have a shred of actual evidence to prove it.

Grace climbed into her car and saw Leigh's car pull away from the kerb a few metres in front of her. Grace watched the red BMW disappear along Stanley Road. Leigh was a brilliant police officer. Grace had plenty of Merseyside's finest in her pockets, and she had no doubt that Leigh knew it, but Leigh herself was incorruptible. She had no family to speak of. An only child, much like Grace, although Leigh's parents were alive and well. They lived in Manchester, where Leigh had been born and raised, and they'd disowned her when she'd become a police officer. A stripper they could deal with – but a copper! Not a chance!

Although Grace knew about Leigh's colourful past, it wasn't a crime to be a stripper. Leigh would hold her head high and brazen it out if the truth ever did come out – Grace was sure of that. Leigh Moss was as tough as nails and as straight as a die. The only way she was going to help Grace was if she believed it was the right thing to do. Grace could only hope that Leigh would realise it was.

Chapter Eighty-One

L eigh Moss stared at the television as Nick Bryce walked into the room.

'Penny for them?' Nick said as he handed her a glass of Pinot.

'What?' she replied.

'I said, "Penny for your thoughts." You've been in a daze since you got here. Was it that bad?' He frowned at her as he sat on the sofa beside her.

'Just the usual,' she replied, aware that he was talking about the shooting incident she'd been called to a few hours earlier.

'So, what's up then?' he asked, his voice full of concern.

'Nothing,' she said, forcing a smile. 'Just thinking.'

'Sounds dangerous,' he replied with a grin.

'Any sign of that Chinese?'

Nick glanced at his watch. 'Should be here soon. I phoned it half an hour ago, but you know what they're like on a Friday night.'

'Wish they'd hurry up. I'm bloody starving,' she said as she took a swig of her wine.

Nick laughed. 'You'll be pissed before the grub even gets here if you don't slow down.'

Leigh stared at him. He was wearing a thin white T-shirt and she could see the outline of his muscles beneath it. He worked out in the gym every day and she liked that he took good care of himself. He was good-looking, but not in that pretty boy kind of way. Not the type she used to go for back in the day. Nothing like Nathan Conlon. Leigh shuddered at the memory of her affair with Nathan, and its chilling end. It had been a long time since she'd allowed him to invade her thoughts, but her meeting with Grace had her rattled, for more reasons that one.

'Do you ever wish we could do more, Nick?' she asked him.

'Do more? How?'

'To stop them?'

'Them?'

'These criminals. The ones who go about ruining people's lives with no thought for the consequences.'

'Don't most criminals do that?'

Leigh shook her head. 'No. Not all of them. I'm not talking about the gangsters who are only interested in taking each other out either. I mean those evil bastards who traffic kids and threaten them into doing their dirty work. We know who they are, but sometimes it feels like there's nothing we can do about it.'

'We do plenty, Leigh,' he reminded her.

'I know we do our job. But mostly it's only ever the little fish we catch, isn't it? Or at least that's what it feels like.'

Nick shrugged. 'I don't see it like that. I think we do the best we can. Remember that big case we worked on with Greater Manchester last year? We got plenty of the big fish then. How many people are better off for them bastards being locked up?'

Leigh looked at him. She wasn't entirely sure they'd got the big fish at all – not the biggest, at least. He was still sitting pretty in his mansion while his minions did the time. Realising she was on the verge of offending Nick, who seemed to be misinterpreting her frustration as criticism, she didn't press him any further. She couldn't blame him for his sudden prickliness. She was his boss now, and even she knew she wasn't the easiest person to work for. Coming from a long line of police officers, Nick took great pride in his job, and he was good at it. He didn't take kindly to anyone questioning his effectiveness, or the effectiveness of the police in general.

Leigh sighed. 'But sometimes, don't you just wish we could act on what we know without thinking about the consequences?'

Nick stared at her. 'What are you on about? Are you talking about becoming some kind of vigilante superhero?' he said before breaking into a grin.

'Don't be soft,' she said as she gave him a playful shove. 'But if you had the chance to take one of them out of the game, with no repercussions. No comeback. Would you?'

'What are you on about, Leigh?'

'I'm just asking a question. Hypothetically speaking. A free pass. Would you?'

'Hypothetically speaking?'

Leigh nodded.

'I suppose so,' Nick conceded with a shrug. 'But there's no such thing as a free pass.'

Leigh was about to respond when the doorbell rang. Nick jumped up to answer it, leaving Leigh contemplating whether she would ever use her free pass or not. It was tempting, if only because the potential recipient had been a thorn in her side for a very long time.

Chapter Eighty-Two

T he sun shone brightly on the day of Paul Carter's funeral. As Michael climbed out of the black funeral car outside The Blue Rooms, he wondered how the world had the audacity to look so bright and chirpy on such a black day. He braced himself for the afternoon ahead. He didn't feel like speaking to anyone. The only people he wanted to be around were his wife and children. But he knew that the club was full of people who wanted to pay their respects to his son, and he owed it to Paul to acknowledge that.

As he wondered whether he had the strength to smile and be polite for the rest of the day, Michael felt Grace squeeze his hand and remembered that she was by his side, and he would be fine. He pushed open the glass door of The Blue Rooms and they stepped inside. The room fell silent when he walked in, and the knowledge that they had all been waiting for his arrival weighed heavy on his shoulders. He felt like the guest of honour at a party he didn't want to be at. Taking a deep breath, he scanned the sea of faces. Some people he knew and some he didn't. Some of them had known Paul since the day he was born and some had hardly known him at all. Still, they knew the Carter family and wanted to pay their respects all the same.

Holding tightly onto Grace's hand, Michael walked through the crowded room. Everyone nodded solemnly as he passed, some of them giving him a gentle pat in the shoulder as he did. He would no doubt speak to them all personally before the day was out, but right now there seemed to be a shared understanding that he needed to be left to his own thoughts. He made his way to the bar where Connor and Jake were already waiting.

'You want a drink, Dad?' Connor asked.

'Whatever you two are having,' Michael said, indicating the two glasses of dark liquid they were holding.

'Grace?' Connor asked.

'I'll have a brandy,' she replied.

Connor ordered the drinks from the barmaid. After she placed them on the bar Michael lifted his glass. 'To Paul,' he said.

Grace, Connor and Jake raised theirs too. 'To Paul,' they chorused before they all took a drink.

The rest of the afternoon passed in a blur. Michael had spoken to more people than he could care to remember, each of them offering their condolences on his loss. Each of them telling him what a good man his son was. He'd smiled politely and nodded at them all. Then there had been the usual line that people trotted out at funerals and he'd lost count of the number of people who'd commented on what a good turnout it was. He'd resisted the urge to punch each one of them in the face. What did it matter whether five or five thousand people had turned up to Paul's funeral? Nothing would bring his son back. At the end of the day, he was still gone. It wasn't like he could enjoy the party.

Michael was enjoying a much-needed moment of quiet at the bar when his ex-wife Cheryl sidled over to him, reeking of Bacardi. She smiled at him, flashing a row of perfect white teeth, and draped an arm around his shoulder.

'It's a good turnout, isn't it?' she slurred.

He gritted his teeth. 'Yeah,' he said before finishing off his drink in one large gulp.

'Where's that wife of yours?' she sneered. 'She should be right here by your side on a day like today, not swanning around holding court. Have you seen her? Working the room like she's at a bleeding garden party and not my son's funeral.'

Michael took a deep breath. There was no way he was going to cause a scene at Paul's funeral. No matter how much Cheryl tried to push his buttons.

'Grace is exactly where I need her to be,' he snapped. 'Talking to people so I don't have to.'

'Where's Connor? I've hardly seen him all day.' She sniffed. 'He should be out here with his family.'

'He's probably in the back with Jake. Leave him alone. This is a tough day for him.'

'For him?' Cheryl screeched. 'And what about me? I'm Paul's mother. It was me that carried him for nine months. Me that gave birth to him. Ruined me figure an' all.'

Using all of his willpower, Michael fought the urge to tell her what he really thought about her mothering abilities. He would like to have reminded her that she'd been a bloody awful mother since the twins had left the womb, but he couldn't. Not today. Instead, he caught the eye of Murf and beckoned him over.

'Everything okay, Boss?' he asked as he reached them.

Removing Cheryl's arm from his neck, Michael shook his head. 'This is a hard day for us all, mate, especially Cheryl. She needs someone to look after her,' he said.

Understanding exactly what he meant, Murf nodded. Taking Cheryl's hand, he started to guide her away. 'Come on, love. Let's get you a drink and something to eat. You can sit with me and the missus,' he said.

Michael gave him a nod of thanks and Murf smiled in return. No further words were needed.

Putting his empty glass onto the bar, Michael walked into the back of the club to find Jake and Connor. The door to Jake's office was closed, so, assuming they were in there, Michael pushed it open without knocking. He saw Connor and Jake sitting at opposite sides of the desk with a half-empty bottle of Johnny Walker between them.

'Dad?' Connor said. 'You okay?'

'Not really,' he said with a sigh as he took a seat on the small leather sofa in the corner of the office.

'I'm sorry I just left you to it,' Connor said apologetically. 'I can't face talking to everyone.'

'Don't worry about it, Son. That's what me and Grace are here for.'

'Drink?' Jake asked, holding up the whisky bottle.

Michael shook his head. 'No, thanks. Your mum hates that stuff, you know? I came home smelling of it once, and I'd only had one with Sean after we'd closed a deal. I gave her a kiss and she threw up all over the kitchen floor. She was shaking for hours after. I've never touched it since.'

'I think it reminds her of my dad,' Jake said.

'Why do you drink it around her then?' Michael asked.

'Well, she doesn't have to kiss me, does she?' he replied with a grin. 'Besides, it reminds me of him too.'

Michael nodded. As much as he hated Nathan Conlon, and everything he had put Grace and his family through, he was still Jake's father. Grace rarely talked about Nathan. When she did, despite everything he had done to her, she had never once badmouthed him to Jake, no matter what the circumstances, and Michael admired her for that.

'Your mum is looking for you, by the way,' Michael said to Connor. 'You're probably better off staying in here out of the way.'

Connor rolled his eyes. 'She's a pain in the fucking arse. It's a pity she didn't have more time for me and Paul when he was alive.'

'Oy! She's still your mother,' Michael snapped. 'You should call round and see her tomorrow, when she's sober.'

'Can't,' Connor said with a shake of his head. 'We're busy tomorrow.'

Jake nodded in agreement.

'Busy doing what?' Michael asked.

'Just business,' Connor replied.

'What sort of business?'

'The usual sort. Since when do you need to know what we're up to?'

'Since the pair of you have been going around causing mayhem, that's when. I've told you to leave things to me.'

'Paul was my brother, Dad. Do you expect me to sit back and do nothing while his killer walks about thinking he's got away with it?'

'So that's what you're worried about. What people might think? This is about yours and Jake's egos as much as Paul. You're letting your emotions rule your heads. You're being reckless and impulsive and that leads to mistakes. One or both of you are going to end up getting arrested or bloody killed.'

'We know what we're doing,' Connor replied petulantly.

Michael shook his head. He knew he was challenging their authority and they didn't like it. They weren't used to it, but he didn't care. 'I'm warning the pair of you to leave it alone. I'll deal with it. Understand?'

The two boys glared at him.

'I said, do you understand?' he shouted.

Connor and Jake nodded.

Michael stood up. 'Good,' he said. 'At least that gives me one less thing to worry about.'

'I just fucking miss him so much,' Connor said suddenly, as a tear ran down his cheek.

Michael walked over to him and pulled him into an embrace. 'I know, Son. So do I.' He looked over at Jake and saw that he was crying too. Michael beckoned him to stand up and pulled him into a hug too.

'I couldn't stand to lose either of you as well,' Michael whispered as he held the two boys close, his hands on the back of their heads. 'Promise me you won't do anything stupid?'

'We won't,' they replied, although even Michael knew it was a lie. It had been two weeks since Paul's death and Grace still hadn't been able to find out who was behind it. He knew that the trigger man was dead, but that gave him little comfort. He wanted to know who paid Zak Miller, because until they were out of the picture, none of his family were safe. He was becoming increasingly impatient himself and he knew how Connor and Jake felt. He wanted to bust some heads open, but he trusted Grace's methods. If anyone could find Paul's killer, she could.

Chapter Eighty-Three

Leigh Moss sat on the chair in her office and groaned as she looked at the pile of paperwork on her desk. She was about to tackle it when the landline started to ring.

'DI Moss,' she answered.

'Hey, Leigh. How are you?'

'Nat?' she replied. 'It's lovely to hear from you.'

DI Natalie Smith was her opposite number in Greater Manchester Police. They had worked on a case together earlier the previous year when they were both sergeants, and, with a lot in common, had got on like the proverbial house on fire. They had kept in touch and spoke to each other every couple of weeks. Leigh felt like Nat was one of the few people who understood her. 'I'm good, thanks. And you?'

'Same old,' Nat replied with a sigh. 'I'm still working sixty hours on a good week. I hear things are crazy in your neck of the woods too?'

'Tell me about it. I'm pulling seventy-hour weeks myself. Sometimes it feels like it's never ending.'

'Wouldn't change it for the world though, eh?' Natalie said with a laugh.

'Nope.' Leigh smiled. She and Natalie were so alike. They both thrived on the adrenaline. They were both much more hands-on than most of the other DIs they knew, because being in the thick of the action was what they lived for.

'It's a shame we can't work together again,' Natalie said. 'Now that was an operation.'

'Yeah, it was.' Operation Goldfinch had been a joint one between Merseyside and Greater Manchester Police, to crack a human trafficking ring. It had been hugely successful, resulting in international headlines and lengthy prison sentences for most of the people involved.

'It still kills me that Ted got away though,' Natalie said.

'Yeah, me too,' Leigh agreed. Ted was the nickname they'd both used for the big player. The one who had orchestrated the whole thing, but had walked away without even a caution. He was well known for being the biggest criminal in Manchester, but he was like Teflon, hence the name 'Teflon Ted'.

'He's at it again, you know,' Natalie said.

'What? No? He never bloody learns, does he? Surely it's only a matter of time before someone is willing to throw him under the bus?'

'Well, it hasn't happened yet,' Natalie replied with a sigh. 'Do you know what, Leigh, there's nothing I wouldn't do to take that bastard down.'

'Nothing?'

'Nothing! He's pure evil. He hasn't one moral in his entire body. You'd think after what happened to his daughter, he'd have developed a bit of compassion, but he only got worse. If only one of his competitors would take him out,' Natalie said with a sigh. 'It would make my job a whole lot easier.'

Leigh sat in silence for a moment with Nat's words thundering around her head. 'You still there, Leigh?' Natalie asked eventually.

'What? Yes, sorry, Nat. I was thinking about a case.'

'Aren't you always?' Natalie laughed.

'Pitfall of living and breathing the job, I suppose. As you know.'

'Yep. Only too well. Well, I'll let you get back to it. But do you fancy getting together for a few drinks next week? I've got some leave coming up and am trying to muster the courage to visit my brother and his new baby in Southport. A night out with you might just give me the push I need.'

'Yes. Thursday any good for you?'

'Perfect!'

'Great. It's a date then. See you next week, Nat.'

'Bye, Leigh.'

Leigh put the phone down and leaned back in her chair. She glanced at the three commendations from the Chief Constable on her office wall and felt a rush of pride. She loved her job more than anything. She had sacrificed everything for it, even her family, and she'd never regretted it for a second. One of the reasons she loved it so much was because she got to make a difference. She got to make the bad guys pay. And she had always done that within the letter of the law, sticking to every rule and following the correct procedures so that a case had the best chance of making it to court and securing a conviction. But no matter how good you were at your job, and how much blood and sweat you poured into a case, there were always some people who were powerful enough, and terrifying enough, to slide under the radar.

Leigh had considered breaking her code of ethics many times, particularly when she was a uniform in the family crime investigation unit and had witnessed domestics that had left women and children battered and bruised, inflicting deep emotional and physical scars that would never heal. But no matter how strongly she'd felt it, it had always been a brief flicker of a thought and she had never once seriously considered acting on it. Not until now, at least. It had been over two weeks since Paul Carter's murder, and she they were no closer to putting the killer behind bars. Leigh had a good idea who was responsible, but she didn't have a shred of evidence to back it up, and where this man was concerned, none of her superiors would sanction an arrest unless her case was watertight.

Leigh sat in her living room and picked up the glass of vodka before downing it in one. The ice in the glass clinked against the bottom as she placed it down on the coffee table. Taking the burner phone out of its packaging, she inserted the pay-as-you-go sim card into the side and switched on the power, watching as the phone came to life. She swallowed hard and contemplated pouring herself another large vodka but decided against it. Better to have a clear head. She wasn't usually much of a drinker, not any more, but she'd needed something to take the edge off her nerves. There was a reason they called it Dutch courage, she thought to herself. Years ago, when she'd worked as an exotic dancer in Nathan Conlon's club, she'd got drunk every single night, or used coke or anything she could get her hands on. It had been the only way to blot out the wandering hands and slobbering faces.

Leigh's hand trembled as she dialled the number. It was one she knew off by heart, having memorised it years ago and never forgotten it. Her pulse quickened and she took a deep breath to calm her nerves. She was about to do something that she never thought she'd even consider. She loved her job. She was damn good at it. She upheld the law and kept the public safe. She was a crucial part of the thin blue line, and she was bloody proud of it too, despite what her family thought. Now she was about to go against everything that had been drilled into her. She was about to betray the very principles she had sworn to uphold. In principle, what she was about to do was wrong. Very wrong. But morally, it was very right. She believed that with every fibre of her being. Just this once she would cross that thin blue line, because it was the right thing to do.

Thinking back to the Crimestoppers phone call and the woman in a state of distress who had whispered that vital piece of information, Leigh pressed dial and lifted the phone to her ear.

'Hello?' the recipient answered on the fourth ring.

'It's me,' Leigh said. 'I have a name for you.'

'Okay. How sure are you?' Grace Carter replied.

'One hundred per cent.'

'I'm listening.'

Leigh said two more words before hanging up the phone. Removing the sim card and snapping it into two, she threw it into her log burner and watched it melt in the flames.

Chapter Eighty-Four

G race had thought about Leigh's phone call on the long drive home from Lytham. She'd just signed the contracts on their new wine bar and had met with the architect that morning to talk through her plans for the place. It had provided a welcome distraction from her quest to find Paul's killer, which continued to lead her down dead ends.

Walking into the kitchen of her home, Grace placed her car keys on the worktop.

'Mummy,' Belle shouted from her seat at the table.

'Hello, sweetheart,' Grace said as she walked over and planted a kiss on her daughter's head.

'I'm eating all my sketti,' Belle said with a big, beaming smile. 'And so is Oscar.'

Grace looked over at her son and smiled as he waved his chubby little hands, which were clutching fistfuls of spaghetti Bolognese, in the air with a huge grin on his face. Michael sat beside him with a spoon and bowl in his hands, trying, and failing, to contain the mess that their son was making.

'I think he's a bit little for that yet,' Grace said as she planted a kiss on Oscar's head too.

'You okay?' Michael said as he looked up.

The look of concern on his face only confirmed that she must look as shell-shocked as she felt. Grace shook her head. 'I need to talk to you.'

Placing the bowl of food out of Oscar's reach, Michael stood up and rushed to her side. 'What is it? What's wrong?'

'Is your dad still here?' she asked.

'Yeah. He's upstairs looking at the door handle in the nursery. You know how he likes to think of excuses to hang around and make sure I'm not on my own,' Michael said with a roll of his eyes.

'Do you think he'd take the kids to his for an hour or so?'

Michael frowned at her. 'Of course he will. But why? What's wrong?'

'Let's speak to your dad and then we can talk,' she replied, while giving him a reassuring squeeze of his hand.

***

Less than twenty minutes later, Pat Carter had loaded Belle, Oscar and their essentials into the back of his Range Rover. Grace waved them all off as he drove down their driveway and out of the gates, while Michael paced anxiously in the background.

'So, what is it?' he asked anxiously as she closed the front door.

She turned to face him. 'I know who was behind Paul's murder. I know who ordered the hit.'

Michael Carter stared at his wife as she passed him a glass of neat brandy.

'Drink that. You're in shock,' she said gently as she passed him the glass.

He took it from her but didn't drink it. She was right, he was in shock. He could hardly believe what she'd just told him. It didn't make any sense to him. If it hadn't been Grace giving him this piece of information, he'd wouldn't have believed it. But Grace was sure, and he was sure of her. If she said her source was reliable, then it was.

He shook his head. 'You're sure?' he asked again.

She nodded.

'But why?'

'I don't know. But I can find out. I can deal with this if you'd rather not?'

'No,' Michael snapped as the anger started to bubble up inside his chest, as though it had been waiting for the shock to dissipate first. 'I need to do this myself. I want to look into that treacherous fucker's eyes when he's begging for his life, and ask him why he killed my son.' He'd almost forgotten about the glass he was holding, as the rage started to burn at his skin, until the thick crystal shattered in his hand. He placed the broken remnants on the coffee table and tried to shake off the liquid now covering his hand.

'Michael,' Grace said as she took his hand. 'You're bleeding. Let me go and get something to clean you up.'

Michael sat on the sofa, waited for Grace to return and thought about the man who had so cruelly betrayed him. He thought about every single time he had saved that fucker's life. Every single time he stopped him from getting a bullet in his head, and this was the thanks he got. Michael couldn't connect the dots no matter how hard he tried. It just didn't add up. But then, what did he know any more? Since Paul had died he hadn't felt sure of much at all. But one thing he did know was that the man who had taken his son was going to pay. His days were numbered.

Chapter Eighty-Five

Michael kissed Grace on her forehead and pushed back the covers of their king-size bed.

'Where are you going?' she asked sleepily.

He looked at the digital clock beside the bed and saw it was just after midnight. 'Can't sleep,' he replied. 'I'm going downstairs, save me keeping you awake tossing and turning.'

'Want me to get up with you?'

'No. You go back to sleep. I'll just watch some telly or something.'

'Okay. Are you sure?'

'I'm sure,' he replied and watched as she lay her head back on the pillow.

He slipped out of their bedroom and walked quietly down the stairs. His heart was racing in his chest, as it had been for the past few hours since Grace had told him who was responsible for Paul's murder. He opened the door to the study, sat at the large oak desk and switched on the laptop. It came to life instantly and he opened his email account, searching for one message in particular. It contained the phone number of Mark Sullivan – a man whose services were not for hire to just anyone, but were exactly what Michael needed. Mark was very expensive, at least that's what Michael had been told – not that he'd be paying.

Michael dialled the number on the screen, wondering if Mark would be up, or would even answer. After a few rings, he did.

'Yeah?' he said.

'Mark. It's Michael Carter. Carrie introduced us.'

'Michael,' he replied. 'I remember. You saved her arse that night, didn't you? What can I do for you?'

'Is it safe to talk?' Michael asked.

'Wouldn't answer if it wasn't,' Mark replied.

'I need you to monitor someone for me. I need to know his every movement. He won't be on social media, but his wife will. I want you to concentrate on her too, because I want to know when she's not going to be home. I also need to know where the CCTV is around his home. I need to get in and out, if not unnoticed, then at least unrecognised.'

'I'm kind of busy right now,' Mark replied, which Michael knew was no doubt true given his usual clientele. And when Carrie had offered Mark's services, she had warned that he would take on a job only when he had the time or the inclination to.

'I'd be surprised if you weren't. You're the best at what you do. But this job is a walk in the park for you, and you know it.'

'Okay. How quickly do you want this done?'

'Take as long as it takes, Mark. But as soon as there is a window when this fucker is going to be home alone for a couple of hours, I want to know. No matter what time of day or night it is, you let me know.'

'Okay. Should be easy enough. I'll get onto it tomorrow.'

'Good.'

'Just give me his name, and I'll do the rest.'

Michael provided the name, and the address.

'I'll be in touch soon,' Mark said before hanging up.

Michael put the phone down and closed the laptop. He'd been introduced to Mark a year earlier, when he'd organised the security for the premiere of a film set in Liverpool. He'd managed to ingratiate himself with the film company's PR rep, Carrie Santangeli, when he prevented her from being caught snorting cocaine off the chest of the film's main star, a well-loved A-lister, whose wife was at home nursing their six-month-old daughter through croup. The company would have moved heaven and earth to cover for their star, and Carrie would have been thrown under the bus. As a thank-you, she had introduced him to Mark, who was also at the party, and who was regularly employed by Carrie and the production company to dig for dirt on anyone who might threaten the reputation of their stars, or to cover any tracks that needed covering. This introduction also came with the promise that should Michael ever be in need of such a service, Mark would be at his disposal. A one-time-only deal. At the time, Michael had shrugged it off, wondering when he would ever be in need of such a service, but now he realised it would be the key to getting his target alone at exactly the right time, and ensuring there would be no witnesses.

While Carrie had been quite open about who she was, and what she did, Mark was an enigma. Michael wasn't even sure if Mark was his real name. All Michael knew was that he'd once worked for the government – perhaps still did – and he was a tech genius. Give him a name, and he could give you their life story – from where their kids went to school to what they ate for breakfast. Give him an hour and he could find out where someone lived just from looking at their Facebook page. The thing was, Mark wouldn't work for just anyone. They had to come with a personal recommendation, which Michael had been lucky enough to receive.

As for the one-time deal, Michael didn't care if he never got the chance to work with Mark again. If he came through on this occasion, Michael would consider the favour returned.

Chapter Eighty-Six

Michael Carter's knuckles were white as he gripped the steering wheel of the stolen car. It had been eleven long days since Grace had told him who was responsible for Paul's death. It had taken every ounce of his willpower not to drive straight over there and put a bullet in the fucker's head, or break every bone in his body. But he'd known that he had to play this one very carefully. He had four children and a wife who were depending on him. If his intended target suspected he was about to be rumbled then he'd be ready with a small army. Michael had to do this cleanly and quickly. There could be nothing to tie him to the crime; he couldn't afford to get caught by the police and lifed off. So he'd waited until the time was right, doing his research quietly and discreetly, involving only those on his workforce whom he trusted with his life. He had to be patient, and wait for exactly the right moment.

Mark Sullivan had phoned him earlier that morning to tell him that precise moment was now. The house was dark except for a light in the front-room window. There was no one in there except for the bastard who'd ordered the murder of his son, and now it was time to make him pay.

Michael took a deep breath as he opened the car door and stepped out into the cold street full of detached, gated houses. Thanks to Mark, he knew where the CCTV cameras were positioned, and he'd made sure he wouldn't be recognised by keeping his head down and his hood up. He jogged over the road. Using the keycode for the electronic gate, which Mark had also provided, he entered the pin and slipped through the gate as it slowly swung open. As he jogged around the side of the house, he took the toolkit from his pocket. He'd put it together especially for the job, with the help of Murf, who'd been a first class burglar in a previous life and whose skill at breaking and entering was second to none. He turned the small scalpel over in his hand, the metal glinting in the moonlight, and closed his eyes. There were so many things he could do with a weapon like that, but tonight he intended only to use it to break in by the back door. He'd thought about bringing a wholly different type of toolkit with him. The kind he'd used a long time ago, before the twins were even born, when he was young and had nothing to live for.

Whenever he thought about the man he was back then, and the pain he'd inflicted on people, it made him feel physically sick. It wasn't that he'd enjoyed the job, but he'd been good at it, and had been able to detach himself from it in a way that, looking back now, frightened him. When Grace had been kidnapped two years earlier, that side of him had come to the fore again. He'd dealt with her kidnappers himself, ensuring that they had felt pain like they'd never imagined. Afterwards, he'd worried that going back to that dark place inside him was going to be the end of him. But then Grace had been there, waiting for him, with their beautiful daughter, and he'd found his way back to the light again.

Less than six months later they were married and just over a year after that, Oscar was born. Michael had made a promise to himself that he would never become that man again. He couldn't afford to. He had too much to lose. So, even though the thought had crossed his mind to make Paul's murderer, of all people, suffer in the most unimaginable ways, he owed it to his other children, and to Grace, not to.

Solomon Shepherd looked up at the man standing before him and suppressed a shudder. He considered himself a pragmatic man. Ever since the passing of his beloved daughter Chantelle years before, he'd not feared death in the same way he once had. He knew that one day he would meet an untimely end – it was a given for men like him, but he hadn't counted on his demise being at the hands of the man now standing in front of him.

Twenty-seven years earlier, when Michael Carter was a fresh-faced newcomer, he'd worked for Sol alongside his father, Patrick. They were two of the best enforcers Sol had ever encountered. They were a force to be reckoned with and with them by his side, Sol had been unstoppable.

Patrick was a legend who instilled fear in anyone who crossed him. But Michael was different. There had been something very special about him. He'd had a talent that Sol had not seen before or since. Sol had no idea what it was, but if he could bottle whatever it was that had made Michael Carter so terrifying, he would have been invincible. But it all came to an end after Patrick got sent down for drug supply and extortion a few years later, and Michael set up with his brother Sean. Sol had been furious at the time, but there was nothing he could do. Michael had been a loyal soldier who had earned his right to strike out on his own.

In the following years, Michael had most definitely mellowed. Sol wondered if it had been the birth of his sons which had had a calming effect. Certainly, since he'd married Grace Sumner, he'd become even more of a family man. Sol had often wondered whether Michael Carter was still capable of the violence he was once renowned for. However, at that moment, he had absolutely no desire to find out.

Michael stood before him for what seemed like an age, staring at him with a calm expression on his face. There was no hint of emotion. Not a trace of the rage that Sol knew must be coursing through every sinew of his body. Sol had seen that look on Michael's face many times before, and it absolutely terrified him. The only thing that gave him some comfort was the glint of metal from the gun that hung loosely by Michael's side. Perhaps that would mean a quick end? It was all he could hope for now.

'Why?' Michael finally said, his deep voice penetrating the oppressive silence of the small room.

Sol blinked in response. He was very rarely lost for words, but what could he possibly say to this man, who he knew had come to seek vengeance for the murder of his son?

'I asked you a question,' Michael growled.

Sol sat up straighter in his chair. He was alone in the house except for Jasmine, who was upstairs in bed after he had given her the hiding of her life because she'd been secretive with her phone. He'd checked and found nothing incriminating on it – but still, he wouldn't put it past her to try and contact Connor. Sol had no weapons close to hand. His phone was in the pocket of the silk robe he was wearing but he would never get to it before Michael had a chance to act. He had no choice but to answer the question, or he would have the information forced from him. Sol considered himself a hard man. There were not many who could break him. But Michael Carter would. Of that he had no doubt.

'The stupid prick got the wrong man,' Sol shrugged. 'Stupid little bastard.'

Michael stared at him. His face remaining impassive. 'You expect me to believe that? Mistaken identity? So, you didn't mean to kill my son? That's poor even for a snake like you, Sol.'

'Oh, I meant to kill your son, Michael. Have no doubt about that. But not the one who died.'

Michael frowned at him and Sol saw the first flash of anger before the cool façade returned. 'What?'

'The bullet was meant for Connor, not Paul. Connor, who'd been screwing my missus behind my back for months and thought I was too fucking stupid to figure it out.'

Michael shook his head. 'No. You've got it wrong.'

Sol laughed. 'Don't fucking tell me I don't know who my own wife is fucking, Michael. Your son is still sniffing around her now, despite what happened to his brother. He's a fucking liability. He should learn to keep his dick out of married women.'

Michael stepped closer to him and much to his anger and annoyance, Sol flinched.

'You're telling me you murdered my son over a woman? Over a woman who obviously doesn't even want to be with you?'

'Not just a woman. My wife!' Sol snapped. 'You know I can't have my wife fucking around with someone, Michael. Least of all some kid less than half my age.'

Michael shook his head. 'You always were too worried about what other people thought of you, Sol.'

The next thing Sol saw was the metal barrel of the handgun moving closer to his face. He saw the flash. Heard the ear-splitting crack of the gunshot. Then there was nothing.

Chapter Eighty-Seven

Michael let his arm fall to his side, the gun in his hand nudging against his leg. He'd thought it would bring him some relief to kill the man responsible for Paul's death, but it offered none. It brought some closure to the whole chain of events at least. No witnesses. The gun would never be found, he would make sure of that. He could have taken Sol somewhere and tortured him. The old Michael would have. But he took no pleasure in that sort of extreme violence any more. And when Paul had died, Michael had made a silent promise to his surviving children, and his wife, that he would be a better man. It was his fault that his sons had chosen the paths they had. They had simply followed in his footsteps, as he had his own father's. Well, now was the time to break that cycle. It might even be too late for Connor, but there wasn't a chance he was going to let Belle and Oscar go down that road. From this day forward, Michael was going to be legit. There would be no more blood on his hands.

Turning around, he put the gun in his jacket pocket and started to head for the door when he noticed the figure standing in the doorway.

'You must be Michael. Connor looks just like you,' she whispered.

As he approached her, Michael noticed the bruising on her neck, the blood congealed around the gash on her lower lip, and the makings of a black eye.

'I thought you were supposed to be at your sister's?' he snapped.

Michael shook his head. He thought he'd done his homework on this one. There was not supposed to be a snip of evidence to connect him to the crime, especially not a witness. According to her Facebook page, Jasmine was visiting her sister in North Wales for her nephew's first birthday, not standing in the living room watching the murder of her husband. This was a complication he could do without.

She nodded. 'I am at my sister's. At least that's what everyone is supposed to think anyway. My sister Rose has even been posting photographs of me from the last time I was there two weeks ago, as though they were taken today.'

Michael rubbed a hand across his forehead. 'Why?'

Jasmine lifted her hand, and it was only then that he noticed she was holding a small handgun. 'I've been planning this for a month now. I can't live like this any more,' she said quietly as she touched her cheek.

'So you were on your way down here right now to shoot him yourself?' he asked incredulously. That was a hell of a coincidence.

'No. I was going to do it later, when he was asleep in bed. But then I heard a noise. I thought someone had broken in. So I came down with this.'

Michael shook his head. He didn't know whether to believe her or not. She was either telling the truth or about to blow his head off. 'You think you'd have actually done it then?' he asked, trying to read her.

She nodded firmly. 'It was either him or me. It was only a matter of time.'

Michael sighed. What the fuck was he going to do with her?

'Would you mind taking me to my sister's?'

'What?'

'My car's at my sister's house. She picked it up from the garage today and drove it to her house for me earlier. I need to be at my sister's house. I already disabled the CCTV before I went to bed, so no one will see me leave. I couldn't possibly have been a witness to whatever went on here tonight, could I?'

'I suppose not. But what makes you think I'd trust you enough to let you walk out of here?'

She smiled at him. 'You may not know me, but I know you, Michael Carter. I know you wouldn't hurt a woman, even if I am armed,' she said as placed the gun on the sideboard next to her. 'Besides, why wouldn't I keep my mouth shut? You have just done me a massive favour and saved me the job of killing that bastard myself. I love Connor. I have done for a while, and I've been desperate to leave Sol for a lot longer than that. But if that wasn't enough to convince you, then how about the fact that I'm four months pregnant with your grandchild? I wouldn't have been able to hide it from him much longer, and then what do you think Sol would have done to me and my baby? And Connor too? Sol would have known it wasn't his. He fires blanks, you know? Had the snip after his daughter died coz he didn't want any more kids.'

Michael shook his head in exasperation. 'Does Connor know?'

'Not yet,' she whispered. 'I haven't been able to see him for a few weeks. Sol's had me on a very short leash.'

Michael stared at her. He knew very little about this woman other than that she was allegedly carrying his son's child. But what choice did he have?

'I'm really sorry about Paul,' she said softly, pulling him from his thoughts. 'I know it was Sol. I'm sorry I caused all of this.'

'It was Sol. Sol was the one responsible for all of this. Not you, or Connor. He can never find out about this. It would kill him.'

Jasmine stood in the doorway looking up at him like a child. 'I won't tell him, I promise. And if you could take me to my sister's, I can lie low for a few days and then when this all blows over, I can tell Connor about the baby. I think he'll be over the moon, don't you?'

'Probably,' Michael conceded. 'Come on then.' He gestured for her to walk out of the door before him. 'Where does this sister of yours live then?'

Epilogue

Grace wrapped her hands around her husband's waist and kissed him full on the lips.

'What was that for?' he said with a smile.

'Just because,' she replied.

'Do you have any idea how much I love you?' he asked her.

'Yes, I do.' Because she did. She felt it every single day. Despite everything that had happened between them, and everything their family had endured, this man was there for her through it all, and she loved him more than she had ever imagined she could.

'What time's everyone coming?' Michael whispered in her ear.

'In half an hour,' she replied. 'And we still haven't finished putting up the balloons, so don't be getting any ideas.'

'Me?' he protested with a laugh. 'You're the one who

dragged me back to bed as soon as the kids were gone this morning.'

She gave him a playful shove. 'Behave yourself and go and hang some banners or something.'

'Yes, Boss.' He gave a mock salute before disappearing into the sitting room where Jasmine's baby shower was due to take place. She was due in three weeks' time, and to Connor's delight was having a boy. Obviously, the child was going to be named Paul after the uncle he would never have the chance to meet.

Grace stared out of the kitchen window into her back garden and thought about how far they had come since Paul's death four months earlier. Belle and Oscar were happy and healthy. She and Michael were as solid as ever. Isla was still very much part of the family, and Grace had even maintained a relationship with Siobhan, who was now living in Lytham and managing Grace and Michael's new wine bar. Isla stayed with them every other weekend. Jasmine and Connor were as happy as any couple Grace had ever seen. Whilst Connor had understandably gone off the rails after Paul's death, Jasmine, and their unborn child, seemed to have calmed him down a lot.

He and Jake were partners again, and had branched out further into a wide range of ventures. Jake had finally come out as gay, and to his relief everyone who knew him had accepted it as a non-issue. No one would dare to cross him or Connor now. After everything that had happened, they were considered untouchable. Grace still worried about Jake though. She wondered if he'd ever really dealt with Paul's death. Neither he nor Connor had been told that

Connor was the intended target that day. Grace, Michael and Jasmine had sworn to take that secret to their graves. It would do nothing but cause more pain and upset. Although she would never admit it out loud, Paul's murder had united them all. The Carter family were stronger than ever and nothing would ever come between them again.

Grace's train of thought was interrupted by her mobile phone ringing. She glanced at the screen but didn't recognise the number.

'Hello?' she answered.

'Grace. It's Tony Webster.'

Grace's stomach lurched. Webster would never phone her on a Sunday unless the news was urgent – and bad.

'What can I do for you?'

'I thought you'd want to know as soon as, that Jake and Connor have been arrested.'

Grace sighed. This was all she needed. Especially as their very expensive but very accomplished barrister, Faye Donovan, was on holiday in Monaco. 'For God's sake! What for?'

Tony paused before he answered. 'Murder.'

The word hit Grace like a punch to her gut. The urge to sink to the floor and rest her cheek against the cool tiles was strong. After everything they had just been through? Now this? Taking a long, deep breath, she ended the call from Webster and dialled Faye Donovan's number, no longer caring that she was about to interrupt her holiday.

To ensure her son and stepson's freedom, Grace Carter was prepared to wage a war the likes of which the city had never seen.

ONE MORE CHAPTER

YOUR NUMBER ONE STOP

FOR PAGETURNING BOOKS

One More Chapter is an
award-winning global
division of HarperCollins.

Sign up to our newsletter to get our
latest eBook deals and stay up to date
with our weekly Book Club!
<u>Subscribe here.</u>

Meet the team at
<u>www.onemorechapter.com</u>

Follow us!
 <u>@OneMoreChapter_</u>
 <u>@OneMoreChapter</u>
 <u>@onemorechapterhc</u>

Do you write unputdownable fiction?
We love to hear from new voices.
Find out how to submit your novel at
<u>www.onemorechapter.com/submissions</u>